GIRL'S ROCI

by the same author
Disappearer
Colin Cleveland and the End of the World
Girl's Rock
The Eternal Prisoner
Rogue Males

Mark Hunter series
Beautiful Chaos
Sixty-Six Curses
Trouble at School
Mysterious Girlfriend
The Beasts of Bellend
Countdown to Zero

Girl's Rock
(Revised Edition)

Chris Johnson

Samurai West

Published by Samurai West
disappearer007@gmail.com

Story and Art © Chris Johnson 2020/2023
All rights reserved

This paperback edition published 2025
ISBN-13: 9798294253622

Chapter One
Riding on the Rocket

'Would you stop sucking your bloody thumb?'

'Sorry, Craig.'

'Don't be sorry; just don't do it. It makes you look bloody stupid, and as I happen to be sitting right next to you, it makes *me* look bloody stupid by association.'

'No-one's looking at us.'

'Everyone who walks up and down this aisle is looking at us. They'll all be thinking you're a retard.'

'Why would they think that?'

'Well you don't see many grown-ups sucking their thumbs, do you? It's generally considered a juvenile pastime. Very popular with babies, it is.'

The speakers are Craig Jenx and Dudley Moz. They occupy seats in the forward cabin of a spaceliner *en route* from planet Gameron to Daedalus Station.

Craig and Dudley both look to be young men of the herbivore persuasion; skinny and unintimidating in appearance. Craig is slightly the taller, with a world-weary air and an unshaven jaw; Dudley is as a boy boyish, regarding the world through mother-me eyes.

'I thought you were trying to give up, anyway,' proceeds Craig.

'I *am* trying to give up,' says Dudley, drying his wet thumb on the leg of his jeans.

'Yeah? And how's that going?' sarcastically.

'It's not that easy,' says Dudley. 'I can *not* suck my thumb whenever I'm thinking about not sucking my thumb, but then, as soon as I stop thinking about not sucking my thumb, before I even know it, I'm sucking my thumb again.'

'Then you need something else to occupy your mouth,' Craig tells him.

'Like what?'

Craig considers.

'You could take up smoking.'

'But that's bad for you!'

'Makes you look good, though,' replies Craig. 'More than you can say for sucking your thumb. That bloody *doesn't* make you look good.'

'I'm not going to start smoking,' insists Dudley. 'It's bad for you.'

'Then smoke those safe cigarettes.'

'Safe cigarettes are for people trying to quit smoking the real thing! Nobody starts on safe cigarettes.'

'Well, *you* could,' says Craig. 'There's not some rule, is there, that says you can't smoke safe cigarettes unless you've already had the dangerous ones?'

'I don't want to smoke anything.'

'It'll give you something to do with your mouth.'

'Can't you think of something else I could do with my mouth?'

'Well, you could try talking a bit more,' suggests Craig. 'It's very popular, you know, talking is. A lot of people are doing it these days.'

'I *do* talk,' retorts Dudley. 'I'm talking to you right now, aren't I?'

'Yes,' agrees Craig. 'You've mastered that one. But now we need to get you talking to other people a bit more.' He pauses, sighs. 'Sorry; I'm nagging you, aren't I?'

'That's alright, Craig. I know you only want to help.'

'I do. What I want is to see you come out of that shell of yours and spread your wings.' He frowns. 'Or is that a mixed metaphor…? No. Birds come out of shells as well, don't they? I was thinking of tortoises. Anyway. This is why we're going where we're going, isn't it? For you, your first taste of independence, and for both of us it's meeting the girls of our dreams.'

'I'm really nervous about meeting her,' admits Dud.

'Most people would be nervous about meeting the particular female you had to go and choose for your idol,' says Craig. 'Krevis Jungle. The scariest-looking girl in the scariest-looking band in Shinjuku.'

'I like strong women.'

'Yeah, I'd kind of got that.'

'But you like the "delicate flowers," don't you, Craig?'
'Where'd you get from? "Delicate flowers"?'
'From you! You always say Mami's a delicate flower.'
'Well, it's a type, isn't it? The traditional Japanese woman. 'Course I'm not saying Mami's weak or anything. She's an independent and emancipated woman and all that—in her own band and running her own record label and whatnot. But underneath she's still that traditional type; that's what I mean. Shy and submissive. Scrupulously polite. Humble...' Craig stares off into the distance. 'See, the thing about women like that is, when they do fall in love with you, they don't do it by halves. They fall for you heart and soul, y'know? They give you everything; calling you "my master" and saying things like "Do whatever you want with me..."'

He heaves a sigh of prospective contentment.

'I'm not sure if she'll be *that* traditional, Craig,' cautions Dudley.

Yes, as you will have gathered from the foregoing, Craig Jenx and Dudley Moz are dedicated music (and musician) lovers. And their particular area of interest is the girl band scene of the Shinjuku district on Daedalus Station. In Shinjuku, the bands are all girls, the fans are all guys. The girls provide the music; the guys provide the adoration.

This situation on Shinjuku is not one that has popped up overnight; in fact, it is the culmination of several centuries of Japanese history. To trace its origins, you have to go right back to the twentieth century, right back to the birth of rock 'n' roll, and more specifically, the advent of punk rock. It soon came to pass that there were more girl bands per square mile in Japan than existed in any other country; and as the years slipped away this ratio only increased, and the girl bands began to outnumber the male bands more and more, until finally there arrived at time when the few remaining male bands just withered away and died of neglect. And this is why in the Japanese district of Shinjuku on space-station Daedalus, there are only female rock bands.

But why should this phenomenon be peculiar to the Japanese race? What balance of gender attitudes and cultural factors have led to this state of affairs? Many of the galaxy's leading ethnologists have pondered this one, but none of them have come up with a more compelling explanation than that arrived at by Craig Jenx himself! His theory, as once propounded to his friend Dudley, I give to you in full:

'It goes back to Feudal Japan, y'see. In those days, when the Samurais got home from a hard day's feuding, the ladies would like entertain them, singing songs and playing the shamisen, right? Well there you go! Since rock music came along the shamisen's been replaced with the electric guitar, but the principle's the same, isn't it? It's all about the women making music to entertain the men!'

(Fortunately for himself, Craig has never gone public with this theory, so he has yet to be assaulted in the street by angry feminists wielding hard-bound copies of *The Female Eunuch*.)

We all have a void in our lives that needs to be filled; we all need that something with which to define our lives, etch out our identities. It might be a belief system, a humanitarian cause or a favourite holoviz drama; just something to embrace as our own. For Craig and Dudley that *raison d'être* is the girl bands of Shinjuku; which is why we see the two young men on this spaceliner bound for Daedalus Station where their promised land is to be found. This is more than just a pilgrimage for the two of them; they are not just visiting Shinjuku; no, they are moving there, bag and baggage. Having endured a positively Kafkaesque immigration process, they have finally had their applications stamped and approved and now they have left their old homes on planet Gameron, and are *en route* to the J-fans' Promised Land.

Daedalus Station is a space-station colony. Originally just an ordinary refuelling and supply station, one of the many bridgeheads of Earth's expansion into space; as time passed more and more people started to settle down on the satellite. In fact, so many people settled there that soon there just wasn't room enough for everyone, and so they were forced to extend the limits of the Station. They built upwards, they built outwards, adding whole new levels to the original structure. More and more people arrived, a whole polyglot society was formed, and Daedalus Station has become just as much a recognised legitimate colony world as any terraformed planet.

The colony is subdivided into districts, districts based around different cultural or ethnic groups, many of which started out as just small settlements, sometimes just a single homestead; but they grew, as these things will, and became the thriving districts that they are today. Shinjuku is the name of the Japanese district of Daedalus Station.

Aside from their resident fanbase, the Girl Bands of Shinjuku have accumulated a cult following stretching across the galaxy. Some of these fans will find the wherewithal to make pilgrimages to their Mecca, while many others will only ever dream of going there. Craig and Dudley, as stated, are actually moving there, transplanting themselves into the Holy Land. Soon they will be walking the streets of Shinjuku; hanging out at the same pubs and cafes as their goddesses; eating the same food; shopping in the same shops. They will become part of the resident fanbase, the fans who go to all the bands' shows, who mix with the band members themselves, and maybe even form much closer relationships…

Even goddess-worship has its carnal side.

Craig and Dudley have found and secured for themselves a two-bedroom apartment in downtown Shinjuku, the area in which most of the girl bands and J-fans reside. Craig would ideally have preferred a flat of his own as he had had on Gameron, but housing is limited on Daedalus Station, and flat-sharing economical. The apartment they have found suits them well: ready-furnished, reasonable amount of living-space, reasonable rent, amenities close by.

And anyway, although he would have preferred his own exclusive space, Craig is to some degree responsible for his friend Dudley. He has a certain obligation to keep an eye on him, and living under the same roof will place him in a better situation to do this. Dudley, as you will perhaps not be surprised to hear, was, until today, still living at home with his parents, in spite of his being in his mid-twenties. And it has been very much due to Craig's encouragement that he has been convinced to fly the nest and relocate to Daedalus Station. It is Craig who has urged him to cut the apron strings and gain his independence; to actually make some changes in his life, and—most importantly—to fulfil his girl band-related dreams.

Dudley's overprotective and frankly obnoxious parents only very reluctantly agreed to let their only son depart, and they have tasked Craig to watch over him, to ensure that Dudley eats well, that he doesn't stay out too late, that he doesn't drink or use recreational drugs, that he doesn't mix with 'fast' young women, that he doesn't go to disreputable clubs and listen to ear-damaging music...

With the possible exception of the dietary arrangements, Craig is firmly resolved in performing the complete reverse of the above stipulations.

'I'm going for a slash,' announces Craig.

He rises from his seat and sets off down the aisle towards the toilet facilities, situated at the far end.

The flight cabin is commodious; three rows of seats, separated by two broad aisles. Craig and Dudley are seated along the left-hand row; Dudley occupying the window seat. The portholes are firmly shuttered for most of the flight, so having a window seat on a spaceliner isn't much of a bonus. For the safety of the passengers the portholes have to be sealed during the time the liner traverses hyperspace. Because, to stare into the swirling abyss of hyperspace with unshielded eyes will inevitably drive any human being insane with terror. Terminally and irrevocably.

There are conflicting theories in circulation as to just why this happens. Some believe that to gaze into the awful grandeur of hyperspace is to open the human mind to all the vastness, all the mystery, all the wonder of the multiverse; to be assailed by the very truths behind reality itself. And this information, so say the theorists, these revelations, are just more than the mechanism of the human brain can cope with; the truths revealed are just too vast and too fearful for the mere human mind to process. The result: horror and total mental meltdown.

That's one theory. Another is that it's just an effect of the lighting.

Coming to the end of the aisle, Craig finds himself in the path of a woman just emerged from one of the toilet cubicles. Light brown pig-tails sprout from brightly-coloured scrunchies; glasses with loud frames; brightly-coloured clothes: a thirty-year-old teenager.

I know this woman, thinks Craig.

He sidesteps to the right to let her pass. The woman sidesteps as well, and then looks puzzled as to why Craig is still standing in front of her.

I know this woman.

Craig steps back to the left. The woman does likewise. Once again she is puzzled to find her path still impeded.

I know this woman.

Craig sidesteps to the right again. The woman mirrors his movement, a look of intense concentration on her face.

Craig sighs, grabs the woman firmly under the arms, and performs a hundred-eighty-degree turn.

The woman looks alarmed at this sudden transposition.

Without a word, Craig turns away from her and heads for the toilet cubicles. The woman likewise turns away from Craig and heads off down the aisle.

I know that woman.

And then it hits him. Of course! It's Fragrance Pie, the novelist! One of Gameron's most renowned citizens. Franny bloody Pie. Who'd have thought they'd be sharing a spaceliner with Fragrance Pie...?

Craig is spot-on in his identification of the woman. She is indeed Fragrance—'Franny' for short—Pie, the celebrated young novelist. (Well, thirty is relatively young for a novelist; especially one as prolific as Franny.)

If Craig Jenx had kept himself more up to speed with the arts and entertainment news, he would not have been so surprised to see Franny Pie onboard this particular spaceliner, because he would have known that their destination, Daedalus Station, happens to be the venue for this year's Intergal Literary Festival. This annual convention, held at a different location each year, enables authors from across the Federation to get together and indulge in their favourite pastimes of talking at great length about their books and about themselves.

Franny is attending the convention this year, in the company of her agent, Lydia Luvstruk.

As she walks down the aisle, Franny smooths her ruffled feathers. Her encounter with Craig Jenx has somewhat disconcerted her, especially the part in which he laid rough hands upon her. He might not have been the most intimidating of men in appearance: skinny, not too tall... And from the lumberjack shirt and that beard-growth indicative of a man who only bothers shaving once or twice a week, Franny has him pegged as the slacker type. Some might dignify him as a 'non-threatening male', but not Fragrance Pie. Franny holds firmly to the belief that there is no such thing as a 'non-threatening male'; that no male is ever entirely 'non-threatening'. Even the most innocuous-looking of them can, in Franny's considered opinion, lose his temper and lash out at least verbally, if not physically; even the most ardent so-called 'male feminist' can let his hormones spiral out of control to a degree that he will not take 'no' for an answer... This is Franny's view. Not a full-blown androphobe, she is nonetheless wary of men. She is cynical of the notion of complete sexual harmony, considering it to be a chimera, an unattainable goal.

Men are at best like carnivorous house-pets: no matter how domesticated they might be, there is always that chance of the wild animal asserting itself and taking control.

Close to the cockpit end of the aisle now Franny looks for her seat. Where is it...? Third from the end of the row, wasn't it? Third from the end... Third from the end...

Ah, here we are! Third from the end.

Expecting to see the composed features of her agent Lydia, Franny is nonplussed at the sight of two Calvarax occupying the seats. The eyes projecting on stalks from the sides of their brown, elephant-skinned heads curve round to face Franny, regarding her with looks of mild inquiry.

Franny's first alarmed thought is that her agent, formerly a single human female, has suddenly transformed into two Calvarax males. Her second, more sensible, thought is that she may have arrived at the wrong seat.

This theory is confirmed when she notices an arm waving at her from across the cabin, over the heads of the Calvarax. Lydia! Franny realises her mistake. Correct though she was about their seat being third from the end of the row, she has been walking down the wrong aisle.

It was that slacker's fault! Yes! When he had picked her up without so much as a by-your-leave, he'd gone and deposited her in the wrong aisle.

Returning Lydia's signal, Franny says a quick 'Sorry!' to the Calvarax, and hurries to rejoin her. A precipitate turn at the end of the aisle and she barrels into a stewardess's refreshment trolley, and with enough momentum to overturn both the refreshment trolley and herself.

The trolley, disgorging its contents, lands loudly on its side with Franny sprawled over it; sprawled uncomfortably rather than provocatively: not exactly a model for *Spaceliner Concession Trollies* magazine. The stewardess looks horrified; the nearest passengers jump up from their seats.

Franny crawls painfully from the recumbent refreshment trolley, onto the carpeted deck, now saturated with spilt drinks.

'Are you alright, Miss Fragrance?'

A polished voice eloquent with alarm and concern. It is Lydia. Her dark hair is coiled and pinned in place; she wears sensible gold-framed glasses, an immaculate designer business suit.

'Yes, I'm all right,' sighs Franny.

She climbs to her feet, pats herself.

'Just a bit wet,' she says. 'Knee hurts a bit. Might have bruised myself.'

'Bruised?' echoes Lydia, aghast. 'This is unacceptable! Bruises on your perfect body!' She turns to glare at the stewardess. 'I will take this stewardess's details and ensure that she is summarily dismissed from her job!'

'No, Lydia; don't,' dissents Franny quickly. 'It was my fault. I wasn't looking where I was going…'

'Of course! You were in haste because you were so anxious to return to me!' declares Lydia. 'Oh, I am so honoured, Miss Fragrance! That you would risk actual bodily harm just to be by my side!'

Two more stewardesses arrive to help clear up the mess, and Franny and Lydia return to their seats.

'It seems you walked down the wrong aisle, Miss Fragrance,'

remarks Lydia. 'Such an easy mistake to make. These spaceliners really should have the aisles numbered and indicated with signposts. As soon as we arrive on Daedalus Station, I will draft a letter to the company to that effect.'

'Oh, it was my fault I got lost,' responds Franny. 'I ran into this man. Every time I tried to get past him, he blocked my way and—'

'Why this is blatant sexual harassment!' exclaims Lydia. 'Identify this passenger to me at once, Miss Fragrance, so that I can report him to the flight security officer!'

'No, no, it was nothing like that,' demurs Franny. 'Although he did—Tokyo Rose!'

Franny has the look of someone who has just remembered something important. Lydia regards her with puzzlement.

'Tokyo Rose? What's that?'

'It's the name of one of those girl bands on Daedalus,' says Franny. 'That man was wearing a t-shirt with their name on it! It didn't really register at the time, because I was only thinking about getting past him. He must be one of those J-fans... But then, this man's a Gameronian; I thought all the J-fans were there on Daedalus Station...'

'Perhaps he is an off-world fan of the Shinjuku girl bands, and being unable to resist the call of his raging hormones, he is relocating to Daedalus Station to be near to the musicians he lusts over,' suggests Lydia, hitting more or less on the truth.

'If that's true, it looks like the appeal of those girl bands is spreading across the galaxy,' muses Franny. 'I'll have to make a note of that.'

'Yes, you must, Miss Fragrance,' quickly agrees Lydia. 'Your idea of making Daedalus Station's Shinjuku girl bands and their libidinous fans the subject for your next novel was truly a stroke of genius. And as we will be attending the Literary Festival at the same station, you will have ample opportunity to conduct all the on-the-spot research that you deem necessary.'

'Yes, I'll be killing two birds with one stone,' agrees Franny. 'I wonder if I should speak to that man I ran into... I want to know what make those J-fans tick...'

'But you have always been deeply cynical of these so-called J-fans, Miss Fragrance,' says Lydia. 'You are sceptical of what some describe as the almost religious veneration these men purport to entertain towards the female musicians in these bands, inclining to the belief that their interest in the girls is primarily sexual...'

'Well, yes that's what I *do* think,' concurs Franny. 'But I won't know for sure until I interview some of these J-fans...'

'I'm confused, Miss Fragrance. Wouldn't it be a tad inconvenient if you were to discover that the veneration of these men towards the girls is sincere after all?'

'I don't think it's a matter of "inconvenient,"' says Franny. 'It simply means that I'd have to rethink some of my ideas about the book.'

Lydia remains puzzled. 'Why would you have to do that? Surely, you can proceed to write the novel according to your preconceived ideas, depicting the J-fans as individuals motivated primarily by fantasies of obtaining sexual gratification with those female musicians, even if there is no evidence to support this. It will, after all, be a work of fiction.'

'Yes, but based on fact!' protests Franny. 'If I misrepresent those J-fans and my critics find out, they'll tear me to pieces; they'll say I'm treating men unfairly.'

'But, Miss Fragrance!' protests Lydia. 'That's what you always do!'

Now it's Franny's turn to protest. 'Lydia! That's not a nice thing to say!

'Naturally I mean this is a compliment, Miss Fragrance! Your deep-rooted cynicism towards the male gender is as refreshing as a spring breeze!'

'Is it?'

'Absolutely! Your cynical portrayal of men is one of the signature features of your fiction, Miss Fragrance! A central *motif* running through your work. Your fans adore it. They would be upset if you were to change. Why, even your male readers admire it.'

'Oh, *them*,' snorts Franny. 'Those men seem to think that just by reading my books they're somehow elevating themselves above other men. That's the trouble with becoming a mainstream success; you can never be sure about all your readers.'

'As long as they pay for your books and don't just shoplift

them,' says Lydia. 'That's what matters in the end. The steady flow of royalties. You're such a runaway success, Miss Fragrance, that they are bound to honour you with the Lifetime Achievement Award at this year's convention.'

'Oh, you're not still going on about that, are you, Lydia?' groans Franny. 'I've just turned thirty; I've only been a published author for twelve years. They're not going to give me the Lifetime Achievement Award, are they? They wouldn't do that unless I was terminally ill or something.' A sudden worrying thought grabs her. 'I'm not terminally ill, am I?'

'Of course not!'

'I just thought… If you'd found out and not told me…'

'Don't even think such things! You're perfectly fit and healthy, Miss Fragrance,' Lydia assures her. 'Why, I've read your medical records—'

She breaks off.

Franny looks at her. 'You've read my—?'

'Yes, it's true you're still young,' says Lydia, quickly changing the subject. 'But even so: twelve novels in as many years, and all of the highest literary quality. Such insightful powers of observation! Such dazzling prose! Yes, no-one deserves to be honoured this year more than you, Miss Fragrance!'

'Yes, they do,' argues Franny. 'There's Betty Mudie, isn't there? She'll be at the convention, and I'm sure they've invited her because it's her they're planning to give the award to.'

'I understand that Miss Mudie is your literary idol,' says Lydia, trying hard to keep the disdain from her voice. 'But sometimes the pupil surpasses the teacher. And you sell a lot more books than she does.'

'Lydia, they don't give out the Lifetime Achievement Award on the strength of book sales. And for my sake, please speak more kindly about Betty Mudie, because I really do want her to receive that award.'

'Miss Fragrance, I would endeavour to be agreeable towards Daedalus Station's most prolific child-murderer, if that was what you wished of me,' declares loyal Lydia.

Mami Rose. Vocalist, guitarist and songwriter for the 'sensational rock' band Tokyo Rose, and in Craig's estimation the most talented and amazing woman in the known universe.

And here he is, in the backstage dressing room, actually sitting next to her!

After years of worshipping her from a distance, admiring every picture, devouring every scrap of video footage of his goddess, here she is before him, and even more glorious in the flesh! A scintillating goddess.

Having greeted each other, they have seated themselves on the settle running along the wall. The other two members of the band are across the room, chatting in their native tongue, but Craig and Mami hardly notice them; they are lost in each other's eyes!

And that's the most wonderful thing of all! She seems to be as thrilled to meet him as he is to meet her. They have long communicated online, but Craig has never been able to really gauge how much of a positive impression he has made on Mami; whether to her he is just another adoring fan, or if she has started to think of him as something more than just that…

And now it seems clear that she *does* have feelings for him!

And just look at her! The most beautiful woman in existence! And *he* is the one she likes!

Framed by a bob of blonde hair (dyed of course), her broad, feline face with those large, sparkling eyes and that expansive, generous smile. Her overbite is of a dazzling whiteness, composed of large, strong teeth. The smile she directs at him is warm, enticing, but with a hint of shyness to it…

Shy! *He's* the one who should be feeling shy right now! But yet, his goddess is demure, and although larger-than-life on stage, here with him, she is bashful and hesitant.

Mami's voluptuous figure is broad like her face. In fact, her large head and broad lines lend her the deceptive appearance of being smaller in height than she actually is. At the moment she is casually dressed in jeans and a woollen jumper. On stage she and her bandmates always wear more elaborate outfits.

'Well here we are,' says Craig. 'Meeting at last.'

'Yes, we meet!' concurs Mami. 'I'm so happy!'

Her voice is full-bodied, musical. (As Craig has always said to Dudley: 'You could cream your jeans just listening to Mami talk.')

'You know I've always liked you,' continues Craig.

'I like you, too!' declares Mami. She continues to gaze at him.

Craig takes her hand, one of the strong-fingered hands he has always admired when watching footage of Mami playing her guitar with consummate skill.

'It's funny,' says Craig. 'I always imagined we'd connect straight away whenever we finally met. And now, unless I've got it wrong here, I feel like we *have* connected.'

'No, you not wrong,' agrees Mami, eagerly. 'We have connect! I feel this, too!'

Mami brushes her hand over his mouth. He gently kisses her callused finger-tips.

'Craig…' she sighs gazing at him with that look in her eyes; that special look that says she would do anything for him.

Their lips meet…

"This is your captain, speaking—'

The voice piped over the tannoy, drags Craig from his daydream.

'We are about to emerge from hyperspace,' proceeds the captain in her reassuringly feminine tones. 'We will then be making our approach to the main terminal of Daedalus Station, arriving on schedule. We hope you have enjoyed your flight, and thank you for flying Galaxy Tours.'

Craig and Dudley exchange looks.

'Well this is it,' says the former. 'Destiny awaits.'

Chapter Two
Jump into the New World

The nine-year-old Japanese girl sits on the floor watching the holoviz with rapt attention. Actually, the girl is only half Japanese; the Asiatic predominates, but there is a hint of Caucasian ancestry in the moulding of her facial features

Asuna, vocalist and guitarist for the pop-punk band Raw Babes in the Country, studies her daughter's profile, idly wondering once again who the girl's father might be. Hina's black hair and eyes, her complexion, come straight from herself, so they are no indicator. But is there anything else, anything else in her features or expression to suggest her paternity...? She still can't see anything. Perhaps Hina's still too young for any distinct resemblance to have appeared. At nine, the child's face is smooth, aglow with youth, but no character has really impressed itself on those features as yet. Still, something's sure to emerge as she gets older, some indicator as to which of the three suspects, those three men Asuna allowed to inseminate her during the course of that week in which she was ovulating; something to indicate which of them is the father of the child.

Not that it really matters. All three of those guys are long gone, and Asuna is doing a perfectly good job of raising her daughter by herself. She doesn't need the father to come back and fulfil his paternal duties; she doesn't even need any money out of him... It would just be interesting to know which one of those three guys it actually was...

Artificial night has fallen over Shinjuku, and the lights are on in the front room of Asuna's apartment, the curtains drawn.

Asuna has a visitor: Machiko, her band's bassist. They have been chatting away, while Hina, undisturbed by the conversation, watches her holoviz anime.

Picture a young woman full of animal spirits and pride of her sex, enjoying the summer of her existence, bursting with health and good humour: this is Asuna. Her cropped hair, dyed ash-blonde, contrasts with her skin which, like her daughter's, is of the tanned 'yellow' complexion.

Machiko's hair is also short in length, but hers is undyed. Her face is more masculine in its lines than her friend's, the features strongly defined. Her complexion is fairer and her figure more of an oblong to Asuna's hourglass.

'Those two J-fans from Gameron should be getting here today,' says Machiko.

'Oh, yeah,' says Asuna. 'They're moving into the Sunshine House apartments, right? Where Vern lives... He knows them, doesn't he?'

'Yes, Vern's been friends with one of them online. I don't think he knows the other one. He likes Mami Rose; I mean, the J-fan Vern knows likes her.'

'And what about Mami? Is she into him?'

'Don't ask me,' replies Machiko. 'Who knows what goes on inside that girl's head.'

'Ha! Yeah, she is a space cadet, that girl,' says Asuna. 'Anyway, what about you and Vern? Still keeping him panting at arm's length?'

'No actually,' counters Machiko. 'I've decided to give him a chance.'

'A chance to get down and dirty with you? Are my ears deceiving me?'

'I've just agreed to meet up with him,' says Machiko firmly. 'For drinks.'

'Well, that's a start. When is this happening?'

'Tomorrow night.'

'And you don't plan on going all the way with the guy?'

'No, not on the first date; I'm in no big hurry.'

'Yeah, I'd kind of noticed that, Machi-chan. You know what the guys call you, don't you?'

'Yes,' sighs Machiko. ' "The Unobtainable." They all think I'm either frigid or a lesbian in denial.'

'Boy, if only they knew the truth!' grins Asuna. 'You're red hot! A dedicated solo flier. Right?'

'Correct.'

'Just can't get enough of yourself, can you?'

'True.'

'A hot body like yours is too good for any mere man, right?'

'Exactly.'

'But, still… You like Vern, don't you? I mean, you seem to get on with the guy.'

'Yes, I like him. He's a nice enough guy to talk to. And… well, you can't help getting a good feeling from knowing how crazy about you some of these J-fans can get.'

'I know! It's a real buzz, isn't it? "We have the power!" '

A loud knock at the door.

'I think I know that knock,' declares Asuna, rising from her armchair.

'It sounds like they're either angry or drunk,' says Machiko.

'Oh, they're drunk alright,' confirms Asuna.

She opens the door to admit a young Japanese man, skinny and not too steady on his feet.

'Hi, Shinji,' says Asuna.

Hina looks round from the holoviz.

'It's the dipsomaniac!' she pronounces.

Asuna is only mildly surprised. Her precocious daughter has developed this habit of suddenly coming out with these English loan words; some of them—like this one—words Asuna didn't even know they'd ever borrowed.

Shinji salutes Hina, who, granting him a smile, turns back to the holoviz.

'Hi, Machiko,' says Shinji, sitting on the step to take off his shoes.

'And when did you start drinking today?' inquires Machiko.

'Teatime or thereabouts,' is the reply.

'Beer?'

'Yeah.'

'And how many have you had?'

Shinji starts counting on his fingers. At least he attempts to, but he looks at his fingers as though they're not in the right place, or that there are too many of them.

He gives up, drops his hands. 'A few,' he says.

'Well, sit yourself down,' invites Asuna. 'I'll fix you some coffee.'

Shinji drops heavily onto the sofa.

'You ever thought of not drinking just for once?' suggests Machiko.

'Hey!' protests Shinji. 'I don't always drink.'

'You always seem to be drunk when I see you.'

'Well, y'know, that's cuz you only see me when I'm out. I mean at shows and stuff.'

'So, when are you not drunk?'

'When I'm at home.'

'But when you're at home no-one sees you. You never answer the door.'

'Yeah, but I'm not too good with people, y'know? Not all the time… And then my pad, it's kind of messy… I don't like people to see it.'

'Well, you could tidy it— but maybe it's a waste of time saying that to a guy.'

'I tidy up once in a whiles. Always seems to get messy again…'

He scratches his head, stretches out on the sofa.

By the time Asuna returns with the coffee, Shinji has fallen asleep.

'Oh, well,' says Asuna, placing the superfluous drink on the coffee table.

'What are you going to do with him?' asks Machiko.

Asuna shrugs. 'If he doesn't wake up before I turn in, I'll just let him crash here. It won't be the first time.'

Talkative taxi driver.

If there's one thing Craig hates, it's a talkative taxi driver. He prefers his cabbies taciturn, or else occupied in a conversation with someone else on their hands-free, preferably in another language.

This cabbie is a cheerful black man, bearded and dreadlocked. And he is at least being informative in his loquacity, treating them to a verbal guided tour of their new home, Daedalus Station.

After landing at the spaceport, Craig and Dudley had claimed their luggage—two suitcases each—and after passing through customs and immigration had proceeded to the taxi-rank outside the terminal building. Here they had immediately been accosted by this cabbie, who had, with scant ceremony, commandeered their luggage and deposited it in the boot of his vehicle; and then, with a bow at once ironic and good-natured, opened the rear door for them. Craig and Dudley had meekly climbed into the cab. There wasn't much else they could do.

Now they are cruising along the raised carriageway, leaving behind the glittering towerblocks of Daedalus Central, and heading out into the suburbs.

'So, are you fellers J-fans?' inquires the cabbie. 'I'm thinking, y'see, cuz of you movin' into the Shinjuku district, that maybe you're part of that girl band scene… Now, am I right, or am I right?'

'You're right,' confirms Craig.

The cabbie chuckles. 'I knew it! I knew it! Yeah, you two, you've got the look of J-fans about yer. An' y'know, I don't mean that as an insult, or nothing.'

'None taken,' Craig assures him. 'You're not into the girl bands, then?'

'I'm sorry to say not. Not my scene,' declares the cabbie. 'I mean, don't get me wrong; I got nothing against it. But y'know, it's just not my kind of music, is all.'

Figures, thinks Craig. Just about wherever you go in the universe, you can count the number of black rock music fans on both hands. Historically, blacks pretty much invented rock music back in the day on planet Earth, but then it seems like they just handed it over to the whites and the yellows, and moved on to other things.

'What kind of music do you like?' he asks, not really caring.

'Garage is what I dig the most,' is the reply.

'The Smut Girls are a garage band!' blurts out Dudley. 'They're my favourites!'

'He doesn't mean garage *rock*, you prawn,' Craig tells him.

The cabbie chuckles.

An illuminated sign ahead announces the Shinjuku exit.

'We're there already?' questions Craig. 'I thought it would be further out.'

'Well, we is at the Shinjuku exit,' replies the cabbie, guiding his vehicle onto the exit ramp. 'But we ain't in Shinjuku yet. Not by a long shot.'

'I don't get it,' says Craig, not getting it. 'Why say "Shinjuku Exit" if it's not near Shinjuku?'

'Because, my good man,' says the cabbie, 'this is as near as the freeway gets to where you is headin'. Y'see, when you're drivin' around Daedalus Station, you gotta think outside the box. This ain't like being on a planet, like the one you guys come from. When you move around Daedalus Station, you gotta think in three dimensions, man. Y'know, like with space travel.'

'Three dimensions?' echoes Craig. And then: 'The road!'

The exit road, illuminated by floating lights, appears to end abruptly right ahead of them. As if to confirm this impression, two red crosses issue a mute warning.

'What about the road?' asks the cabbie, unconcerned.

'It stops up ahead!' cries Craig. 'Hit the brakes!'

'Now, why would I go'n do that?' returns the driver. 'If I stop here, we ain't never gettin' to where you fellers want to go. You can't just walk it.'

'There's nothing there!' yells Craig, seeing only a yawning abyss in front of them. 'We're going to fall!'

'I know there's nothin' there, man,' replies the cabbie. 'Down is the way we needs to go, y'see?'

Craig doesn't have time to say whether he sees or not, because at that moment they leave the road and all he can do is wail in terror, with Dudley making it a duet. Locked in terrified embrace, they prepare for the freefall. And for a few tense seconds they *do* plummet; but then something kicks in, the car lifts, and then, remaining on the horizontal plain, begins to descend smoothly, slowly.

The cabbie chuckles. 'Oh, man! The looks on you fellers' faces! I wish I'd taken a picture. Boy-oh-boy! You thought your number was up, didn't you? Oh, ye of little faith! I mean how could I off you two in this here ve-hi-cle without killing my good self at the same time? Do I seem like the suicidal type to you?'

'Well, no,' admits Craig.

'I should think not,' says the cabbie. 'But seriously, it's like I already said: here on Daedalus, you gotta think in three dimensions when movin' around. An' y'see, the only way to get to the Shinjuku district from the freeway, is this way: straight down. That is why they call this the Shinjuku Drop.'

'How far down is it?'

'About two miles.'

'And everyone has to go up and down like this when they're going in and out of Shinjuku?'

'Well they do if they're travellin' overground. But there's also the subway system. Subway'll take you anywhere on the Station.'

'Doesn't that make taxicabs redundant?'

''Course it don't. I mean, yeah, most folks'll take the subway travellin' between districts. But we're still needed for local travel. Then we do the spaceport runs like this one, cuz you wouldn't want to have to haul your luggage through the subway system.'

They continue to descend. They are descending a kind of well; vast buildings surround them. The buildings show very few lights. They look functional and are wrapped in pipes and conduits.

'So, is this Shinjuku?' wonders Craig. It doesn't look like the pictures he's seen.

'Nope, we ain't there yet,' is the answer. 'This here's the buffer zone. All the districts have these places. Y'see, it's from here that they regulate all the utilities.'

'Utilities?' echoes Craig.

'Yeah, man. The water, the electric; the drainage, the recycling.' Those things don't come outta thin air, do they? Hell, even the thin air don't come out of thin air; they have to make that, as well! This is a space station, man. Doesn't come with a ready-made air supply, does it? Not like one of those fancy terraformed planets you fellers come from.'

Finally, they reach the ground. Back on its wheels, taxi moves off along an unmarked road, more like a tunnel, boxed in by the irregular shapes of the buildings. There is no streetlighting here.

Squinting, Craig thinks he sees human shapes by the roadside; some standing, some sitting.

'I can see people!' he announces.

'Yep. Them'll be the homeless folk,' says the cabbie. 'You'll find them in all the buffer zones. Gangs as well. They hang out in these places. Yep, it ain't too safe around here. I mean, we're okay in the cab, but you wouldn't want to be out here at night on foot, if y'know what I mean.'

'Then what about the people who work in these buildings?' asks Dudley. 'Isn't it dangerous for them getting in and out of work?'

'No, that ain't a problem. The good people that work these plants, they can commute without even steppin' outside. Tunnels take 'em in and out of the buffer zone.'

A haze of light appears ahead of them.

'Is that the end up ahead?' asks Craig.

'Yes, my man, we is nearly through the buffer zone,' replies the cabbie. 'Then we will be arriving in Shinjuku, your spiritual home! And now to be your temporal home, to boot!'

'This is intolerable! Do you have any idea who my client is?

Fragrance Pie, you dolt! Fragrance Pie! The greatest living author in the Galactic Federation! You must have been advised which flight we were arriving on, surely? Yet there was no chauffeured limousine waiting for us at the spaceport! Not a sign of one! We were forced to arrive here in a common-or-garden taxicab! And now, here we are and no sign of a reception committee! What an insult this is to my client! But, perhaps that idiot taxi-driver brought us to the wrong hotel? Yes, that would be the only plausible explanation! Well, girl? Speak up! Are we in the right place or not? Is this or is this not the Excelsior Hotel, venue for this year's Intergal Literary Festival?'

'This *is* the Excelsior...' confirms the discomforted receptionist.

'Really? This is the Excelsior, is it? Well, where's the reception committee?' demands Lydia Luvstruk.

'There has been no reception committee scheduled for today...' announces the receptionist, hesitantly.

'No reception committee?' echoes Lydia. 'Has there been some administrative error? Did you know that Fragrance Pie was arriving today?'

'Probably...'

'"Probably"?' Lydia pounces on the world.

'A great number of authors are arriving at the Excelsior at the moment...' explains the receptionist. 'Lots of them. And... and well, we can't organise reception committees for all of them...'

'I should think not,' says Lydia. 'But my client—'

Franny, deeply embarrassed by all this, intervenes.

'Let's not make a fuss, Lydia,' she says. 'I wasn't expecting a reception committee. I didn't even *want* a reception committee. You know I don't like fuss, Lydia...'

Lydia turns to her client, her severe expression melting instantly into a simpering look. 'Of course, Miss Fragrance! Do you think that I don't know you better than I know myself? I know you would not have cared for the fuss and attention of a reception committee: the bouquets, the flashing cameras... And had there been one, I would have instantly demanded that the proceedings be terminated. But there *wasn't* a reception committee, and this I just can't help interpreting as a deliberate slight upon your greatness!'

'Oh, nonsense, Lydia,' chides Franny. 'You heard what this lady says: They've got dozens of authors arriving here at the moment. It just wouldn't be practical to have reception committees waiting for all of us.'

'Very well.' To the receptionist: 'Kindly present us with the keys to our rooms. And make sure that our luggage is taken up immediately.'

The receptionist obeys. Having been provided with their passkeys, Franny and Lydia cross the vast lobby towards the row of ornate lift doors, the bellboy who has charge of their luggage following in their wake. As they reach the lifts, one set of doors opens and a man steps out; a lantern-jawed, muscular man with a military buzz-cut. Upon seeing the two women, he stops in his tracks, a grin spreading over his face.

'Well well well, if it isn't Fragrance Pie!' he says.

Franny pulls a wry face. 'Hullo, Henry. It's good to hear that your conversation is still as fresh and original as the dialogue in your books.'

The man's face clouds over. 'What's that supposed to mean?'

'Oh, don't worry about it,' says Franny, turning to the lift doors.

'Yeah, how about I *do* worry about it?' retorts Henry, interposing himself between the women and the lift. 'I didn't come here for any of your smart-talk.'

'Then what *did* you come here for?' steps in Lydia. 'This is a *Literary Festival*. Isn't the Macho Idiots' Convention somewhere down the road?'

'Oh, funny,' sneers Henry. 'I got my invite, the same as everyone else.'

Henry Rollix is indeed a writer. A resident of planet Stratus, he is renowned for his bodybuilding obsession, his aversion to alcohol, and his pathological hatred of law enforcement officers. His fans describe his angry, opinionated prose as 'raw energy writing.' His critics have other names for it.

'An administrative error, I'm sure,' says Lydia. 'But would you kindly stop obstructing the lift? We have only just arrived, and Miss Pie would like to go up to her room to refresh herself.'

'And has "Miss Pie" got herself a guy since last time we met?' inquires Henry, adopting a superior grin.

'No, she hasn't,' answers Franny for herself.

'So, you're still in the market, are you?' says Henry. 'How about you and me meet up and talk about it later?'

'Certainly!' agrees Franny brightly. 'In the bar at ten, over a couple of G 'n' Ts?'

The eyebrows and mouth contract again. 'You know damn well I don't touch that poison.'

'So, you're still on the wagon, are you?' returns Franny. 'What a pity, but I really only like men who can handle their liquor.'

Lost for a comeback, purse-lipped Henry just watches as Franny and Lydia walk past him and into the lift.

Shinjuku!

From the commercial district centre with its glass and chrome architecture and holographic billboards, to its satellite love hotel and red-light districts, Craig's eyes devour the streets as they drive through them. Here it all is: the forests of illuminated signs in Kanji, Hiragana, Katakana; the ubiquitous vending machines standing wherever there is room for them, dispensing everything from soft drinks to soft porn—everything just as he imagined it would be.

Shinjuku: his new home.

And the home of Mami Rose, the girl of his dreams.

The taxi pulls up.

'Here we are, my fine fellows,' announces the driver. 'Nirvana. Shangri-La. The Promised Land. Your new apartment building.'

They emerge from the idling taxicab. Sunshine House looks just like any of the several other apartment buildings lining this street; a flat, unadorned facade, chessboarded with windows.

The cabbie has opened the boot, and Craig and Dudley take their luggage. Craig produces his credit card; the cabbie scans his fee.

'Bless you, my brethren,' he says. 'Your new lives await you. Make sure you both have yourselves a good time, now. Life is for living, right?'

And with this, the taxi departs. The retreating tail-lights seem like an extension of the driver's smile.

'I wonder if we'll see him again,' muses Dudley.

'If this was a book or a film,' answers Craig, 'every time we get in a taxi from now on, it'll be him.'

Towing their luggage, they enter the apartment building. They find themselves in an empty foyer. No reception desk. No smiling clerk. No potted plants. Just a couple of vending machines and a row of mailboxes. They espy a door with a sign over the lintel. The sign is written in characters undecipherable to Craig and Dudley.

Acting on the supposition that these characters translate into English as 'Manager's Office', Craig knocks on the door.

'Is this where we get our keys from?' asks Dudley.

'Well I'm hoping it is,' says Craig.

The door remains closed.

'Maybe there's no-one home,' suggests Dudley.

'Well there bloody well should be,' says Craig. 'We'll be buggered if we can't get into our own apartment.'

'Try knocking again.'

Craig is about to do this when the door opens. Craig sees no-one and wonders if the door has come ajar from his knocking on it. But then he looks down and he finds himself being studied impassively by an extremely small and extremely old Japanese woman. Audience laughter from a holoviz set issues from the room within.

'Ah, hello,' says Craig. 'Are you the manager?'

The woman does not answer. She continues to regard Craig expressionlessly.

'We're Craig Jenx and Dudley Moz,' proceeds Craig. 'We're the new tenants for room 16.'

No response.

'On the third floor...' adds Craig, vaguely hoping this might clarify things.

Still no response.

'Do you speak English?' he asks, slowly and precisely.

Not a flicker.

'I guess not,' decides Craig. 'Me no speakee Japanese,' slowly and precisely again. 'Only speakee *Inglese. Comprendez?*'

'You should have brought a translator,' speaks up Dudley.

'No, *you* should have brought a translator,' retorts Craig. To the woman: 'We need our keys. Keys.' He mimes turning a key in a lock. 'We need to get into our apartment. Apartment.' He points to the ceiling.

Without a word or a flicker of a change in her expression, the woman closes the door in Craig's face.

'Hey, wait a minute!' protests Craig.

He hammers on the door.

'Come back, you daft old bat! We need our keys! Keys! KEYS!'

'I don't think just saying "keys" over and over is going to make much difference,' advises Dudley. 'Not if she doesn't speak English.'

'Well she ought to speak bloody English' protests Craig. 'She's the building manager; not everyone she meets is going to be Japanese, are they?'

'Maybe she's not the building manager,' suggests Dudley. 'You only assumed she was. Maybe she's just another tenant.'

Craig points to the lintel. 'A tenant wouldn't have a sign over their door, would they?'

'It might just be one of those joke signs,' says Dudley. 'You know, like "Wit's End" or something.'

'People only put those things outside houses, not apartments,' returns Craig.

'Well, what are we going to do?' asks Dudley.

'I suppose we'll have to try and speak to someone else who lives here,' says Craig. 'Get them to act as interpreter. If not…'

'What about your friend that lives here?'

'Oh yeah, Vern! I told him we'd be here today.'

'Then let's go'n see him. What number is he?'

'I don't know what number he is, do I? I always spoke to him online. I know his email address, but I don't know his bloody apartment number!'

'Then just email him. Let him know we're here.'

'Yeah… Trouble is, he doesn't always check his mail. We could be waiting till tomorrow for him to get back to us.'

The old woman's door opens again and the old woman wordlessly holds out two electronic keys.

Craig takes the keys. They both bear the number 16.

Again without a word, the old woman shuts the door.

To be sharing a room with Fragrance Pie! And for a whole week!

Of course, technically, there's no reason at all for them to be sharing a room. The Excelsior is a large hotel, and in spite of all the conference guests, there would have been more than enough vacancies for herself and Miss Fragrance to occupy separate suites. But Lydia just couldn't resist the chance. She wants to make the most of this opportunity of having her adored client all to herself for a week! She wants to be there to see Miss Fragrance when she sits up in bed each morning, adorably tousled and sleepy, myopically groping for her glasses on the bedside table... She wants to be there to see Miss Fragrance each time she emerges from the bathroom, fresh and glowing from her ablutions...

Opportunities like this don't come along every day. Lydia is determined to make the most of this one.

A fool proof plan, this booking of a single suite, but for one potential problem: Miss Fragrance is a remarkably sagacious and perceptive lady: will she smell a rat?

'Oh. So we're sharing a room, are we?' says Franny.

You see? So perceptive! The moment she opens the bedroom door of their suite, and sees the two beds, she instantly divines that they cannot both be there for her own personal use!

'Indeed we are, Miss Fragrance,' confirms Lydia, deciding on a nonchalant attitude. 'I hope this will not be too inconvenient?'

'Well no, not at all,' replies Franny. 'I just thought that in a hotel this size you could have got us a two-bedroom suite, or even separate rooms.'

'And I would have done just that, Miss Fragrance,' Lydia assures her. 'But alas, when I came to make the booking, all the single rooms and two-bedroom suites had already been taken.'

'All of them?' Franny, incredulous. 'But this hotel's massive!'

'So it is, Miss Fragrance,' agrees Lydia. 'But the turnout for the conference is high this year. And in addition to that there are other guests unrelated to the conference staying here...'

'Yes, I see,' says Franny. (Yes! She's bought it!) She smiles brightly at Lydia. 'Well as long as you don't snore, I'm sure we'll get along just fine.'

'Oh, I can assure you, Miss Fragrance, that I do not snore!' Lydia hastens to assure her. 'Not a single stertorous breath will issue from my lips—'

'I was joking, Lydia,' Franny tells her, smiling.

'Of course you were!' Lydia laughs merrily. 'Your lively sense of humour is one of your trademarks, Miss Fragrance!'

At this juncture, Lydia's phone buzzes.

'Excuse me, Miss Fragrance!'

She takes her phone, looks at the screen. Lance Buzklik! What does Lance Buzklik want? How dare Lance Buzklik call her up here! Didn't she leave word at the office that she would be incommunicado to all her other clients for the duration of the convention?

'If you will excuse me, Miss Fragrance, I must take this call,' apologises Lydia. 'I will only be one minute.'

'Take as long as you like,' says Franny. 'You're my agent, Lydia, not my personal attendant.'

'Thank you for your generosity, Miss Fragrance. You are as understanding as always.'

Lydia leaves the bedroom, and, carefully closing the door behind her, crosses the spacious living room to its furthest extremity. Here, she answers the call.

'And what the fuck do you want you little piece of shit?'

'What?' comes an incredulous voice.

'Yes, it's you I'm talking to, Buzklik. There's no-one else on the line, is there?'

'You can talk to me like that!' aghast.

'Oh, yes I can, Buttlick. Especially when I left word at my office that I was *not* to be disturbed while I'm away at this convention. You were told that, weren't you? Yes, you were. But you just thought that you could ring me anyway, didn't you? You just thought, with your laughable delusions of adequacy, that the embargo my assistant informed you of somehow didn't apply to yourself, didn't you? You just thought that you were some glorious exception to the rule, didn't you? Well let me tell you something Buckshit: you are not exempt; in fact I issued that ban on calls especially with you in mind.'

'But this is important!' protesting.

'I don't care how fucking important it is. You can wait till I'm back in my office.'

'But you're supposed to be my agent!'

'Yes, and you're supposed to be a writer. But you're not a very good one, are you? Only one novel published, and that one only because I edited some sense into it. Well, I haven't got time to write all your books for you, so if you're struggling, get yourself a fucking ghost-writer, and then maybe I can get you published. Now don't fucking call me again.'

Lydia terminates the call.

Franny appears in the bedroom doorway.

'Everything alright?'

Lydia turns to her, grinning broadly.

'Everything is wonderful, Miss Fragrance! Nothing to concern yourself with! Just some silly client of mine wanting some advice about his next book…'

Lance Enders props up the bar of the Excelsior, nursing his sixth (or is it seventh? Damned if he can remember!) bourbon on the rocks.

'If only I hadn't gone to Shinjuku that night…' he slurs, addressing the silent barman. 'No. What am I sayin'…? Changed my life, that night did. No, I don't regret it… 'Cept of course my work life would be a helluva lot less complexica- complex- complicated if I hadn't a been there…Yeah, I know what you're thinkin': "Smart-looking guy in a smart-looking suit; he musta been slummin' it." Right? No. No sirree. It was business. Although I guess maybe you could say I was slummin' it on business. I had to meet this guy, y'see. An' we needed somewhere nice an' private to talk. Now, this guy, *he* liked slummin' it. He liked the Shinjuku prostitutes. Said the Asian whores y'get here in Central weren't the same thing. I dunno; artificial or somethin'. So I meet this guy at his favourite Japanese cat-house in Shinjuku. Place was like a Geisha House, 'cept the ladies did a lot more than Geishas do; cuz Geishas don't go all the way. Did you know that…? You did.

'Anyway, my meeting with this guy turned into a big argument. Doesn't matter what it was about; in fact I can't even tell you what it was about. I'd have to kill you if I did. So anyway, I walked out on this guy. I walked out and I walked off and cuz I didn't know the damned district, I got myself well and truly lost. I mean it was no big deal; I was just walkin' to work off steam, an' I had my phone, so I could call me a taxi whenever I wanted. Anyway, I decided I needed a drink. Next bar I come to I'd call in and get me one of these—Say, this glass is empty! Pour me another one, barkeep.

'So, I come to a place. I could hear music comin' from inside. Muffled, but you could tell it was a live band playin', not just music piped through the speakers. I went in an' the bar was almost empty. The music was comin' from a back room, an' most people were in there watchin' the band. First I thought I'd just sit myself in that nice quiet bar and have me a nice quiet drink, but then—an' I still don't know what it was—somethin' made me decide to mosey on in to that back room and have a look at the band. So in I went, paid the few lousy bucks that was the door-fee, an' I joined the crowd. It was a rock band, an' the band were all girls, cuz this was Shinjuku...

'An' then... Well, an' then it just zapped me. Like a revelation or somethin'. It was like I'd never heard real music before. Well I guess I hadn't. I mean you know the kinda music that gets into the download charts: that synthetic shrinkwrapped stuff. But this, this was the real thing. An' the fact that it was being played by girls... Yeah I know there's some who'll say it shouldn't make no difference what sex the musicians are; but it does: it makes a helluva difference. The crowd, they were all guys; every one of 'em. Not a girl in sight except the ones on the stage. They were Shinjuku guys o' course. Slackers 'n oddballs, white 'n yeller, all wearin' jeans and check shirts. An' then there was me, the guy in the designer threads, an' I was mesmerised just like the rest of 'em.

'It was like a revelation. Yeah, I know what you're thinkin': "What a corny line!" Right? Yeah, I know it's a corny line, but there's no other way to describe it. Those girls... The band was Tokyo Rose, y'see... Y'don't know 'em? They're one of the biggest in the Shinjuku scene; been around a long time. An' there they were, up on stage, lookin' all cute an' all, but they were makin' a really big noise with those guitars, an' those drums. An' I just felt like I was looking at the Meaning of Life or somethin'; like there were all the answers, up there on that stage, in those girls, in that music: the duality of human nature; instinct versus intellect; the problem of good, the nature of evil; the yin and the yang... It was just all there, my friend. The whole goddamn shebang. That's how it felt—even though most of their songs seemed to be about food.

'But it was the drummer who mesmerised me the most. I mean they were all beautiful ladies, but you can't help summing 'em up, deciding which one you like the best. Itsumi, her name is. She's one helluva drummer. She was so cute, so fulla life. Me, I'd never really looked at Asian girls before, but I was sure lookin' at this one now…!

'Yep, so that's how it all started. That's how I became a J-fan, like all those Shinjuku guys. At first I thought they wouldn't even accept me: a swanky guy from Central, workin' for a high-profile PR company, livin' in a condo… But no, they were cool about it. So were the girls from the bands. An' as for Itsumi: well, we really hit it off. We were just… nah, I won't say "made for each other." The corniest line in the book, right? But… I dunno. We just clicked, y'know?

'An' that's what's landed me in the mess I'm in right now. Y'see, I already have a ladyfriend here in Central. Not only that, but she works for the same company as me. Her name's Natalie. You've probably seen her around. We're all here, organising this dumb convention. She's about so high, dark brown hair, usually wears this red skirt-suit. Really classy dame, she's got this "don't gimme any bullshit" look about her. An' that's just how she is: a real go-getter. We've been together about six years, now. An' thank Christ we never decided to move in together! Things would be a lot more complicated now if that'd happened…

'An' what's up with you, buddy? Yer head's movin' around an' your face is all twitchin'… You epileptic, or somethin'? Not that it's any o' my business… But yeah, Itsumi knows about Natalie, but Natalie doesn't know about Itsumi. So, I've been havin' to juggle my private life of late, if you know what I mean. Cuz boy, if Natalie ever found out I was seein' another girl, she'd go ballistic! She can be one major bitch-queen, I tell yer. Yep, she'd rip my balls off—'

He looks at the bar-tender with sudden comprehension. 'And she's standin' right behind me, ain't she? That's what you been tryin' to tell me, ain't it?'

The bar-tender nods his head in solemn confirmation.

Lance swings round on his chair. His blurry eyes focus on Natalie, taking in the deep crease-line between scowling eyebrows, the compressed painted lips...

'Hiya, Nat...' he says weakly.

'So her name's Itsumi, is it?' says Natalie. 'I knew there had to be someone, you sneaking rat. I'm not stupid.'

'Honey...'

'And don't you dare say "I can explain", Lance Enders.'

The very words that are perched on the tip of Lance's tongue. He swallows them with a gulp.

The girl in the white dress seems to appear from nowhere.

Suddenly she is just *there*, standing in the open doorway of the apartment. Craig looks at the girl. The girl looks back at Craig, unspeaking.

She's not Craig's type, this girl. For a start she is obviously not Japanese. Her long hair is blonde, her eyes a pale blue. Once a white man like Craig has allowed himself to become fixated on Japanese women, all non-Oriental women start to look a bit plain by comparison; unappetising; unattractive. And this girl, in Craig's estimation, looks very plain. Her pale face is expressionless, her figure stringy.

The only enigma about this girl is her sudden presence.

'Can I help you?' inquires Craig.

'No,' says the girl. 'What about you?'

'What about me what?'

'Do you need any help?'

'Oh! With the moving in, you mean? Well, thanks for the offer, but we're okay. Place is already furnished and neither of us have brought that much stuff. Not much moving in to do, really.'

'Oh,' says the girl.

Her voice, although quite low, is as expressionless as her face.

'Dud,' calls out Craig. 'We've got a visitor.'

Dudley sticks his head out of his bedroom, sees the girl. They exchange expressionless looks. Dudley then turns to Craig, hoping for guidance. Dudley is unused to dealing with girls.

'Our mew neighbour,' announces Craig. 'Say hello.'

'Hello,' says Dudley.

'I'm Craig, this is Dudley,' proceeds Craig. 'What's your name?'

'Stacey,' says the girl.

'Nice to meet you,' says Craig. 'We've only just got here, so you're the first neighbour we've met. I mean, I assume you're a neighbour? You live in this place, yeah?'

'Yes, I live downstairs,' confirms Stacey. 'You're the J-fans from Gameron, aren't you?'

Craig is surprised. 'Yes. How did you know that?'

'I know Vern. He lives downstairs as well.'

'Oh, you know Vern? Is he in? I'd like to say hello.'

'Yes, he's in,' answers Stacey. 'He might be out, though.'

'So he's either in or he's not in,' summarises Craig. 'Well, we'll go down and see for ourselves after we're all set up. What's his number?'

'Ten.'

'I've got a problem with my suitcase,' says Dudley to Craig.

'What sort of a problem?' asks Craig.

'It won't open,' says Dudley.

'It *will* open,' Craig tells him. 'You're probably just doing something wrong.'

'Well, can you help me with it?'

Craig sighs. Clearly Dudley, out of the family nest for the first time, still expects to have every little problem sorted out for him.

'Alright. Look—' He turns to address Stacey, but the doorway is now empty. The girl has gone.

'Oh. Just a flying visit, was it?' murmurs Craig. To Dudley: 'Weird girl, wasn't she?'

'A bit,' agrees Dudley

Craig follows Dudley into his room.

The apartment has sprung no surprises upon its new tenants. Both of them have seen holographs of the place, and they have arrived to find it identical to those images in every respect. Opening the front door, you find yourself in a long, narrow corridor, with two doors on either side. The doors on the right give access to first the small bathroom and then the small kitchen; the doors on the left are those belonging to the two small bedrooms. The end of the corridor brings you out into the relatively spacious living area.

Craig has appropriated to himself the first bedroom, the one adjacent to the outer corridor; his belief being that Dudley will feel safer inhabiting the inner bedroom, with Craig a buffer between himself and the outside world.

The suitcase having been successfully opened, Craig is in the kitchen boiling a kettle of water for a cup of tea when he hears a knock on the still open front door.

'Hello?' calls a new voice.

Craig steps out to find a man in his thirties standing in the doorway, and recognises him as Vern, his internet contact.

'Hello!' he says. 'Vern, right?'

'That's me. And you're Craig. Stacey just told me you'd arrived.'

'Yeah, she popped in a minute ago.'

A smile spreads over Vern's face. 'He fooled you, did he? Yeah, he usually does with people who don't know him.'

'"He"?' echoes Craig. 'You mean that girl was a bloke?'

'Was and is.'

Craig smiles. 'Yeah, he fooled us. So he's a tranny, is he?'

'Yeah, but not full time,' answers Vern. 'He's not always cross-dressed. Just when he feels like it.'

'And was the hair a wig?'

'Oh yeah. His real hair's short. Dark as well.'

'And what's his name when he's not in drag?'

'It's still Stacey. Stacey's a boy's name as well as a girl's. It's what d'you call it...? Bisexual? Unisexual?'

'I think it's unisexual. Hang on a minute. If he's a friend of yours, does that mean he's a J-fan?'

'Oh yeah, he's one of us.'

'Likes girls so much he wants to be one, does he? Least he doesn't try to look like a Jap girl; that'd be sacrilege or something!'

Vern joins them for tea. As they chat (with Dudley for the most part being a silent and occasionally thumb-sucking auditor), Craig assesses his new friend. Not with regards to appearance so much; Craig is not overly concerned about the looks of potential rivals; his experience tells him that women aren't nearly as bothered about a guy's looks as guys are about a girl's. Craig's assessment of male acquaintances has always been an assessment of their personality, their social skills. In terms of charm and conversation, Craig's own social skills are erratic at best; he has his good days and his bad days. Thus, he always finds himself assessing any guy he meets in terms of whether his social skills are more or less finely-honed than his own. In the case of Vern, he decides that he doesn't have much to feel inadequate about. Vern can keep a conversation going, but he's no sparkling raconteur, no great comedian.

Craig is glad about this; he feels sure he can become good friends with Vern!

Chapter Three
French Toast Rendezvous

'Oh! That me!'

Mami Rose is impressed to see the large poster of herself adorning Craig's bedroom wall; a photo of her on stage with the lights making a halo of her hair; it has become one of the most popular images of her amongst her following.

'Well I wouldn't have anyone else's picture on my wall, would I?' answers Craig, smiling his most dashing smile.

Mami, the real Mami, dressed in the same cute pale-blue jumpsuit she is wearing in the picture, throws her arms around Craig, and looks into his face with adoring eyes.

'No...' she says. 'You love only me!'

Their lips join in a prolonged kiss. When they part, Mami's eyes are filled with that look of sweet surrender.

'Just take me,' she begs. 'Do whatever you want with me...'

Craig looks at her.

'Get undressed, Mami,' is his command, gentle but firm.

Obediently, Mami unbuttons her jumpsuit, pulls it down from her shoulders, down past her hips... She is not wearing any underwear. Now she steps out of the jumpsuit and she stands before him in all the glory of her voluptuous body. Craig drinks in the sight of those ripe curves, the small, apple breasts, the dense thatch of pubic hair.

She looks at Craig, a hesitant smile on her face.

'You're beautiful...' Craig tells her.

He arranges her facedown on the bed. Tears form in his eyes as he admires for the first time the magnificent hemispheres of her buttocks. He has never seen them in the flesh before, but he has dreamed about them; those buttocks you could lose yourself between.

Genius songwriter and musician, peerless vocalist and live performer—and the best arse in the universe.

Reverently, Criag moves in to kiss the soft flesh, to inhale the delicious odour of Mami Rose. Long has he dreamed of this moment. For him this is an epiphany. This is his holy grail. He kisses and he kisses...

...And Mami goes and farts in his face.

'Sorry!' she sings out.

Oh, Mami!

'Oh, you're sorry, are you?' says Craig, with mock severity.

'It just come out,' says Mami, wriggling her bottom. 'Couldn't hold in.'

'Well I'm afraid you're going to have to be punished for that,' Craig tells her.

'Oh, no! Please not punish!' pleads Mami, wriggling some more.

Open-palmed, Craig fetches her a slap across the buttocks.

Mami yelps out with surprise.

'Oh no! Please!'

Craig slaps her again. And again. He keeps on spanking her until she is laughing, crying, pleading for him to stop.

Finally he desists. Both of them are now thoroughly aroused. Craig kneels on the bed behind her, and guides himself between her legs, penetrating deep inside her.

Mami moans with pleasure.

Craig commences thrusting into her... At first slowly, and then faster and faster... Mami's groans of pleasure grow louder and louder...

...And then Craig, the masturbator, lying on his solitary bed, discharges.

(Come on! You didn't actually think all that was really happening, did you?)

Kenichi just had to get out of his apartment. The walls were closing in on him. Easy enough to happen in a pokey five-mat apartment like his. It's early, just past dawn, the holographic sun still rising above the rooftops. It's also quiet; not much traffic this early in the day. Not many people, either. Kenichi prefers it this way. The more people around, the more eyes there are to look at you, to judge you, to laugh at you and hold you in contempt.

It's to avoid those eyes that he has been holed-up in his apartment for so long. But as always happens, sooner or later he starts to feel trapped, boxed in; he starts to crave fresh air and freedom over safety; so here he is, aimlessly walking the early-morning streets.

Right now, casting his eyes across the street, he sees his friend Shinji emerge from the front entrance of an apartment building.

What the fuck? Shinji doesn't live in that building—Wait a minute! That's where Asuna lives! Yeah, Asuna from Raw Babes in the Country: her apartment's in that place! What the fuck?

If anyone had been looking, they would have seen the storm clouds gather over Kenichi's face. Locking his sites on Shinji, he stalks across the road. Shinji, blissfully unaware of the fury closing in on him, saunters along the pavement.

Kenichi grabs him by the shoulder and spins him round.

'Whaddaya think you're doing?' he demands.

'Hey, Kenichi!' says Shinji, smiling.

The two young men are similar in appearance, both skinny and weak-chinned. Kenichi is slightly shorter in height, and his mouth, too wide and drawn down at the corners, makes him the more ugly of the two.

'Don't "Hey, Kenichi!" me, jerkwad!' retorts Kenichi. 'I saw you, y'know! Don't think I didn't see, cuz I fucking did.'

'Saw what, man?' asks Shinji, confused.

'*You*, dumbass,' is the reply. 'You just now, coming out of Asuna's apartment building. I was right across the street: I saw you. So don't try and deny it!'

'I'm not denying it, man,' even more confused.

'So you admit it!' crows Kenichi. 'You admit you were with Asuna last night?'

'I dunno about "with her," man,' says Shinji. 'I just crashed on her sofa, is all.'

'You expect me to believe that? You expect to believe that you went round Asuna's place last night, and all you did was sleep on her sofa?'

'Well, yeah…'

'I wasn't born yesterday!'

'I know that, we're the same age—'

'Don't get smart with me!'

'I wasn't being smart, man.'

'So, you're saying that nothing happened? You didn't fuck her?'

'Fuck her? Jeez, man! I dunno if I could've even if she'd wanted me to. I was like, completely wrecked, y'know.'

'Completely wrecked, huh?'

'Yeah, man. I'd been to a few pubs, lookin' for someone to hang out with. I kind of turned up at Asuna's. Machiko was there. I sat down on the sofa, an' I guess I must've passed out, cuz the next thing I know I'm lying there with a duvet over me an' it's morning.'

'And then what? Did you walk into Asuna's room with the hard-on you woke up with? Give her a personal wake-up call?'

'No, man! I couldn't just walk in there like that! You don't do that to a lady. No, I just took the painkillers and drank the glass of water she'd left out for me, and then I went to the bathroom for a piss and I was out of there. Asuna and her kid weren't even up.'

'Is that so…?' reluctantly mollified.

'Yeah, man,' confirms Shinji. 'An' why are you like so uptight about it, anyway? I mean, Asuna's not your girl; you don't even have the hots for her, far as I know. I mean, yeah, we all like all of 'em, don't we? But you don't have a thing for Asuna especially, do you…?'

'No, I don't…' concedes Kenichi.

The simple truth is, Kenichi's interrogation of Shinji has been fuelled partly by sexual jealousy, the idea that his friend has been getting some when he, Kenichi, hasn't been; but most of all by his inherent paranoia.

Kenichi is paranoid. Chronically. He knows it. His friends know it. But there's nothing anyone can do about it. Medical science has still yet to find a drug that can comprehensively cure paranoia.

His constant delusions of being deceived, despised and discussed by his friends help to make Kenichi's existence a misery for himself. He would do anything to be able to change the irrational way in which his brain works.

And he can also make life very difficult for his friends, with his constant accusations and suspicions, his over-reaction to the slightest criticism, real or imagined. His behaviour has lost him all the friends of his youth. And his attempts to make new friends have always ended in failure, his endeavours sabotaged by his own mental condition. It is only since he has stumbled on the Shinjuku girl band scene that he has found a group of people who will actually put up with him. Both his fellow J-fans and the girls in the bands have welcomed him, a fact for which Kenichi, in his rational moments, is insanely grateful. And he has bonded with the alcoholic Shinji, seeing in him a fellow-sufferer, albeit with different symptoms.

'You're still crushing on Itsumi, right?' queries Shinji.

Kenichi's drooping mouth droops further. 'Nah. I fell out with her…'

'Man, you're always falling out with people!' exclaims Shinji. ''Cept, half the time, it's only you who thinks you've fallen out. The other guy's usually cool about it. What's it about this time?'

'Oh, she said something to me online, and then I said something to her… You know how it is…'

'Sure, I know. I bet Itsumi doesn't even think you two have fallen out at all, man. I bet it's just you.' He pauses, hesitates over what he wants to say. 'Still, you might wanna think of switching your sights onto someone else. I mean, Itsumi's pretty tight with Lance right now.'

'I know that,' mutters Kenichi.

'They've been steppin' out quite a while now.'

'I know that,' growls Kenichi.

'An' that dude's got money. Lives in Central, has a high-salary job, lives in a condo…'

'I know that!' shouts Kenichi.

'Just checkin,' man, just checkin,'' says Shinji. 'Y'know, I need me some hangover food. What say we go'n find some place that's open and get us some breakfast?'

'Sure... Why not?'

They set off.

Krevis Jungle is so called for a very good reason: She has a dense growth of hair extending between the cleft of her buttocks; a bum fringe, to use the colloquial term. Craig—and anyone else who's interested—knows this for a fact because the members of the Smut Girls sometimes post porny pictures of themselves on their website. This fact sometimes pisses off Craig. Not because he has any prudish aversion to nude photography; but because his favourite band, Tokyo Rose, don't do the same thing... Of course, he understands that Mami and her bandmates just aren't that type who would go in for doing porny pictures; that some girls are up for displaying themselves like that, some girls aren't...

But still... Craig's just a bit jealous of Dudley for being lucky enough to know what his girl band crush looks like butt-naked, while he, Craig, is deprived of that same important knowledge.

But then, Craig has his sanguine plans to rectify this situation in the very near future; he hopes to become intimately acquainted with how Mami Rose looks in her birthday suit; hopes that those bedroom fantasies of Mami offering herself up to him will soon be transformed into carnal realities.

Dudley has already affixed a large poster of his beloved Krevis Jungle to the bedroom wall, as Craig sees when he enters the room. Not one of the nudie shots; Dud's not one to put anything like that on his wall. (In fact, muses Craig, the only kind of guy likely to adorn his bedroom walls with porny pictures is going to be a guy who has given up all hope of ever entertaining an actual living breathing woman in said bedroom.) The image on the poster is still a provocative one. Krevis, with her trademark moody pout, wears thigh-boots and bondage gear; the general effect is that of a dominatrix who would be more than capable of dealing with an uncooperative client.

Dudley sits on his bed, pulling on his socks.

'What do you want for breakfast?' asks Craig. 'We've got nothing, nothing, and nothing.'

'Nothing?'

'Absolutely bugger all,' confirms Craig cheerfully, as one imparting good news. 'Except the instant tea and coffee we brought with us. So you can have your caffeine fix, but if you want some grub, we'll have to go out and find it.'

'Okay,' says Dudley. 'We can find a supermarket, can't we? There must be one nearby.'

'Well, yeah. But I was thinking that today we could just find a café or something to have breakfast, and after that we can do the grocery shopping. This is our new neighbourhood. We ought to start checking out the local eateries.'

'Sure.'

The bush. The muff. The fig-leaf.

That's what it comes down to, muses Craig. If you're madly in love with a girl (and for that matter, even if you're not), and you've never seen her naked, you always wonder about what kind of bush she's going to have. Is she going to be well-thatched or lightly-spruced? Is it going to cover a wide or fairly small area? Does she have a full, natural growth, or does she prune and shape it? Depending on the girl's race, you might speculate as to the colour of the thatch…

Personally, Craig has always preferred a dense and widespread bush on a woman, so naturally his fantasies of Mami Rose always depict her thus adorned. As to whether that hair will continue across the perineum and along the buttock crevice, as with Dudley's inamorata, Craig doesn't really mind. He's never really had a thing for bum fringes, and if he discovers that Mami comes equipped with one: fine, he will soon learn to revere them; if not: also fine.

But what if Mami turns out only to have a light sprinkling of pubic hair? Or even none at all? Will he be able to cope with the disappointment?

Craig and Dudley step out of Sunshine House and into the artificial daylight. The synthetic air is fresh (all pollution being rapidly expunged) and the temperature is at its regulated norm.

'Our first morning in Shinjuku,' says Craig, as they stand and survey the view.

Traffic is fairly light, but there are plenty of pedestrians. And they are all Japanese. This racial uniformity seems strange to both the young men, accustomed as they have been to the much more heterogeneous population of Gameron City.

Craig notes the spot across the street where he thinks he saw that Lolita girl and her guardian the night before. He hasn't told Dudley about this incident as yet. Could it really have been them? But why would they be watching the apartment? Perhaps he had only imagined that. Perhaps it wasn't even those two at all. He'd been going by nothing more than relative stature and a pair of twin-tails.

'Which way do we go?' asks Dudley.

'I know no more than you on that subject, Dudley,' answers Craig. 'But my understanding has always been that just about everywhere in Shinjuku is well-supplied with eateries, so whichever way we go, I'm sure it won't be long before we find somewhere to supply us with breakfast.'

They set off.

At the next corner they find themselves on a shopping street. A lot of the shops are electrical stores. This part of downtown Shinjuku abounds with electrical stores; it's renowned for them. Likewise, you will also find areas of town specialising in second-hand book shops, in clothes shops, in otaku culture, etc, etc.

'That reminds me,' says Craig, noting these electrical stores. 'After we've got some grub in, we'll need to go shopping for a record player.'

The Shinjuku music scene is a vinyl music scene. The girl bands release all their albums, singles and maxi-singles on good old-fashioned analogue. Coincidentally, the electrical stores around here all specialise in retro-electrical goods; all the most obscure media playback devices, games consoles, cyberspace terminals, and all the parts you'll need to maintain them can be found in these shops.

Before them now is a diner, a plate-glass frontage revealing the rows of tables within, most of them unoccupied.

'This'll be our local eatery, then,' observes Craig. 'Unless there's one closer to the apartment in the other direction. Come on: let's see what the grub's like.'

They step inside. An arm waves from across the room. It's Vern, their neighbour from last night. Seated next to him is a thin, pale young man.

'Here for your breakfast, are you?' asks Vern, when Craig and Vern join them. Craig confirms that this is the case. 'Sit yourselves down.'

Craig and Dudley seat themselves facing Vern and the pale young man.

'Who's your friend?' asks Craig.

Vern laughs. 'Don't you recognise him? You only saw him last night!'

Craig looks again at the youth, and realisation dawns. 'Oh yeah, you're Stacey, aren't you? Without the wig and the dress.'

'Hello,' says Stacey.

Craig calls up the holographic menu. He slides it across to Dudley. 'Pick what you want.' To Vern: 'You seem very cheerful, my man. Are you one of those "first thing in the morning" people?'

'Uh-uh, it's not that. I'm just cheerful because I've got something to be cheerful about.'

'You won the Galactic Lottery or something?'

'Pretty much. I've got myself a date with Machiko.'

'What, as in Machiko the bassist from Raw Babes in the Country?'

'There's no other Machiko around here,' affirms Vern.

'Actually, there are probably lots of them,' advises Stacey.

'Okay, there are probably lots, but there's only one *I'm* interested in, and she's the one I've got a date with!'

He claps his hands with glee.

'Nice work,' says Craig. 'So you've obtained yourself a date with the Unobtainable One. How'd you manage that?'

'I just asked her. Simple as that.'

'You've been asking her for months,' Stacey reminds him.

'Well, yes I have, but this time she's said yes.'

'Perseverance pays off,' notes Craig. 'And you just found out this morning?'

'Yep. Email was waiting for me when I got up.'

'Nice one. And what sort of "date" is this going to be. The teenage sort? Meet in front of the station; look round the shops;

lunch in a fast-food place; maybe take in a film; that sort of thing?'

'No, it's an evening date. Just a "meeting up in a pub" date.'

Craig takes out his phone. 'Myself and Dud here are both hoping for life-improving emails like the one you've just got,' he says. 'Dud's announced his arrival to—Hello! New message!'

A religious silence falls over the company as Craig eagerly reads his mail.

'Well?' prompts Vern.

A heavenly radiance spreads itself across Craig's face. Somewhere, an angel quire sings. Controlling his voice, he calmly announces: 'You're not the only one with a hot date for tonight.'

Dudley looks at him.

'Mami Rose?' he asks.

'Mami Rose,' confirms Craig.

And if he had been a cartoon character Craig would have ricocheted around the room like a champagne cork.

Chapter Four
Sex on the Beach

Dancing the pavement two-step.

Craig sighs. He moves to the left. So does the person in his path. He moves to the right. His antagonist does the same. Just like his encounter with that woman on the spaceliner.

And then he looks at her face.

It *is* the woman from the spaceliner! That author woman! What's her name again? Fragrance Pie!

Recognition is mutual.

'You!' she exclaims.

'What is it, Miss Fragrance?' A tall woman, with a look of the boardroom about her, stands by the author's side.

'It's that man I told you about,' Franny tells her. 'That J-fan on the spaceliner!'

Windowed eyes narrow. 'The man who assaulted you?'

'Do what?' protests Craig.

'Molestation at the very least,' declares the woman.

'Now, Lydia,' cautions Franny. 'I wouldn't call it molestation.'

'But he dared to lay his hands on you, Miss Fragrance!' insists Miss Luvstruk.

Night has been instituted but the street in which they stand is bright with a medley of artificial light.

'I only picked her up so that we could get past each other!' he says. 'Otherwise we'd have been dancing the two-step all day!'

'I was right!' says Franny, suddenly smiling. 'I was right! He *is* one of those J-fans! The fact that he's right here in Shinjuku proves it! You're a J-fan, aren't you?'

'Yes, I am,' firmly. 'And I'm now a resident of Shinjuku. More to the point, what are you doing here? I assumed you'd come to Daedalus Station for that book festival.'

'Literary Festival,' Lydia corrects him.

'Whatever. So, what are you doing here? You're a long way from Central.'

'I'm here researching my next book,' Franny tells him.

Craig looks unimpressed. 'How exciting. And what's this magnum opus gunna be about?'

'You!'

'Me?' alarmed. 'You can't just go'n write a book about me! Not without getting my permission! And you *won't* be getting my permission, because I don't want to be in your stupid book! Find someone else to libel!'

'I don't mean *you* you,' explains Franny. 'I mean *you*. You Shinjuku J-fans. That's what my book's going to be about.'

'Really?' says Craig. 'Well, knock yourself out. Assassinate our characters as much as you want. I'd love to stay and help you with your research, but unfortunately I'm on my way to an urgent appointment, so if you don't mind, I'll bid you and your lawyer a fond *adieu*.'

'I'm a literary agent, not a lawyer.'

'Really? Fascinating.'

Craig steps neatly round the two women and continues down the street.

He becomes aware of footsteps matching his own. He looks back. It's them! They're following him! The author has a determined look on her face.

'What the bloody hell do you still want?' demands Craig. 'I told you I've got somewheres to be. I am not available for interviews at this juncture. Kindly piss off.'

'You're going to a gig, aren't you?' accusingly. 'One of those girl band live shows? Then I shall tag along. I need to see one of these shows. It's for my research.'

'I'm not going to a gig,' growls Craig.

'Although I can guess in advance what it'll all be like,' proceeds Franny. 'You men with your eyes out on sticks drooling over those half-naked girls and their stone-age music.'

'I'm not going to a gig,' again.

'You men pretend to worship these girls as goddesses, but really you'd like to jump on stage and get inside their sweaty underwear, wouldn't you? That's what it's all about, isn't it?'

'I'm not going to a bloody gig!'

Franny stops in her tracks. 'Wait a minute. You're not going to a gig?'

'No. There aren't any gigs on tonight. I'm meeting someone for a drink.'

Craig doesn't elaborate as to just *who* he's meeting. Fragrance might consider a J-fan's meeting with his girl band idol to also be worthwhile research material.

'No gigs tonight?' says Franny, deflated.

'None. If that's what you came here to see, you should've checked the local listings before traipsing all the way out here.'

And with this, Craig turns his back once again on the two women and marches onwards.

Franny calls after him. 'You do know there's a world outside of your cosy little girl band scene, don't you?'

'Yes, I am aware of that fact!' Craig throws back at her.

'What about planet Deveron? Aren't you even worried about that? Have you even heard of planet Deveron?'

'Of course I've heard of planet bloody Deveron!'

Thankfully, Craig is passing beyond shouting-distance; the author and her agent are swallowed up by the evening crowd.

'Have I heard of planet Deveron?' ponders Craig. 'Deveron, Deveron... Oh yeah! Deveron! One of those rogue planets, isn't it? There was something about it in the news... Rumours of a military build-up or something… That Pie woman thinks us J-fans have our heads buried in the sand. Like we don't think about anything else except the girl bands… Of course I've heard of bloody Deveron. Actually, where *is* Devron? Is it in the same sector as Daedalus Station…?'

Craig can't remember.

Craig knows Machiko from Raw Babes in the Country, of course. That is to say he knows what she looks like; he has seen pictures of the girl, live footage of her performing with her band. Given this, it may seem strange that when, at that very moment, she walks right past him, he fails to recognise her.

But there are extenuating circumstances. For one thing it's after dark, and for another Craig is distracted at that precise moment, dredging up his scanty knowledge of planet Deveron.

Machiko is also on her way to a pub date. Two fateful encounters are to take place this evening: Craig's meeting with his idol Mami Rose, an event occurring not much more than twenty-four hours after his arrival on Daedalus Station; and Vern's date with Machiko, an event for which he has been angling for several months now.

Two J-fans meeting two girl band members for drinks at the pub. And no, not at the same pub; that would be stretching coincidence too far.

Machiko, in granting Vern this long sought-after date, feels that she has been pretty damn magnanimous. Throwing a bone to a lovestruck fan. As J-fans go, Vern is one of the more 'normal'; he exhibits no eccentric personality traits; he has no apparent psychological hang-ups; he has no drug or alcohol dependence. He's just a fairly average guy, averagely intelligent, averagely good-looking; no movie star but an affable and sociable young man. Many would describe men like Vern as 'boring', but it's a kind of boring that's fine with Machiko. *She's* the star. *He* doesn't need to be interesting.

Maybe it's not an entirely selfless act, this gesture of hers. If it turns out she gets on with the guy, if there's any kind of rapport that builds up between them, then yeah, maybe she'll agree to meet him again, and maybe they'll become an item.

But whatever happens, she is *not* going to let him climb between her legs. Not on the first date. If that's an old-fashioned attitude, then fine, she's old-fashioned. Of course she knows enough about men to know that *he'll* be hoping for the evening to end with them in bed together. Well, he'll just have to wait, won't he? Machiko does not like feeling pressured into doing anything; in fact, she detests it.

If Vern's feeling horny, he can just go home and relieve himself when he gets there, can't he?

That's what Machiko will be doing, as per usual; and if it's good enough for her it's good enough for him!

Sex on the Beach is a cocktail bar in upper downtown Shinjuku. A neon sign above the door announces the name in big pink letters. It's not surprising she has arranged to meet Craig at this place: Mami is notoriously fond of elaborate cocktails; she has written several songs on the subject.

Craig has already scoped the joint online, so he knows the layout of the place. He walks inside. The place is not too busy. Almost immediately he spots Mami. She is sitting alone in a booth. Her eyes meet his. Her face lights up! She smiles! She's recognised him! He wasn't sure if she would.

She gets up from her seat to greet Craig.

And then, confronted by this smiling vision, this Japanese goddess, Craig does something unexpected; something unexpected to himself as well as to Mami; something outside all of those previous fantasy scenarios of his first meeting Mami; something he didn't think he was capable of doing at all:

He faints!

Yes! Dizziness overwhelms him, his vision fades to black, and he feels himself falling…

…And then Mami's face swims into focus, a concerned expression written on its features. For a split-second Craig's memory is confusion; then he remembers. He realises he is lying on the floor of the cocktail bar, and Mami is kneeling over him.

He fainted! Talk about embarrassing!

'Sorry,' he says weakly.

'You are okay?' asks Mami in her deliciously sweet voice.

'Yeah... I just... I just...'

'You faint,' supplies Mami.

'Yeah, I guess I did,' confesses Craig. 'Kind of embarrassing really...'

'Don't be embarrass!' says Mami. 'You just happy to see me!'

'Well, it's one way to break the ice, I guess!'

Craig gets up from the floor and sits with Mami in the booth, and they are soon talking happily. They have clicked. Just as Craig has always anticipated, they have clicked straight away. There is that instant rapport between them, that communion of souls. There had been nothing false about their online connection; it had always been a genuine bond, not a wishful illusion, as so many computer relationships prove to be when translated into the real world.

They talk and they drink cocktails. Mami speaks in her quaint imperfect English. They smile into each other's faces while touching each other, bridging the gaps in verbal communication with the non-verbal kind. And then it's back to Mami's place and before you know it, she is facedown with her breath-taking big bottom in the air, presenting herself to her destined lover...

...And in case you haven't worked it out yet, this is another one of Craig's fantasies. The real Craig Jenx hasn't even got to Sex on the Beach yet; he has had to make an emergency stop at another drinking establishment in order to fortify himself with a double vodka and sparkling ginseng mixer.

And this because, with the eagerly-awaited, long fantasized-about encounter with his goddess now mere minutes away, Craig, out of the blue, has been struck with an attack of nerves!

Dudley Moz wouldn't believe this if he could have seen it. Dudley has always attributed to his friend all the confidence and ease in social situations which he lacks in himself. And for that matter Craig himself finds it hard to believe; an attack of nerves has never been something he has anticipated. He doesn't understand it. It's completely out of character!

Yet, here he is, sitting in a bar, in danger of being late to his fated appointment, and having to fortify his nerves with this double-helping of Dutch courage. And hence this new fantasy with the built-in fainting scenario.

For Christ's sake get a hold of yourself, Craig Jenx! This is your dream come true, you fucking idiot. Are you going to spite yourself by not even showing up?

What's the worst that can happen...?

No! Don't think about worst case scenarios, you fucking idiot! Not right now! Think positive! Just sail in there and assume that everything is going to go exactly the way you've always pictured it! Why shouldn't it? You're crazy about her and she's crazy about you, right?

I mean, she *must* be, mustn't she? What about that gif she once sent you with all the hearts rising up from the bashful-looking cartoon girl who looked like her? And what about that time she signed her email 'love Mami'? Yeah! She wouldn't have written that if she didn't mean it, would she? Yeah, maybe you've had loads of other messages from her that she hasn't signed 'love Mami', but the fact she wrote it even once means that she meant it, right? She's just a bit bashful, is all! Like the girl with the hearts in that gif.

She likes you! She must do! I mean, she wouldn't have arranged to meet up with you like this if she wasn't even a little bit in love with you, would she? And only the day after you first arrived here! You see? She couldn't wait, could she? She couldn't wait to actually meet you in person!

So, what have you got to be nervous about, stupid? You're the man, aren't you? She's the delicate Japanese flower! You can have her falling head over heels if you just go in there and be your usual charming self! And as for looks, you may not be a film star or an athlete, but you're not fat, bald or ugly, are you? And even if you were, girls like Mami are the last people to judge men by appearances! It's your personality she'll be interested in! So you've just got to go in there and be funny and entertaining and dashing! Yeah! Make her laugh and let her know how much you like her! That's what she'll be wanting from you!

Now, get your shit together, Craig Jenx! Accumulate it into a neat pile. Look at the time! You're going to be late at this rate! And you should never keep a lady waiting! Nothing can go wrong, so just get a move on and meet your destiny at Sex on the Beach!

With this resolve, Craig rises from his table and makes boldly for the exit.

He then performs a neat about-turn and heads back to the bar.

Maybe just one more vodka and ginseng, and *then* he'll be ready to meet his destiny…

Machiko's face is not what you might call a typically Japanese one: a long face, with a strong jaw, a nose almost Roman; and with its androgynous qualities enhanced by the short hair-cut, it could, at least at first glance, be mistaken for a Caucasian visage. Her complexion is as pale as any Northern European's, but the colour of her hair and her eyes, and the epicanthic fold of the lids of the latter indicate her Asian ethnicity.

Such is the face of Machiko, Raw Babes in the Country's 'unobtainable' bass-player, and the face with which Vern has fallen in love. (The face, along with the accompanying body and—we trust—the personality that goes with both.)

And that face is right in front of him right now! Here he is, sitting at a table one-on-one with the girl of his dreams. Perhaps because he has been on speaking terms with his idol for some time now, Vern hasn't been afflicted with the same attack of nerves which are delaying Craig from reaching *his* rendezvous. In fact, Vern was the first to arrive at the pub, determined as he was not to create a bad impression by turning up late.

'I know what you all say about me,' says Machiko

'What who says?'

'You. You J-fans.'

'What do we say about you?'

'You say I'm frigid, right? You say that just cuz none of you guys has ever got lucky with me, right?'

'Well, y'know, *some* of the guys might say that… *I* never thought that.'

'You didn't, huh?'

'Uh-uh. Not me.'

'And what did you think, Vern?'

'Well… I suppose I just thought that you're not into casual sex. That you're… That you're just waiting for the right man to come along.'

'The right man, huh? And… you think maybe *you* are that right

55

man...?' smiling.

'Well... I...' Nervous laugh.

'You would *like* to be that right man, wouldn't you?'

'Well, yeah... Sure I would...'

'And you think you're in with a chance?'

'Well... I'm *here*, aren't I?'

'Yes, you are here. The first J-fan I have ever agreed to go on a date with. But let's get one thing straight, right? Whatever your chances may be in the long run, you will not be getting intimate with me tonight. This evening doesn't end with you and me having sexual congress. Is that understood?'

'Loud and clear. You don't do sex on the first date. You like to get to know a guy first. I'm totally with you there. But... y'know...'

'What do I know?'

Well, I mean... This isn't like a blind date, is it? This isn't like two people meeting who've only talked online before... We already know each other pretty well; we've known each other for more than a year now...'

'Yeah, we're not total strangers. But this is still our first time alone together, and I just want to see how things work out, see how we get along... So we don't go all the way tonight. And that is non-negotiable. Understand? So don't waste this evening trying to get me to change my mind, okay? Let's just talk, okay?'

'Absolutely. Talking's fine with me. And I won't mention sex at all. Not once.'

'We can talk about sex all you want, Vern. I'm just saying don't try and talk me into bed. Not tonight.'

'Oh. Okay. So you don't mind talking about sex stuff?'

'No. Why should I? I have no hang-ups about sex. Look, I've already said I'm not frigid. And I've never been raped and I wasn't sexually abused when I was kid. That's another thing you guys wonder about, isn't it? These things get back to me, you know? But you're wrong: I've never had a bad experience; I have no trauma, no hang-ups. And it's not that I'm into girls, either. I'm just not in any major hurry to have sex with a guy is all.'

'So you've never... I mean, have you—'

'Yes, I'm a virgin. That's what you're asking, right? I've never had good sex; I've never had bad sex. I've never had sex with a male. I'm kind of conceited, you see. I think I am too good for any male.'

'I get that. You don't think much of guys, then?'

'No, it's not that. Not exactly. I just think my body's too good to be shared with just any horny guy who wants to ride me.'

'What... so you like your own body?'

'I love it. I just love to take myself to bed and make myself feel great. I don't need any male to assist me with that. I can turn myself on, I can send myself to heaven; I don't need any male to find that kind of satisfaction. I suppose I'm selfish. I like to keep my body to myself.'

She laughs.

'What is it?' says Vern.

'Your face, Vern! You look very surprised!'

'Well, I *am* surprised. I'm hearing about a side of you I'd never guessed about before. I didn't know you were so... sexed up.'

'Yes, I'm sexed up. Why shouldn't I be? I don't need to have been with a male to be sexed up.'

Machiko excuses herself to go to the toilet, leaving Vern with a lot to think about. He'd always imagined himself having to prompt Machiko into even *thinking* more about sex, to inspire in her some kind of sexual awakening... But now he finds out she's already *wide* awake!

We should be fair to Craig Jenx here. Not all of his fantasies involving Mami end up with her facedown on his bed, buttocks ascendant. Criag fantasises about sex because most people do, what with it being pretty much built-in. Even when it's not at the front of our minds it's at the back of our minds. (Multi-tasking women will be better than men at dealing with this sometimes-annoying problem.) So yes, of course he has those dreams of intimacy with Mami's hindquarters; but as much as that it's just being with his idol that Craig has fantasized about; meeting her, talking to her, developing a rapport with her, embracing each other so that they are cocooned in mutual love, shut off from the rest of the universe...

Craig has been without anything like that kind of

companionship for some time now. Up until a couple of years back, he had been in a stable relationship with a girl, a white girl back on Gameron. She was, like him, a fan of the local punk scene; he had met the girl at a gig, and it had started, as these things often start, as a drunken one-night stand. But then they had decided to become an item; they had similar outlooks on life and similar interests, and basically they got along... And things had gone swimmingly for about five years; but then deterioration had begun to set in; they had started to argue more often, to find fault with each other, and sex between them had become perfunctory and unsatisfying... And then, by mutual consent, they had finally decided to call it a day.

Even though breaking with her had seemed the right thing to do at the time, Craig had felt the loss. Her presence in his life had obviously been beneficial to him, and without her, he had felt aimless and unmotivated... It was then that he had discovered the Shinjuku Girl Band scene, and as people often take up a new hobby to compensate for the end of a relationship, Craig had leapt into this new music scene with avidity. From the get-go Tokyo Rose had been his favourite band, and from the start he had found Mami to be the most attractive member of that band. He hadn't fallen in love with her instantly; the infatuation had sort of crept up on him, and then before he knew it, she had become the only girl for him. Although she lived light-years away and he had never actually met her, he had found himself pinning all his hopes on Mami. He had stopped looking around him in Gameron City for a new girlfriend, and, as has been said, he had soon developed a complete lack of attraction for any girls who didn't happen to be East Asian in general and Japanese in particular.

So, Craig is hanging all his hopes on Mami Rose, and not just his hopes of getting back his sex life. He knows that first impressions count and he wants to make the best first impression he can with Mami.

And by arriving at Sex on the Beach both drunk and half an hour late, it cannot be said that he has gotten off to a good start in this noble endeavour.

Half an hour late!

Only now, under the neon pink letters, does he look at his watch and see how hideously late he really is. If only he'd known he would need to fortify himself with a drink or three—then he could have taken his Dutch courage at home before setting off and he would then still have arrived here on time.

Will she be pissed off with him? He doesn't think of Mami as the impatient type, and nor, if she is annoyed at his tardiness, does he think her the type to express that annoyance. Still, just knowing that she *might* be annoyed underneath, even if she doesn't show it…

And then another thought hits him.

What if she's not even there? What if she's got fed up of waiting and has already left? He can't see her leaving out of ire, but he can see her taking his non-arrival as a snub, and going home upset at having been stood up…

He walks into the bar.

The décor of Sex on the Beach evokes the South Seas. Booths and bar counter fashioned from bamboo; fake palm trees; holographic tropical birds; lilting ukulele music providing the soundtrack.

Craig looks around.

She's there!

Sitting in the very booth in which he had placed her in his fantasy. She looks bored, prodding with the drinking straw the contents of her half-empty glass.

Heart pounding, he crosses the room towards her. She doesn't look up until he is standing right before her.

'Mami?'

She looks up.

'Craig, yes?'

Craig's heart sinks. It's wrong. Her first words, her first look, and already it's all wrong. Her smile is perfunctory; she speaks his name with no trace of enthusiasm in her voice.

It's just wrong.

'Yep, it's me, and I'm really sorry I'm late!'

'That's okay!' she says. 'I only just get here.'

Late herself! And she doesn't sound like she thinks it's any big deal! And why is she sitting there looking so bored if she's only just arrived? Hasn't she been anticipating this evening as eagerly as he has?

Or has she just agreed to this meeting out of a sense of duty?

Craig slides into the booth. She offers her hand and he takes it. The handshake is weak, an empty formality. Where's the hug? Where's that eager embrace of the two people who share a warm online relationship meeting in the flesh for the first time?

Craig feels his air-built castles come crashing down on top of him. Only when they fall do these vaporous constructions born of blithe optimism become solid enough to cause pain.

This is all wrong.

'So you arrive in Shinjuku yesterday?' says Mami.

'Yes,' replies Craig.

She looks older in the flesh. Maybe she's not wearing much make-up… And her hair is too long. Mami always has her hair cut in a bob, and Craig always prefers it when it's a short bob, less than chin-length. He thinks it looks more cute that way and he has told her this in the past, and she had sounded pleased about his preference. But here she is, with her hair grown to way past chin-length. In fact it's so long you can't even really call it a bob anymore… Has she done this deliberately in defiance of his preference? Is the length of her hair a silent message from her to him?

This is all wrong.

'So you move into Sunshine House?' she continues.

'Yeah. That's where we are.'

'You and your friend?'

'Yeah. Dud.'

Craig really wishes he had a drink in front of him. Of course it would be a simple matter to go to the bar and avail himself of one, but somehow he thinks that he can't just get up from the table when he's only just got here and met Mami; when they've only just exchanged a few words…

'I am happy you have moved to here,' says Mami, with a slight smile.

'Thanks,' says Craig, thinking her words sound more dutiful than sincere.

This is all wrong.

Where's that glowing smile of hers? That warm generous smile he has seen in so many images; the smile he has dreamed of basking in?

This is all wrong.

Things are not going the way he envisaged them and Craig struggles to adjust to this very uncomfortable reality. The alcohol has done him no good at all; all he feels is light-headed; any false confidence the drink had given him has by now completely evaporated. He doesn't feel nervous; not now; he just feels dejected. He has been with Mami for about a minute and already he feels like the evening is completely unsalvageable.

It feels like she just doesn't like him. And it feels like she arrived here all prepared to not like him. So why did she come? Why did she agree to meet him? Was it indeed just something she considered to be an obligation? What's happened to the Mami he had exchanged all those flirty emails with online? The Mami who once signed herself 'love Mami'?

This is all wrong.

The atmosphere is all wrong.

But is it just that he's reading it wrong? Is the awkwardness just in his own head? Or is the atmosphere really there and being felt by both of them? In gauging atmospheres a person can be either perceptively sensitive, or can be morbidly sensitive. The former person generally gets things right, the latter type more often gets them wrong. Which is he being tonight: Perceptively sensitive or morbidly sensitive?

And the irony of it all is that Mami Rose has written about this very subject. Tokyo Rose's song 'Human Shrinkwrap' (which I'm sure I don't need to tell you all is the opening track from their album fifth album 'Getting Blood from a Stone') is a song about the barriers that get in the way of human communication, and how even the best of friends cannot always fully express themselves to one another.

Now if only it could have occurred to either Craig or Mami to bring up the subject-matter of that song and to wryly apply it to their current situation...! I think this might have done something to if not completely break the ice, to at least make it very hazardous for skating.

The idea does not occur.

'You don't have a drink yet,' says Mami. 'They make nice cocktails here.'

'Yeah, I should go'n get one,' agrees Craig, glad that the opportunity has presented itself. 'What do you recommend?'

'You should have a Sex on the Beach like me.'

'Yeah, okay,' agrees Craig, and heads for the bar.

It goes without saying (but I'll say it anyway) that Dudley Moz, listening to records back at the apartment, is envisaging what a great time his friend must be having right now. Of course, for the maximum ironic effect I should have presented this the other way around: I should have first described Dud mentally picturing what a great time Craig must be having, and then flipped the scene to show Craig having anything but a good time. (This will be something for the screenwriters to consider in the unlikely event of this book ever being filmed.)

But yes, like Craig himself, Dud has been sanguine about his friend's meeting with his idol. He has always considered Craig to be much more attractive to women than himself; more confident, more witty and charming; and therefore that anything might go seriously wrong with Craig's rendezvous with Mami has never entered into his calculations. He firmly believes that nothing but good will stem from Craig's finally meeting up with Mami Rose. To Dud, Mami seems just the kind of girl Craig needs; the kind of girl to put him back on the right track.

Of course he can't help but feel a pang of jealousy. He wouldn't be human otherwise. Craig gets himself a date with his girl band idol only the day after their arrival on Daedalus Station, while he, Dudley, is still waiting for a reply to the message he has sent to his own idol. And so here he is spending the evening alone, consoling himself with his favourite music.

He's not too concerned that Krevis hasn't got back to him yet; not concerned enough to be worrying about it. She's probably just very busy at the moment, he thinks. The Shinjuku girl bands are notorious workaholics.

All things considered, Dud has had an enjoyable first day in his new home. They had had breakfast at that diner with Stacey and Vern; and after that they had been directed to the local supermarket and stocked up on groceries. When these had been unpacked and stored in the kitchen of their apartment, they had gone out for a stroll, to explore their new neighbourhood, and to buy themselves a record player from one of the electrical stores. And they were lucky enough that in the first shop they had tried they found the very thing they wanted: a high-quality record player and matching twin speakers with authentic twentieth century bodywork. Some of the technology inside the device is a bit more modern: for one thing the stylus is self-cleaning, and for another the stylus arm can be deployed automatically, which is convenient for Dud, who happens to have a very unsteady hand for putting needles on records!

At lunchtime, Craig and Dud had met up again with Vern and Stacey by appointment at the Osaka Noodle Bar, a renowned eatery amongst J-fans, on account of its being owned by the father of Itsumi, the drummer for Tokyo Rose—and that the girl herself sometimes worked at the counter when she wasn't busy with her band. And she had actually been serving today when Craig and Dud had arrived! Even though Itsumi had never been the main crush of either of them, being the first girl band member they had actually met face-to-face, meeting her was still very much a 'moment.' Itsumi has a square, chunky face that Craig had said was more characteristically Korean than Japanese. Itsumi had known who both of them were and had been very friendly and welcoming when Vern had introduced them to her.

And they had also made the acquaintance of two other J-fans at the noodle bar: Kenichi and Shinji. Itsumi actually *was* Kenichi's main crush, but the poor guy was in a depression because it seems that Itsumi is currently hooked up with some rich J-fan from Daedalus Central. Kenichi and Shinji both didn't have much luck with girls, it seems, Craig later remarking that they both had that 'involuntarily celibate' look about them.

Dudley's thoughts are interrupted by a knock at the door.

Who could it be? Not Craig obviously; he would just let himself in.

Somebody selling something? Dudley is still not sure how things work in this apartment building. There is no reception area to speak of; just an empty foyer and an elderly manageress who keeps herself shut up in her room. Can random callers just walk in, take the lift and start knocking on doors?

The knock is repeated, and Dudley has almost decided not to

respond to it, when it occurs to him that the caller might be Stacey. The cross-dressing boy is quiet like himself, and he feels he is starting to get along with him.

He goes to the door, opens it.

Standing on the threshold is not Stacey at all but a tall, robust Japanese woman, her hair long and thick and with razor-sharp bangs.

Krevis.

Krevis from the Smut Girls.

Krevis. Right here.

'Hi there!' she says, grinning brightly. 'I thought I'd just answer your email in person. Surprised you, yes?'

And here Dudley does what Craig wishes he could have done on meeting Mami.

He faints.

Craig Jenx is not a happy bunny.

Even though his long-anticipated first meeting with Mami started badly, he cannot deny the fact that since then, all things considered, things have started to go downhill. In fact they have gone so far downhill and at such a rapid speed that they have reached the bottom of this metaphorical declivity and have crashed, crashed beyond any hope of a re-ascent being practicable.

It happened like this: the conversation had been proceeding along awkwardly enough, but it had been proceeding. He had soon realised that Mami's command of English was even less advanced than he had been led to believe from the written English of her online communication. (Had she computer-translated her messages?) He found himself often having to rephrase sentences he had spoken in order for her to understand them. This wasn't so bad, although of course in his fantasies he had always imagined any gaps in their verbal communication being filled with simian touching and stroking; but with the ice still thick around them, they had advanced nowhere near to the touchy-feely stage of social grooming.

Things might just have slowly started to improve, but then the fatal interruption had occurred.

The arrival of this interruption was signalled by Mami's face lighting up with one of her dazzling smiles, one of those very smiles he had always imagined being favoured with himself.

But the glowing smile was not directed at Craig—the lucky recipient was someone Mami had just espied walking into the bar.

'Carl!' she had called out.

And 'Carl' it was. Carl was another J-fan, a young man of roughly the same age and appearance as Craig himself. Mami had immediately risen from her chair and hugged Carl like an old friend—the very embrace Craig had dreamed of receiving but had not received.

Carl, it turned out, was a resident of Shinjuku, but he had been away for several months, backpacking around the galaxy. He had just got back today.

Whoopee.

Any hopes Craig had entertained that once all the greetings and 'Long time no see!'s had been exchanged that this Carl entity would be gently but firmly dismissed were soon dashed to the ground. Mami had promptly invited interloper to join them at their table! And without even stopping to ask Craig if this was okay with him!

'I called round yours and were out,' Carl explained. 'But then someone told me I'd find you here.'

(Craig decided on the spot that he would very much like to learn the identity of this 'someone,' so that he could thank them personally for their generous sharing of information.)

Craig's last forlorn hope had been that Carl, on learning that Craig was newly arrived in town and in the middle of his first ever meeting with Mami, would belatedly exercise some degree of tact and take his departure.

He had done nothing of the kind, the bastard.

Carl has been here over an hour now and clearly intends to stay the full course. Craig's increasingly blunt hints have been wilfully ignored.

Carl is now officially Craig's most hated enemy.

The two old friends have been chatting away non-stop, only occasionally remembering Craig's existence and throwing him a conversational bone. Craig has become the gooseberry at what he had originally considered to be his own first date.

Another reason Craig has for hating Carl is that he is, it turns out, proficient at speaking Japanese, and it is only out of deference to himself that the two have been conducting their conversation in English.

Well thank you very much.

And the worst thing of all is that Mami was so obviously glad of her friend's arrival on the scene. She reached out to him as though to a lifeline, clearly seeing his advent as a reprieve.

'You meet many girls when you were travelling?' asks Mami slyly.

'Sure, I *met* girls,' answers Carl. 'You can't really avoid 'em, what with them making up sixty percent or whatever it is, of the galactic population. But I didn't get lucky with any of them, if that's what you mean.'

'No?' Mami sounds sad.

'Nope. Not a one.'

'That too bad,' says Mami.

'Well, you know. None of them could hold a candle to you Shinjuku girls. Especially that… now what's her name…? Mami Rose!'

'Oh, you!' She slaps him playfully.

Carl turns to Craig. 'What about you? Got a girlfriend?'

'I've only been here a day,' answers Craig pointedly.

'Yeah, I guess you have,' agrees Carl. 'Got your eye on anyone?'

You know fucking well who I've got my fucking eye on you fucking piece of shit.

Out loud he answers 'No,' hoping this will wound Mami.

He sees no sign of his shot having hit home.

'You know what?' says Mami, looking from Carl to Craig. 'You two kind of look the same! Don't you think so?'

'Yes, we do!' and 'No, we don't!' exclaim Carl and Craig simultaneously.

Mami giggles.

It occurs to Craig that a lesser person than himself would probably walk out of this situation right about now, would probably have done so already; walk out in both bitter defeat and as a non-verbal protest, a parting shot. But Craig is not a lesser person than himself. He is made of the strong stuff, and he resolves to stay the course and to drink the bitter cup right down to its dregs. And it's a bitter cup which has little umbrellas in it, which try to insert themselves into your nostrils every time you take a drink.

By comparison, the evening has been much more successful for Vern, a character for whom we care much less than we do for Craig. (Speaking for myself at any rate. Try as I might, I know I cannot control the reader's sympathies.)
 'I've had a really nice time tonight,' says Vern.
 'I know,' replies Machiko. 'You keep telling me.'
 'Do I? Sorry.'
 'It's okay. I had a nice time too.'
 They have left the pub now, and Vern is being a gentleman and walking Machiko home, even though this is taking him somewhat out of his own way. They have left the brightly-lit streets behind and are threading their way through a neighbourhood of apartment buildings and small businesses.
 'You've got cats at home, haven't you?' asks Vern.
 'Yes, I have five,' says Machiko. 'You like cats?'
 'I love them,' replies Vern, who up until this moment has always considered himself more of a dog person.
 Vern believes he has made progress. He knows he is not the world's most witty or charismatic man, but he's a nice enough guy, isn't he? As J-fans go, he might be considered 'boring,' but at least he's not a screw-up like Kenichi, or an alcoholic like Shinji… And anyway, boring means safe, doesn't it? Boring means dependable. And that must be what Machiko wants. Yeah, she wants a nice, safe, dependable guy. That must be why she agreed to have this date with him!
 And now, well now Machiko has consented to let him walk her home. And when they get there…? Sure, she said from the get-go that she didn't want to sleep with him tonight, but that was a couple of hours ago, wasn't it? She's got to know him a lot better since then, and she might have relented and changed her mind…
 They arrive at Michiko's apartment block, pausing before the illuminated façade of a soft drinks vending machine.
 'Thank you for walking me home,' says Machiko.

'Not at all,' says Vern. 'Sooo…'

' "So" what?'

'I was wondering…'

'Yes?' interrogatively.

'If I could maybe come up and see your cats…?'

Machiko cocks her head on one side.

'You want to see my cats, huh?'

'Sure. I mean, if you don't think it's too late…?'

'No, I guess it's not too late,' allows Machiko. 'Alright. You can come up and see my cats. I'll even make you a cup of tea. But *that's it*, alright? And when I say you go you go, understand?'

Vern raises his arm in an oath-swearing gesture.

'Absolutely. I'll say hello to the cats, and we can drink our tea and I'll be off. Scout's honour.'

'Okay then,' says Machiko with something of a sigh in her voice. 'Let's go up…'

Sex on the Beach pinkly flashes its illuminated name, the light blinking across the pavement. They have just issued from the bar, two of them tipsy and merry, the third inebriated and sullen. He has been unable to elevate his mood, unable to take up conversational arms and win the damsel's heart with any show of verbal dexterity. He has played the fifth wheel right to the end.

And now he hates Carl, is angry at Mami, and despises himself.

Mami addresses him: 'Thank you to come out and see me tonight.'

Thank you to come out and see me. She makes it sound like she invited him out. But then, maybe that's what she does think. She was the one who set the time and the place, wasn't she?

'Yeah, it was nice to meet you,' mutters Craig.

An awkward smile from Mami. 'Er, we go this way.' She points down the street.

We go this way. Meaning your home lies in the opposite direction and then there's no need for you to walk me home because I've got someone else to do that.

'Yeah. I'll be off then.'

He turns on his heel.

'See you, pal,' calls out Carl.

The words make Craig wince.

Looking back, he sees Mami and Carl walking down the street side-by-side.

Jealousy and suspicion take swift possession of Craig. Is he just walking her home? Or is he *going* home with her? Is he going to be invited by Mami into her apartment? Or will he just go in with her anyway, armed with that cocky attitude of his that clearly thinks no girl can say 'no' to him?

Craig turns and starts to follow them.

He follows them through the multi-coloured streets of nocturnal Shinjuku, past the nightclubs, the live houses, skirting the red-light district, and then onto quieter, darker streets.

They stop before a modest apartment building. Is it hers or is it his? They stand beneath a streetlight, chatting merrily. Craig, across the street, wrapped in shadows, watches with bated breath. He has no idea where the conversation is going; they are speaking in Japanese.

Another minute and then they embrace. As they separate, he kisses her, briefly but on the lips.

And then they part, Mami entering the building, turning to give Carl a final wave before disappearing inside.

Carl sets off down the street, walking with a light step.

Craig releases a pent-up breath.

One small consolation.

He turns and begins to retrace his steps. At the risk of getting lost in the unfamiliar district he decides to avoid the garish bustling streets, to keep his battle-wounds hidden in the shadows. And those wounds start to bleed salt tears. As he pursues the route he hopes will take him home he cries; cries like he has never cried since he was a child, a deluge of absolute misery and desolation.

Chapter Five
Days Like Building Blocks

Tomoki is crying. He is crying because some bullying boys (now driven off by Hina) were teasing him for being a crybaby. And not just a crybaby, but a crybaby and a sissy who sleeps in the same bed with his mother. All of which is true of course.

The setting is Hoko Park in Shinjuku. A cheerful morning, the verdure basking under the artificial sunlight, the sound of birds singing in the trees. (And it *is* just the sound. There is no wild bird population on Daedalus Station: they'd only keep flying into the roof!)

The two youngsters stand under the leafy shade of a maple, Tomoki wiping his streaming eyes and nose with the backs of his grubby hands, while Hina stands before him resting a comforting hand on his shoulder. Tomoki is only five, so the nine-year-old Hina towers over him in both height and precious life experience.

Hina is the mixed-race daughter of Raw Babes in the Country front-woman Asuna; we have met her before. Young Tomoki is the son of Klitzy Normous (real name Minami) from the Smut Girls; we haven't met Tomoki before—or his mum for that matter.

'Don't worry about it,' Hina is saying. 'If those boys bother you again, *I'll* sort them out for you, so don't worry.'

'But then they'll just tease me even more for hiding behind a girl!' blubbers Tomoki.

'Nothing wrong with that!' retorts Hina, referring to the hiding and not the teasing. 'I'm stronger than you are. The strong protect the weak.'

Hina delivers this maxim with profound gravity.

'But boys are s'posed to be stronger than girls!'

'Says who?' demands Hina.

'*They* do!'

'"They do"? You mean those bullies? You shouldn't listen to them!'

'Who should I listen to?'

'Me, silly!'

'Just you?'

'Yes, just me.' She pauses. 'And your mum.'

'Mum?'

'Yes! She's tough, your mum. I bet *she* doesn't go around telling you boys should be stronger than girls, does she?'

'No…' concedes Tomoki.

'There you go then.'

Hina, as mentioned previously, is a Eurasian girl; all the candidates for her paternity being white guys. Tomoki, on the other hand is a full-blooded Japanese lad. There is no mystery concerning the identity of his father—only his current whereabouts.

'You know that those boys wouldn't have started teasing you if you hadn't gone and told people about how you sleep in the same bed as your mum,' says Hina.

'But I didn't know!' protests Tomoki. 'I thought everyone sleeps with their mums!'

'Then you were very silly to think that, weren't you?' Hina tells him. 'For a start lots of kids have dads as well as mums and on top of that they have brothers and sisters as well. How could you fit all of them into one bed?'

'I didn't think about that,' confesses Tomoki, looking down at his sneakers.

'Then you need to remember these things,' pursues Hina sententiously. 'Everyone's different. We're the same, us two, because we haven't got dads or brothers and sisters, but other people *do* have dads and brothers and sisters.'

'So it's only people like us with no dads or brothers and sisters who sleep with their mums?' asks Tomoki, hopeful that he has grasped the situation.

'No,' is the disheartening answer. 'Not everyone with no dads or brothers and sisters sleep with their mums. I think it's just you. *I* don't sleep with my mum.'

'Don't you?' Tomoki looks at her with disbelief.

'No.'

'Why not?'

'Because my mum likes to sleep with other people a lot of the time, so there wouldn't be room for me. But I am allowed to watch sometimes.'

Confusion writes itself on Tomoki's cherub face. 'You watch your mum sleeping? Isn't that a bit boring?'

'No, it's not boring.' She adopts an airy tone. 'But you wouldn't understand; you're too young.'

'I'll be as old as you soon!' defensively.

'No you won't!'

'Yes I will!'

'No you won't! Because when you're as old as me, I'll be even older! So there!'

Hina shows all the makings of a great stateswoman: she has already mastered the art of the incontrovertible argument.

That front room will surely haunt Vern's dream for the rest of his days.

Machiko's front room, the room to which he had been banished after *it* had happened. Not even daring to switch on the light, he had just sat there, sick with fear, awaiting the pronouncement of his fate.

And the cats. The cats had all been staring at him with luminous eyes, and to him in his highly-strung state of mind at that time, those eyes seemed to be full of accusation and feline disdain. As though they knew precisely what had occurred in that other room.

You pig.

That was what she had said to him. You pig. Not the most explicit or scatological of insults, but the delivery of those words had been imbued with every atom the speaker's feelings of anger, betrayal, and contempt.

Looking back, Vern hates himself all the more because he knows at that time, while he sat there in that darkened room, his feelings had been much more those of fear for the consequences of his actions rather than repentance for those actions themselves. Selfishly, he regretted what he had done because of it earning him from Machiko feelings completely the reverse of those he had hoped to inspire. And most of all he feared the consequences taking the form of the loss or his reputation and even his liberty.

But then had come the reprieve. Of sorts.

Machiko had emerged from the bedroom wrapped in her silk

dressing-gown. *That* silk dressing-gown. She had switched on a standard lamp, sat herself on the sofa facing him and had coolly delivered her verdict, speaking in formal Japanese.

'I will not be pressing criminal charges against you,' she had said, and, as if sensing the immense feeling of relief immediately felt by Vern, she had quickly proceeded: 'But that does *not* let you off the hook. Don't you dare think that because I'm not calling the authorities it means you haven't really committed a crime. You have committed a crime. You have committed about the worst crime you could commit against me short of taking my life. Don't you ever forget that. Don't you *dare* ever forget that.

'Your arrest, trial and imprisonment will not serve to make me feel better. And I still have enough regard for you that I don't wish to see you suffer that form of punishment. Nevertheless, you *will* still be punished. I have to revenge myself for this event before either of us can move forwards. But I will let this remain between the two of us. Your crime will not be made public knowledge. I don't want to cause your banishment from Shinjuku. You can remain here, and you can pursue your interests as you have always done. Your friends will never come to know about this.

'But I *will* have my revenge. You have violated my body and you have betrayed my trust. The betrayal hurts me more than your physical assault. I invited you up here because I thought I could trust you; I believed your words but you planned all along to take advantage of my trust in order to satisfy your physical desires.'

'No! I didn't, I—'

'Silence! I did not give you permission to speak. Discuss this matter we will, but not right now. I deny you that right. From now on, you will speak when I give you leave and only when I give you leave. Your punishment for your crime will be inflicted by your own guilty conscience. I am sure that you have one; I don't believe I have misjudged you that badly. Your own conscience will punish you, and I shall make sure that this happens. I shall do everything I can to ensure this result. And then, one day, when I am satisfied that you have suffered enough, then and only then will I forgive you and let your punishment end. How soon that day will arrive I cannot say. It is too soon to predict such things.

'Do not judge by appearances. My words may sound calm and

collected but my mind is still in turmoil. At this moment your presence in my home is hateful to me. I have said all I need to say for the moment, so you may leave. I will call you when I am ready to.'

Vern, shaking with reaction, tears streaming down his cheeks had opened his mouth to speak.

'Not a word! I did not give you permission! Get out of here!'

And she had pointed an imperious arm to the door.

Out of the apartment building, Vern had thrown up beside the vending machine; the vending machine before which they had stood when he had told her how much he wanted to go up to her apartment to see her cats...

Anyone who has walked the streets on a sunny afternoon while fizzing nicely under the influence of alcohol or any other intoxicants, will know that this can be a very pleasant experience; one that leaves you wondering why it is that convention dictates that you're only supposed to indulge in these things at night.

Actually, there are some good reasons for this. These substances are called 'recreational drugs' and most adults do their recreating at night for the simple reason that they have other things to do during the day.

Additionally, if you start drinking, sniffing, smoking or any other way absorbing narcotic substances during the day, by the end of the evening, unless you decide to retire to bed at an uncommonly early hour, you are going to be completely wasted, if you are even still conscious.

But nevertheless, the fact remains that to be pleasantly buzzing while under a sunny sky (even if it is an artificial sun in a holographic sky) is an agreeable experience.

Just ask Craig Jenx. Here he is in exactly the situation described above. He jauntily threads the streets of Shinjuku, his mood chemically-enhanced, a smile on his face and a spring in his step. He hasn't forgotten his disastrous encounter with his goddess Mami Rose just two nights ago; of course he hasn't. How can he just forget something like that? No, he hasn't forgotten it, but now, thanks to psychostimulant influence, he can look back upon that disaster with a calm mind and unclouded judgement.

He felt absolutely wretched to start with. Positively suicidal. He pictured himself ending it all and leaving a suicide note firmly pinning the blame for his self-destruction on Mami. And his misery had only been exacerbated with his discovery that while he was out, Dudley had been favoured with a surprise visit from his own goddess, Krevis Jungle, and with her had enjoyed all the good fortune that he, Craig, had singly failed to obtain. It was enough to drive anyone into the airlock without a spacesuit!

However, spur of the moment thoughts of suicide, unless acted upon swiftly, can often subside. With Craig the thoughts had subsided by the following afternoon, and were replaced with the decision that perhaps his only option was to pack his bags and leave. After his experience, Shinjuku and the whole Shinjuku girl band scene had become hateful to Craig; he felt as if he had tried to enter a world which, instead of greeting him with open arms, had instead turned a cold shoulder to him. He was not welcome here, ergo he should just leave. And as for Dudley, well Dudley could just stay and enjoy his good fortune and the full price of the rent. Dudley clearly had no need of Craig's help and guidance anymore; he had that Asian Amazon with the hairy arse crack to hold his hand for him now.

But once again, with the dawn of the following day, this frame of mind had given way to another, better one, and he had decided that maybe the situation was not irretrievable after all, and that he would regret it for the rest of his life if he just threw in the towel and went back to Gameron right now. His first attempts to try and 'patch things up' with Mami (who herself was doubtless blissfully unaware that anything even needed 'patching up') were not the most well-advised. He had sent her emails. Angry emails. Angry emails in which he had demanded an apology from his idol; an apology for her cold reception of him, and for allowing a third person to interrupt their tête-à-tête.

Mami had offered no response to these demands. Later, Craig had come to realise that perhaps he had been unreasonable in his demands and unkind in the tone of making them.

Scratch that one. Try another approach.

He had Mami's number and had attempted to ring her up. She had answered but only to say that she was in the middle of a rehearsal and couldn't talk right now. Craig hadn't believed this excuse for one minute. Like she would have had her phone switched on in the middle of a rehearsal. She obviously just didn't want to talk to him! (Actually, Mami's band *had* been in the middle of a rehearsal at that time; one which Craig's phone call had interrupted on account of Mami having indeed neglected to switch off her phone.)

Craig's conclusion was this: perhaps the angry tone of his emails had led her to think he only wanted to call her up so he could shout at her, berate her, and in other words cause a 'scene' something which most Japanese people preferred to avoid like the plague. Yes, Mami seemed just the type of person who would find such a situation distressing. In fact Craig could easily imagine her bursting into tears.

But he'd only wanted to apologise! Not to shout at her!

Craig had languished and cried some more after this—but then memory had come to the rescue; he had remembered the beneficial effects of recreational drugs, in terms of lifting one's moods. Although never completely dependent, he'd sometimes done drugs with his previous girlfriend back on Gameron, when they were out gigging or clubbing, or even just for chilled nights in…

In this instance, to think was to act for Craig Jenx, and having procured himself some uppers had under their influence started to feel a lot more positive about the whole Mami Rose situation.

This is what he should have done at the time! thinks Craig, as he drifts through the bustling streets of uptown Shinjuku. Yes, he should have popped some pills before going on that date. Such an important first date demanded careful preparation to ensure that everything would run smoothly. Preparation, that's what it was! Psychostimulant preparation! Mood-enhancing preparation! *That* was where he had gone wrong.

He was a fool to have turned to alcohol like he did. The effects of alcohol in terms of mood-enhancement, are always uncertain, unreliable. With booze, you can easily be knocked off your stride; the smallest setback, and your buzz is gone. But with psychoactive drugs, the effects are more powerful, more certain. When you get that high you feel like you're Captain Invincible! (If there ever was a superhero of that name; and if there was, he almost certainly wouldn't have used street drugs.)

If only he'd felt like he feels right now, he would never have allowed himself to be relegated to fifth wheel status on that fateful night. He would have out-talked and out-shone that bleep-fucker Carl without even breaking a sweat! (At least without breaking a sweat in addition to any sweat he might already have broken as a side-effect of the drug.) He would have dazzled Mami with his native wit and eloquence and she would have forgotten that that back-packing, multi-lingual bastard was even there!

And it's still not too late to bring about that happy state of affairs; to set things back on the right track. Tomorrow is gig night. Tokyo Rose are playing at the Loft, Shinjuku's most renowned punk rock live house. He doesn't have to negotiate any second meeting with Mami: he will see her at the gig! And this time he will be prepared! This time he will shine! He will shine so brightly that all vestiges of that lousy first impression he must have made on his goddess will be erased from her mind!

Machiko's cats.

He remembers crouching down to pet them. As soon as they'd entered the apartment and Machiko had switched on the lights, there they had been, mewing and milling around as they waited for their owner and her guest to divest themselves of their shoes. And then Machiko had gone into her bedroom to change and Carl had felt duty-bound to make a fuss of them; having given the cats as a reason for wanting to come up to the flat. He was not a great cat-lover but at least he wasn't allergic to the little flea-bags.

And then Machiko had emerged from her room wrapped in that silken Chinese dressing-gown. She would put the kettle on for some tea, she said. Vern's eyes had followed her as she crossed the room to the kitchenette; the sight of her naked calves and feet had seemed to promise further delicious nudity beneath that dark silken robe. Machiko, the woman who he now knew revelled in her own nudity, her own body; she would have been sure to take off all her clothes before putting on that dressing-gown…

And it turned out he'd been right about that one.

Janitor robots have cleaned up the vomit he had deposited beside the vending machine that night.

Carl looks up at the modest apartment building with feelings very different from those occupying his mind the last time he was here.

He has been summoned.

He has lived through internal hell these past two days. Machiko had said she didn't want to make a pariah of him by telling everyone of his crime; but he feels he has become one all the same. He would have dearly loved to have unburdened himself to someone: Stacey, Asuna, Sayako... Amongst his friends are some of the least judgemental people in the world, but even so, he just doesn't know how they might react to his confessing to committing a rape... He could soften the description to 'date-rape'; compare himself favourably to the psycho who had raped and murdered Naoko Yamaguchi on that same eventful night... But the commission of that much more horrendous crime does nothing to mitigate Carl's own feelings of guilt; it just makes him feel all the more culpable, as though by association he is just as guilty of that other crime as the real assailant is; just as reprehensible.

And now he has been summoned, and arriving at Machiko's apartment building he hesitates. Overwhelmed with guilt, yes; but there's some self-pity in there as well; he wouldn't be human if there hadn't been.

Maybe, just maybe, Machiko won't be too hard on him today. Maybe she will have relented and maybe she herself might even be that person he's looking for, the shoulder to cry on, the person he can unburden himself to. Hey, maybe she's even changed her mind completely and she's already prepared to grant him forgiveness...?

Buoyed up by this hope, he enters the building and makes his way up to her apartment.

Her severe expression when she opens the door puts a damper on his hopes, as do her first words.

'You're late. When I tell you to get round here, I mean for you to come *straight* round here. Asap. Don't dawdle on the way.'

'I didn't, I—'

'I didn't say you could talk!' snaps Machiko. 'Get your shoes off and come inside.'

None of the cats advance to greet him this time. In solidarity with their owner, they stay where they are and just stare at him with unfriendly eyes.

Having removed his shoes, he stands there uncertain. Machiko has seated herself on the sofa.

'First of all you can make me a cup of tea,' she says. 'Everything's in the kitchen. You should be able to find what you need.'

Nodding his compliance, Carl crosses the room to the kitchenette. A cup of tea. As Machiko made for them both that evening. Just before it all went wrong…

As Machiko must have done he fills the kettle and switches it on. As Machiko must have done he finds two mugs. As Machiko must have done he spoons green tea into the teapot…

When the tea is poured, he places the mugs on the tray and carries it through to the front room, setting it down the table.

'Yeah, I didn't ask for two cups of tea,' says Machiko. 'One's enough for me.'

Carl now realises his fatal mistake; but he can't say anything: he hasn't been given leave to speak. He stares hopelessly at the second mug, the dead ghost of his sanguine hopes.

Machiko affects a sigh. 'Just take the other mug back and pour the tea down the sink.'

Carl obeys.

He returns to the living room, hovers awkwardly.

'You can sit down,' says Machiko.

He sits. They are now sitting just as they were that night, face to face. This time full daylight instead of lamplight illumines the room, and Machiko is dressed not in that fatal dressing-gown, but in casual jeans and t-shirt.

Machiko sips her tea, silently studying Carl, who, unable to meet her gaze, stares at the weave of the carpet.

'Did you know Naoko Yamaguchi?'

Silence.

Machiko sighs. 'You can answer when I give you a direct question.'

'No, I didn't know her,' answers Carl, listlessly. 'I'd heard of her, that's all.'

'Strange that that should happen on the same night,' says

Machiko.

Carl detects no question-mark, and does not respond.

'But then, I guess it's not that much of a coincidence,' reflects Machiko. 'I mean people are getting raped all the time. People are getting murdered all the time, right?'

'I guess so.'

Pause.

'That killer did just what he wanted to do, and you did the same, didn't you? You made your fantasy come real, didn't you? Just like he did. You'd always dreamed of raping the "Unobtainable" Machiko, of forcing yourself on her, overpowering her, yes?'

Carl looks up sharply, seems about to voice a protest, but Machiko silences him with a look.

'No denials, please. I accept your aggressive sexuality. I expect it. You're a male. But you thought you could bring your fantasy out into the real world. You thought you could force yourself on me and make me like it, didn't you? Just like in your dreams.

'You males. You just can't control yourselves. No, I'm wrong. You *can* control yourselves; you just don't want to. You do just what you want and then you blame it on "uncontrollable urges"; you blame it on the other person. So how does it feel to be one of them, Carl? Because you are one of them. You're one of the perpetrators, yes? One of the aggressors?'

Silence.

'Answer me!'

He forces himself to look at her.

'I'm not exactly proud of myself, you know.'

He hopes something in his words, his expression, will inspire some sympathy, some pity. Machiko's face remains expressionless.

'You think I'm being too hard on you? Is that what you're saying?'

'No, I—'

'Well, yes, I *am* being hard on you. This isn't meant to be nice, okay? This is your punishment. It is what you deserve. Remember that.'

Silence.

'One thing,' continues Machiko. 'From here on, officially, we are an item. That's the story we'll put out. It will be an excuse for your coming round here, for your attendance upon me. Okay?'

'Okay,' mutters Carl.

'What was that?'

'I said okay.'

'Yes? You don't sound very happy. I thought that was what you always wanted: for us to be an item? Isn't that what you've always dreamed of? Being the one J-fan who could obtain for himself Machiko, the "Unobtainable"? Well, you've made it. First you helped yourself to my virginity and now we're officially dating. That's what you wanted, yes? Yes?'

'Not like this,' says Carl.

'Not like this. Well, just keep on remembering whose fault it is that it's "like this." Just keep on remembering that.'

Those thoughts he had of an early reprieve are but a distant memory. His gaoler is implacable, and there looks to be very little chance of Carl obtaining any measure of feminine sympathy and support from the woman he raped.

Life can really suck like that sometimes.

Thus far in this history, we have only been introduced to three of the Shinjuku girl bands. We know of Tokyo Rose, the veterans of almost fifteen years; an eclectic band with nine long players under their belts and enough forty-fives to make a very respectable singles compilation (forthcoming.) Tokyo Rose is comprised of Mami, vocals and guitar, who we have met; Otome, bass guitar and chorus, who we haven't met; and Itsumi, drums and chorus, who Craig and Dudley have met but we weren't there when it happened. The band's image is what its three members basically are: three cute, fun-loving Japanese girls, who are always polite, always smiling, who love to talk about food and who will look at you blankly if you bring up the subject of politics.

Tokyo Rose are the band that features Craig's idol, so let us next look at the band that features Doug's: the Smut Girls are a raucous garage rock ensemble, famous for their aggressively obscene song lyrics and for posting porny pictures of themselves online. The band's line-up is: Klitzy Normus (real name Minami), vocals and guitar; Dudley's idol Krevis Jungle (real name Aoi), bass and screaming; and Goldie Shower (real name Haruna), drums and screaming. The band's image is of three big-haired, thunder-thighed bad girls who look as much like a street gang as a rock band (which in fact they are.) Thus far we have only been introduced to the bass player and the singer's son.

The third band of whom we have cognisance are Raw Babes in the Country, whose effervescent punk-pop tunes provide a charming contrast to their lyrics about women tortured and raped by serial killers, young girls abducted by sexual predators, daughters abused by their fathers etc, sweetly sung in the first person. They have recently cut their fifth long-player and their renown places them second only to Tokyo Rose in the Shinjuku scene. Raw Babes in the Country are: Asuna, vocals and guitar; Machiko, bass guitar; and Yumi, drums. On stage they always wear colourful matching outfits, hand-made to professional standards by drummer Yumi, who is also the only member of the band to whom we haven't been introduced.

These are the three bands we have met thus far, but of course they are far from being the only Shinjuku girl bands. It takes more than just three bands to create a music scene that gets itself noticed. (Although now that I say that, it occurs to me that perhaps it doesn't take that many more. About half a dozen bands and the right amount of music press hype can usually do the trick!) There are several dozen Shinjuku girl bands all told, some better than others, and covering most of the sub-genres of rock music between them; but we cannot concern ourselves with all of them, as this will only lead to an excess of subplots and a *dramatis personae* that reads like a Japanese telephone directory.

There is however one more band I would like to introduce into the narrative at this stage, and that band is the Cosmic Rays. Their music has been described a college rock, which considering that the band were formed while its members were all attending university would seem to be an apt description. All three of them were studying physics, and on account of this the band's lyrics are confined mainly to the subjects of astro- and theoretical physics. The band's line-up is as follows: Sayako, vocals and guitar; Rei, bass guitar and chorus; and Mei, drums and chorus. Some observers have erroneously claimed that it is the Cosmic Rays' gimmick to appear on stage wearing lab coats. Not true. The three

girls wear those lab coats all the time, not just on stage.
Let's go and meet them.

Rei and Mei, the rhythm section of the Cosmic Rays, are twin sisters, and in fact *identical* twin sisters. They even wear the same clothes (under the ubiquitous lab coats), style their hair the same way, and wear identical glasses. (Front-woman Sayako also sports glasses, leading to the further misconception that the spectacles are also a part of the band's image, along with the white coats. But in fact, the glasses are not an affectation at all: all three of the girls are blessed with genuine cases of astigmatism.)

The best way of telling Rei and Mei apart is to be in the room when the Cosmic Rays happen to be performing; Rei will be the one wearing a bass guitar and Mei will be the one sitting behind the drum kit. Failing this, then you just have to study the girls' faces. Their bodies may be identical but their personalities are not, and these can be adduced to some extent from the expressions on their respective faces. Rei inclines to be taciturn, so with her it's more an *absence* of expression which distinguishes her facial features. Mei on the other hand is one of those many scientists whose prodigious intelligence is housed in a filthy mind, and this can be discerned in the salacious gleam of the eyes, and the drool often to be seen issuing from her leering mouth whenever she is thinking dirty thoughts.

Here they are.

Side by side and harmoniously in step, the twins make their way along the pavement of a bustling thoroughfare in downtown Shinjuku. Their white lab coats attract little attention from passers-by—the girls are well known in this neighbourhood.

They stop at a private door beside one of the street's many electrical stores, enter and ascend to an apartment above the shop which happens to be the residence of Sayako, the principal Cosmic Ray.

The twins find their band leader in her private laboratory. This laboratory is very cramped as laboratories go, the room having been designed to be a dining area; much of the available space in the windowless room is taken up by an accumulation of makeshift electrical equipment.

Sayako has her hair in a sensible black bob, and as previously mentioned wears spectacles. But the most notable feature of this lady at the present time is the pronounced bulge of the midriff projecting between the unbuttoned frontage of her lab coat. Sayako is seven months pregnant. And in fact, in just two days from this time, the Cosmic Rays will be playing their official 'Last Show Before Maternity Leave' at the Shinjuku Loft.

And if you are wondering how the J-fans feel about one of their goddesses being up the duff, the answer is that, with the exception of one, they love it! The white guys in particular are unanimous in their opinion that only a Japanese woman can still manage to look cute when her midriff has ballooned out like a veteran toper's beer-gut.

Sayako raises her eyes from the viewer of the electronic device she stands before. She greets her friends with a slight bow, which the twins return in unison.

'Are you still tracking the subject?' inquires Rei.

'Indeed,' replies Sayako. She pats the device she has just been studying. 'The Semen Detector is still functioning with precision.'

'Where's the horn-dog got to now?' chuckles Mei.

'If by "horn-dog" you are referring to the subject, he has just reached the Sirius system,' replies Sayako.

'The Dog Star,' says Mei, wiping the drool from her mouth. 'Good place for a horn-dog.'

'He has made impressive time,' remarks Rei. 'In five months, he has already traversed two sectors of space.'

'Yes, the subject does indeed seem determined to distance himself from this station by the widest possible margin,' agrees Sayako. 'I cannot but feel sorry for him. He has made all these great efforts to attain some secure location where he believes I will be unable to trace him, and yet with the Semen Detector functioning I can locate him wherever he goes.'

'But you still have no intention of pursuing him and bringing him back?' asks Rei.

'None,' confirms Sayako. 'It would be a fruitless endeavour. By the very act of his flight the subject has made his position clear: he has no desire to fulfil any parental duties. I am merely utilising him as a guinea pig to test the device. I should be grateful to the subject for impregnating me, and affording us this opportunity to field-test the Semen Detector.'

'Ought to call it the Alimony Chaser,' sniggers Mei. 'All the same, these horn-dogs. Soon as you tell 'em you've got a bun in the oven: *whoosh!* You won't see 'em for stardust!'

Mei chuckles her approval at these manifestations of selfless paternal spirit.

'Indeed,' agrees Sayako. 'But I cannot blame the subject for this. Although the decision to engage in unprotected intercourse was mutual, this decision was based on an error entirely my own. I believed I was still two days short of the commencement of the ovulation period of my menstrual cycle. I miscalculated. The error was mine. And in addition to this, when I discovered that I was incubating an infant, I made the decision to proceed with, rather than terminate, the process—this without consulting the biological father. I cannot condemn the subject's electing to decline parental responsibilities to which he had never acquiesced.'

'The subject was, however, your designated boyfriend,' points out Rei.

'True, but we had mutually defined our relationship as "casual" rather than "serious." The subject was a J-fan who revered me as a rock musician, while as a heterosexual male desired my body. For my own part, I was gratified both by his adoration and the physical intercourse we enjoyed. We had never agreed to sexual reproduction, and my decision to embrace maternity upon discovering my ovulation had been successfully fertilised was, I confess, a completely illogical one. I can only conclude that what is called "the maternal instinct," the basic desire for self-replication and perpetuation of the species, was somehow able to overcome my customary scientific detachment.'

She fondly caresses her womb.

'Is the infant awake?' inquires Rei.

'I believe not,' replies Sayako. 'I feel no movement at this juncture.'

The three lab-coated ladies move through into the living room and seat themselves.

'How is the other research progressing?' asks Sayako of her rhythm section.

'It isn't,' replies Mei.

'We have made no progress,' confirms Rei.

'This makes no sense,' declares Sayako, sighing heavily.

'Yes it does,' argues Mei. 'We're all physicists and here we're trying to research a biological subject. It's not surprising we're not getting anywhere.'

'I did not mean that it was our lack of progress which made no sense. I am referring to the original object of research.'

'The pains of childbirth,' says Rei.

'Yes. Why should there be pain? Why should human childbirth be such an ordeal? There is no logical sense to it!' Sayako sounds almost angry at this enigma.

'Maybe not, but it's always been that way,' says Mei.

'Then it's time the process was changed!' declares Sayako. 'I know I will be accused of selfishness. And I confess that I do not look forward to the physical distress involved in the final stage of childbirth. However, my desire to find a solution is to ultimately benefit all women everywhere in Federated space—not just myself. And I am convinced the solution does exist. There must be some way to obviate these pains of childbirth. They serve no purpose; they are entirely obstructive. Simple logic decrees that a woman should be able to give birth with all the ease and dignity with which she performs her bowel movements.'

'Yeah, but even *that* can hurt sometimes,' points out Mei.

'Only if something is amiss organically,' declares Sayako. 'And these problems can be rectified. This just proves my original thesis. The pains of childbirth must indicate some organic malfunction, a malfunction that can be corrected.'

'Perhaps it would be better if we consulted with some of Daedalus Station's senior obstetricians,' suggests Rei. 'They may be able to offer advice.'

'Agreed,' agrees Sayako. 'But I will stipulate only female obstetricians. I am as distrustful of male obstetricians as I am of male gynaecologists.'

The twins readily voice their agreement.

It seems to be Craig's day for running into people he didn't particularly want to run into. First that Lolita Rabbit kid and her guardian; and now it's that author, Fragrance Pie.

This time, however she is not blocking his path, she is on the holoviz. Craig has called into a pub for liquid refreshment. The holoviz display fills the upper section of the wall facing him. The broadcast is of some afternoon talk show, and the guests, presumably in connection with that Intergal Literary whatsit, are Fragrance Pie and Henry Rollix.

Now Craig has never been a fan of Fragrance Pie; even less so since having met her—but Henry Rollix he despises as a pretentious, self-published shit-head; a macho idiot who fancies himself a serious social commentator.

The two authors appear to be in the middle of a heated argument, the hostess vainly trying to quell the rising storm.

'...Look, it's all about the reader relating to the author's work,' Franny is saying. 'People always like to read something that resonates with their own experience. I would have thought even you could see that.'

'Yeah, well I *don't* see it,' replies Rollix, with evident pride of his poor vision. 'People want to learn something when they pick up a book. That's what they want. They want to know what the author can tell them. People like writers who've actually got something to say.'

'Then they wouldn't pick up your books, would they?' retorts Franny. 'You haven't got *anything* to say! Nothing worthwhile, anyway.'

'More than you, bitch!' snarls Rollix. 'All your books tell people is how much you hate men!'

'I do not hate men!'

'Oh yeah? Then what about last night when I—'

'Oh, I see! Just because I don't want a caveman like *you* in my bed, I'm a man-hater, am I?'

'Sure you are! You've got an icebox between your legs!'

'How dare you!' A new protagonist steps onto the set. Craig recognises her as the woman who started laying into him that night he bumped into Franny. Her secretary or something. This time her wrath is directed at Henry Rollix.

'I will have you know that my client is *not* at all cold between the legs!' she storms. 'In fact she is very hot, moist and slippery in that area! Just not for a cretin like you!'

'Cretin?' echoes Henry, pronouncing it 'Creetin.'

'Yes: Cretin! And it's pronounced "Kretin" you cretin!'

'Don't get smart with me, bitch!' snarls Henry.

Lydia snatches up a vacant frame chair and brings it down on Henry's head.

The shot switches to the uncomfortable hostess.

'Well, we appear to have run out of time!' she announces, laughing nervously. 'So I would like to thank our two distinguished guests for dropping by this afternoon, and we shall certainly be keeping a close eye on events at the Intergal Literary Festival, which officially opens tonight and is of course being held right here on Daedalus Station! Well, I hope you can all join me again tomorrow for some more light afternoon chat. Goodbye for now!'

The lights dim and the credits hastily roll.

Following this the afternoon news is announced.

News anchor's not bad-looking, muses Craig, sipping his drink. Is she African or Asian? Craig ponders this, studying the newsreader's enlarged features. Well, she's dark enough to be African; her complexion is very dark. But the features... Yes, they look more Asian to Craig. Her hair's straight, but of course doesn't prove anything; afro hair can be straightened... Eyes are epicanthic... Maybe Indonesian or Sumatran...?

Only very slowly—so engrossed is he in his attempts to determine the newsreader's racial provenance—does it begin to register in Craig's mind that what the woman is saying is actually quite important: she's talking about Deveron, that rogue planet everybody's worried about. It seems like a Federation goodwill ambassador has managed to convince Deveron's military government to sit down to peace talks with the neighbouring colonies...

Ha! Craig knew it was all just a flash in the pan! Nobody goes to war these days! These military states, they just like to show off; polish their hardware and flex their muscles; but it never leads to anything! And there was that Pie woman having a go at him the other night just because he had more important things like Mami Rose to think about...

Chapter Six
Watchin' Girl

Osaka, the capital city of the Japanese prefecture Kansai, is famed in J-fan circles as being the city from which Japan's two formative female punk bands emerged back in the twentieth century. Given this fact, some have speculated that the Osaka Noodle Bar is intentionally so named on account of this connection, what with the restaurant belonging to the family of Itsumi, Tokyo Rose's drummer, someone who would be very conscious of the roots of the music scene of which she is a part. But in actuality the naming of the noodle bar has nothing to do with this at all. For one thing, the name was chosen by Itsumi's father, the restaurant's proprietor, who has no particular interest in punk rock. The simple truth is that the name was selected more or less at random. Within the environs of Shinjuku you will find any number of streets, parks, and small businesses bearing the names of cities or prefectures in old Japan. Shinjuku itself takes its name from a district of Tokyo, the Japanese capital.

Regardless of the origins of its name, the Osaka Noodle Bar is of great interest to the J-fans on account of Itsumi's presence there. And right at this moment, in the growing artificial dusk, the eatery is of especially great interest to one J-fan in particular; our paranoid friend Kenichi, who has stationed himself at the mouth of an alley across the street and is keeping the establishment under intense but furtive surveillance.

So intense is his surveillance that he doesn't even notice his friend Shinji coming up beside him until he speaks.

'Watchya doin', man?'

Kenichi nearly jumps out of skin.

'Don't do that you jerk!' he says. 'And get out of sight! You're ruining my stake-out!'

'Get out of sight of what?'

'Of the noodle bar, jerkwad!'

Obligingly, Shinji moves further into the alley.

'Why're you staking-out Osaka's?'

'Because!'

'Oh, right. Because.' Shinji nods his understanding.

Kenichi turns his attention back to the bar. The lights have been switched on behind the plate-glass windows. Osaka's is a modest eatery: the serving counter, supplied with stools for customers, spans the entire length of the room to the left of the entrance; adjacent to it, two rows of tables. The place is quiet at the moment; just a couple of customers sitting at the counter; none of the tables are occupied.

A moment passes, then Shinji ventures to ask, 'Because of what?'

'Because of Itsumi,' replies Kenichi, not looking back.

Shinji peers over his friend's shoulder, stretching his skinny neck.

'Yeah, I don't see Itsumi, man,' he says. 'That's her mum working the counter.'

'I know it's her mum,' growls Kenichi. 'Itsumi's not there cuz she's getting ready to go out.'

'Going out, is she?' says Shinji. 'Going out where?'

'That's what I intend to find out,' is the succinct reply.

'You mean you're gunna follow her?'

'Yeah, I'm gunna follow her.'

'Yeah, dude, they call that stalking, y'know.'

Kenichi searches his mind for a suitable comeback to this.

'Shut up,' he says, having searched in vain.

'How d'you even know she's going out tonight?' pursues Shinji.

'Because she told me,' is the reply. 'I was in there before, and she was just going off duty. She told her mum she was going out for the night.'

'And she didn't say where?'

'No.'

'And you wanna find out?'

'Yeah.'

'Why? And don't say "because".'

'I wanna see if she's meeting up with that Enders guy, that's why.'

'What if she is meeting up with him? Makes sense for her to be meeting up with him. He's her guy.'

'Says who?'

'Well… everyone. Including her. And him.'

'Yeah, I know they *were* an item. But who says they still are? How many days is it since they last hooked up, huh?'

'Don't ask me, man. I'm not the one doing the stalking. You tell me.'

Kenichi looks back now, grim satisfaction written loud on his face. 'They haven't met up since *Monday*.'

'Yeah, that's only three days, dude. Don't read too much into that.'

'I'm not saying they've split-up. But maybe things are on the rocks. Maybe they've had a fight or something.'

'Yeah, but don't get your hopes up. I know *I* haven't heard anything about a fight. And anyhow, isn't she meeting up with the guy tonight? That's what all this is about, right?'

'I don't know what she's doing, do I? Maybe she's meeting the guy just so's she can officially dump him. I mean what does she see in the guy, anyway? What's he got that I haven't?'

'Money. A job. A car,' answers Shinji. 'He lives in a swanky condo that probably has one of those luxury king-size beds that goes around on a pedestal, while you've got a crummy five-mat apartment and a futon…'

Kenichi glares at him. 'And that makes all the difference, does it? Having all that money to throw around? Newsflash, dipshit: it's personality that counts, not what's on your bank balance.'

'Yeah, I hate to tell you this dude, but you've got a lousy personality,' Shinji informs his friend. 'I mean, y'know, it really stinks. Really.'

'Shut up,' says Kenichi.

The glob of sputum, hurled as a liquid message of provocation and contempt, falls short of its intended target, alighting sadly on the asphalt, missing even the toe of the target's boot.

'Nice try,' says Klitzy. 'I sure hope you can shoot your wad further than you spit.'

Even some of Herman's gang laugh at this one.

'Shut up, bitch!' snarls Herman, enraged.

The Stormtrooper Gang has rolled in from across town to face-off with the Smut Girls, the meanest bitches in downtown Shinjuku!

There's a rumble going down!

The chosen arena is out in the Buffer Zone; a colosseum of pipes and girders and raw concrete surround the gang-members and their bikes. The perfect place. Less chance of the cops crashing their little party way out here.

The Stormtrooper Gang—coal-scuttle helmets, swastika armbands and Nazi regalia alongside studs, leather and ripped denims—have the advantage of numbers. There are a round dozen of these morons. Spread out behind their leader, they casually handle bicycle chains, nail-studded baseball bats… Herman the German (Japanese of course) confronts the Smut Girls, officer's cap with a cracked peak sitting jauntily on his head, his girl Eva (in forage cap) hanging on his arm.

The Smut Girls number just three: leader Klitzy Normus, flanked by her rhythm section Krevis Jungle (on her right) and Goldie Shower (on her left.) The girls sport identical Bettie Page hair-cuts; their bodies are sculpted to the same robust, big-boned configuration; they wear identical biker boots, fishnets and black faux-leather shorts and ripped sleeveless t-shirts emblazoned with their collective name. Even the arrangement of the facial features is very similar, but Klitzy's face bears the stamp of authority; with Krevis, the plunging eyebrows and the thickness of her lips lend her that surly-aggressive look that has so captivated Dudley Moz; while Goldie's eyes and the slight smile upon her lips suggest a refined cruelty in the disposition of that young lady.

Three against a dozen; and if the odds aren't already stacked against the girls there is the added fact that unlike the Stormtroopers, the Smut Girls are unarmed.

'Last warning,' says Klitzy to Herman. 'Get out of here. This is not your territory.'

'It is now,' replies Herman. 'We're moving in so you bitches can move on out. So why don't you get on your bikes and haul your fat asses outta here? That's *your* last warning.'

'Yeah, scram you porny whores!' adds Eva, glaring spite at them.

'Porny whores, huh?' responds Klitzy. 'So, what does that make you, sweetheart? Look at you, draped on his arm like that. You're not even a whore; you're just a fashion accessory.'

'Fuck you, bitches!'

'Just ignore them, honey,' Herman tells her. 'They won't be talkin' so smart when we've finished with 'em.'

Herman signals his men, who start to close in.

'Better get running, ladies,' says Herman.

'Yeah, I don't think so,' snorts Krevis.

'Okay girls,' says Klitzy. 'Let's just take out this trash, then we can get on with something more interesting.'

'That does it!' rages Herman. 'Take those bitches out!'

The Stormtroopers charge.

The fight doesn't last long. The Smut Girls, moving like lightning, instituting their own personal *blitzkrieg*, swiftly disabling their opponents with lethal unarmed combat skills. The Stormtrooper Gang even help them along by inadvertently taking out some of their own number with their flailing bats and bicycle chains. Klitzy deals with Herman herself, teaching him a salutary lesson about turf rights by way of punching him repeatedly in the face until he collapses insensible, puffy-faced and dentally depleted.

And then only the Smut Girls are left standing; them and non-combatant Eva, who has backed up to the Stormtroopers' bikes, shaking with fear.

'Oh look,' says Goldie. 'There's one left. Leave her to me.'

Smiling wickedly, Goldie advances on the terrified girl.

'Get back, you psycho,' she stammers. 'Leave me alone!'

'No way, sister,' says Goldie. 'You're kinda cute.'

Goldie grabs Eva, pulls her into a tight embrace and fastening her lips against the other girl's in a violent kiss. At first Eva struggles, cries muffled protest; but then comes that sweet surrender, and she responds to the kiss, twining her fingers round Goldie's sleek hair.

'Okay, girls, let's take off,' says Klitzy. 'And if these losers ever decide to mess with us again, we won't go so easy on them.'

And so, treading over the prone bodies of the Stormtrooper Gang, the three girls mount their bikes, Goldie taking her prize along with her.

Klitzy returns straight to her apartment where Tomoki, her five-year-old son, is watching anime.

'Oh, my little darling!' she says, throwing her arms around her boy. 'Have you missed your mummy? Have you missed me?'

'You're all stinky!' protests Tomoki, trying to free himself from her embrace.

'That's because mummy's been working up a sweat fighting some bad guys!' she informs him.

'You should take a shower!' says Tomoki.

Klitzy looks hurt. 'But don't you like mummy when she's all sticky and sweaty? Doesn't it make you feel all comfy-cosy?'

'No!' definitely, still pulling away.

'No?' Klitzy straightens up. 'Well, when you're older you'll soon learn to like ladies when they're like this… Well, you win! I'll go'n take a shower and then I'll make my little man his din-dins, okay?'

'Okay,' says Tomoki, mollified.

Klitzy plants a huge sloppy kiss on his cheek and then retires to the bathroom to wash the blood off her knuckles.

The darkness is thickening when Itsumi emerges from the alley beside the noodle bar and sets off down the street. She is dressed casually: boots, cycle shorts, hoodie. Her hair is pinned up, save for two loose strands framing her square, smiling face.

Having no reason to look behind, she doesn't see two figures hurriedly cross the street and start following her at a distance.

'Now we'll see where she's going,' affirms Kenichi.

'Yeah, but what are you gunna do when she gets there?' inquires Shinji. 'I mean if she's meeting Lance Enders, what can you do about it, man?'

'We can get as close as we can and listen in on what they're talking about,' says Kenichi. 'I wanna know if they're breaking up.'

'And what if they're not breaking up? Not much you can do about it, right?'

'I can clobber the jerk.'

'Yeah, I reckon he'd clobber you. You're a skinny little kappa;

he looks like he works out, y'know?'

'What's that got to do with it? You sayin' Itsumi likes the guy just cuz he goes to the gym?'

'Well, some chicks like a buff bod. Plus the guy's not Asian, so that means he's probably got a bigger dick than you do. Chicks definitely go for that.'

'Shut up!' snarls Kenichi.

Tailing their subject leads the young men into the heart of uptown Shinjuku, home to the big department stores, the fast food chains, and expensive restaurants.

'Why's she meeting the guy here?' wonders Kenichi.

'Because he's loaded, I keep tellin' you,' replies Shinji. 'He's probably booked a table at one of those fancy French restaurants.'

'Don't be stupid,' retorts Kenichi. 'Those places have dress-codes. Itsumi's wearing boots and cycle pants. She'd've dressed up if she was going to one of those places.'

'Yeah, you're right,' concedes Shinji. 'Y'know, I think that might be your first non-stupid deduction of the evening.'

'Shut up.'

But an uptown restaurant is not Itsumi's destination. They arrive at the Shinjuku Underground Station and they see Itsumi enter its portals.

'She's not meeting him here at all!' exclaims Kenichi. 'She's going to Central to meet him!'

'Looks like it,' says Shinji. 'What you gunna do?'

'Follow her—what else? I'm not giving up now.'

Keeping their quarry in sight, they enter the station. She buys a ticket from the automatic vendor; the boys do the same.

The Daedalus Station Underground, a network of tunnels threading the very infrastructure of the space-station, provides a link between all the various districts of the colony. It's fast, convenient, but not always a safe place to be late at night.

Right now in the early evening the station is fairly busy. Kenichi and Shinji follow Itsumi down the huge escalator and along the maze of graffiti-decorated tunnels linking the numerous platforms. Sure enough Itsumi leads them to the departure platform of the Daedalus Central line.

The next train is due in five minutes.

The two J-fans lurk at the platform entrance, not wanting to be seen by Itsumi, who has seated herself on one of the benches.

'Remind me,' says Shinji. 'Why am I here? That dayrider ticket just took a big chunk out of my credits, y'know?'

Kenichi sighs. 'You're here because—' He breaks off, turns a perplexed face to his friend. 'Yeah, why *are* you here?'

'Beats me. I guess I just sort of tagged along.'

Kenichi shrugs. 'Well, I never asked you to tag along. Go home if you want.'

'Nuts to that! I paid out for this stupid ticket, so now I'm gunna use it!'

'Fine then. Just quit complaining.'

'Really? That's great!'

'Yeah, I guess…'

Stacey frowns under his blonde wig. Vern has just announced Machiko and himself are an item.

And he doesn't sound that thrilled about his own good news.

'I'm happy for you…' says Stacey, tentatively this time.

'Yeah…'

'So it happened after your date? And that was the same night that Dudley hooked up with Krevis.'

'Did he?'

'Yeah, she turned up out of the blue at his apartment. I think they clicked pretty much straight away.'

'Knowing her, she probably laid him as soon as she was in through the front door.'

'Well, I don't know exactly what happened, but it worked out.' Pause. 'Yeah… So it looks like the only one things didn't work out for that night is Craig.'

'Why? What happened? He met Mami, didn't he? Did something go wrong?'

Vern looks interested now, pleased even. Stacey frowns again. His friend's reactions are all wrong this evening; he doesn't seem like himself.

'Yeah, something did. Carl turned up—you've heard he's back, right?—and sort of crashed the party. Carl's a nice enough guy but he can be pretty tactless. He should have realised those two wanted to be alone.'

'Huh,' snorts Vern. '*He* may have wanted them to be alone; doesn't mean *she* did. Have they met up since then, Craig and Mami?'

'I don't think so… It's only been a couple of days…'

'Yeah, that guy won't be making it with Mami,' declares Vern with satisfaction. 'Ha! And to think the only reason he moved out here from Gameron was cuz he wanted to get with her! What a waste of credits!'

'It's not nice to gloat, Vern,' admonishes Stacey. 'I thought Craig was your friend. Dudley says he was really cut up about it afterwards; Craig, I mean. He seems better today, though.'

'Does he?' challenges Vern. 'Well he won't be so chipper as soon as he finds out Mami's shacking up with Carl.'

'We don't know that she is, Vern.'

'She will be. I'm pretty sure those two have been together before. Craig'll just have to get used to being a gooseberry.'

'You're sounding really bitter, Vern,' says Stacey. 'I don't understand. You ought to be over the moon now that you're dating Machiko. Is something wrong? Something you want to talk about?'

'Nothing's wrong.'

'Are you sure? Because you really don't seem yourself—'

'Look, can you just drop it, Stacey?' cuts in Vern. 'Actually, I'd like to be alone right now. I'm really not in the mood for company this evening.'

'Okay, Vern,' says Stacey, rising from his chair. 'I'll leave if that's what you want. I hope you feel better tomorrow. And if there's anything you want to—'

'Yeah, yeah…'

'Okay. See you, Vern.'

Stacey departs.

Shinji's backpack contains his 'essential supplies,' to wit alcohol. The lengthy underground journey from Shinjuku to Daedalus Central has allowed Shinji to polish off one can of beer and commence a second. And with these, clearly not his first drinks of the day, he has quickly become very merry and sits singing the words to Raw Babes in the Country songs.

Kenichi, seated next to him, is annoyed. And it *can* be annoying to be in the company of a merry, drunk person when you are neither merry or drunk yourself. He would like to be to able to silence Shinji by telling him that his singing could alert Itsumi to their presence; but as the girl happens to be seated several cars forward of them, this would not sound like a valid remonstrance. Their own compartment is empty save for two or three other commuters, and those two or three other commuters have been studiously ignoring the singing drunk man.

'That was good,' sighs Shinji, having drained the contents of the second can. 'Nothing like a beer to freshen you up.'

The train starts to decelerate.

'Look, we're nearly there,' says Kenichi. 'So lay off with the crooning when we get out of the train.'

'Sure, I know,' answers Shinji readily. 'Can't be singing while we're tailing.'

One thing tailing *does* involve though, is walking, and Shinji's ability to perform this useful function is brought into serious question when he attempts to get to his feet.

Kenichi grabs his arm to steady him.

'Well this is just great!' he snaps. 'You can't even stand up, you piss-head!'

'Relax, man,' replies Shinji. 'It's just a dizzy spell from standing up too fast. I get that sometimes.'

Kenichi releases his arm. Shinji sways, but remains vertical.

'Can you walk alright?'

'I can walk, I can walk.'

'You'd better. Cuz if you start slowing me down when we're following Itsumi, I'm gunna leave you behind. Got that?'

'Yeah, I hear you.'

The train pulls into the terminus. Kenichi is out on the platform the moment the doors slide open. Shinji follows unsteadily. Kenichi looks down the length of the train. Passengers are spilling out onto the platform. He espies Itsumi emerging from a forward carriage.

Yes, there she is!

'Come on!'

He grabs Shinji's arm and they hurry in pursuit, weaving around the other disembarking passengers. Keeping her in sight, they follow her up the escalator. Here at Daedalus Central Terminus the crowd of commuters is much more dense. But Kenichi has fixed his paranoid, obsessive mind on following the girl he thinks he loves, on following her to whatever her destination might be, and he is doggedly determined not to lose track of her. He keeps her in sight.

Finally they emerge from the station building, into the neon night of Daedalus Central. Itsumi makes straight for the taxi rank.

'She's getting in a cab, dude,' says Shinji. 'End of the line for us.'

'No it isn't,' declares Kenichi. Grabbing his friend by the sleeve he drags him to the next cab in the rank and jumps inside, depositing Shinji on the seat next to him.

'Follow that car!' he orders.

'What car, my man?' answers the cabbie, making no move.

'The cab in front of you that's just pulled out!'

'Oh, *that* car. Whatever you say, my friend. The customer is always right.'

The cabbie is our old friend the dreadlocked rasta guy. Humming a tune, he steers his cab out onto the thoroughfare, the other taxi just three cars ahead of them, its roof-sign marking its position.

'You know, that's very clichéd, my friend,' he says. (The translator built into his vehicle enables him to communicate freely with the two Japanese men.) '"Follow that car!" Yes, that is very old. And then, my comeback, just as clichéd, is supposed to be "I've been waiting all my life for someone to say that to me!" Well, I do not care to be that clichéd, and anyways it would not be the gospel truth, on account of the fact that you are the third passenger I have driven who has said that to me.'

'Is that so?' says Kenichi, in no mood for banter.

'It is indeed so,' replies the cabbie. 'And who might it be that you are so anxious to follow, my man?'

'It's… just a friend of ours,' says Kenichi.

'A friend, huh? Well, it is not for me to pass judgement, but when you start tailing your friends that seems to me to be a very strange kind of friendship.'

'We're just looking out for her,' chips in Shinji. 'Itsumi, I mean.

The girl we're following. There's nothing sketchy going on.'

'I am glad to hear that, my man,' replies the man. 'You guys have come up from Shinjuku, am I right?'

'That's right.'

'And the lady you're so interested in: she's Japanese?'

'Yeah.'

'And what brings her to Central?'

'We don't know,' says Shinji. 'That's why we're tailing her!'

And he bursts into laughter.

'Shut up,' says Kenichi.

The vast skyscrapers of Daedalus Central are humbling to visitors accustomed to architecture on a more modest scale. The leading taxi now pulls before a particularly imposing towerblock. The pursuing vehicle glides smoothly to a halt behind. Itsumi steps out of her taxi, and without sparing the second cab a glance, walks briskly up the steps leading to the building's brightly-lit portals.

'And there you have your answer, my good friends,' announces the cabbie. 'Your lady-friend's destination is the Excelsior Hotel.'

'Why would she be meeting him at a hotel?' wonders confused Kenichi.

Shinji laughs again. 'Hotels have bedrooms, dude!'

'Yeah, and so does Enders' condo,' Kenichi reminds him. 'So why splash out on a hotel room?'

'I take it you fine gentlemen are not regular viewers of the news broadcasts?' says the cabbie. 'That hotel is booked solid. It happens to be the venue for this year's Intergalactic Literary Festival. And all these smartly-dressed folks you see drifting in, are here for tonight's opening ceremony. Ah, yes; there's your friend, just going in!'

'Come on. Before we lose her!'

Kenichi quickly pays the driver, and ignoring his 'Have yourselves a nice evening!' bundles Shinji out of the car. They hurry up the stairs to the entrance. The entrance is guarded by several sturdy-looking men in tuxedos, one of whom politely obstructs their progress.

'May I see your invitations?'

'Invitations?' echoes Kenichi, looking up at the man's expressionless face. He wears dark glasses and has a translator clipped to his ear.

'Yes. Tonight's party is invitation only.'

'Tell him we're with the press,' stage-whispers Shinji.

'We're with the press,' says Kenichi.

'Then I'll need to see your press cards and authorisation.'

'Tell him we're not going to the party,' stage-whispers Shinji.

'We're not going to the party,' says Kenichi.

'Only party attendees and hotel guests are authorised to enter this evening.'

'Tel him we *are* staying at the hotel,' stage-whispers Shinji.

'If you are guests at this hotel,' says the doorman, not waiting for the repetition, 'then I will need to see your key cards to verify this fact.'

'Tell him we've lost our key cards,' stage-whispers Shinji.

'Okay, you two: beat it,' says the doorman, losing patience.

Crestfallen, the two J-fans retreat.

'That's it, then,' says Shinji. 'Shame our cabbie didn't hang around. We could have got a ride back to the station.'

'We're not giving up yet!' declares Kenichi. 'What's Itsumi doing at some literary convention? I wanna find out!'

'But we can't get in, man!'

'We can't get in the *front*,' corrects Kenichi. 'So we just have to find some other way.'

Lance Enders sits at the desk in his temporary office at the Excelsior. Comes a knock at the door and his colleague Roland sticks his chubby head into the room.

'Hey, Roland. What's up?'

'Someone to see you.'

'Who is it? I'm busy here.'

'Japanese girl, I think. Not sure what she wants; her English isn't that good.'

Roland looks alarmed. 'What's her name? No, forget it; just show her in.'

His worst fears are confirmed when into the room walks Itsumi.

Roland closes the door on them.

'What the hell are you doing here?' he demands in a strangled (and Japanese) voice.

'I came to see you, of course!' replies Itsumi, smiling brightly.

'But you shouldn't have come here!'

Itsumi looks confused. 'Why not? You gave me that VIP ticket for the convention.'

'Yeah, but that was before— Look, you can't stay here! Natalie's here! She might see you!'

Another confused look. 'Your girlfriend? But she doesn't know me.'

'That's just it! She *does* know you now! I mean she knows *about* you!' Lance scratches his hair in frustration. 'Look, it'll take too long to explain, but I kind of let things out when I was drunk a few nights back.'

Itsumi is unconcerned at this news. 'And what did she do when she found out?'

'Tore me a new one, pretty much.'

'But then you made up?'

'Are you kidding? After she'd finished letting me have it, she just walked off. She's been totally ignoring me for the past few days, not to mention bitching about me to everyone else behind my back. Thanks to her my reputation around here's in the toilet.'

'So what do we do?' asks Itsumi. 'I came a long way to see you.'

'I know you did, honey,' says Lance, relenting. 'And it's my fault for not keeping you up to speed with what's been going on… I tell you what: here's the key to my suite; it's up on the thirty-first storey. You take yourself up there, watch the holoviz or something, order whatever you want from room-service, and I'll join you in say a couple of hours. I can't come right away cuz I've got to finish up here first. How does that sound?'

'Sure! Let's do that.'

Itsumi takes the key card and exits. But instead of heading for the lifts, she bends her steps towards the ballroom. And why not? There's a party going on; she might as well check it out now that she's here!

Kenichi and Shinji find what they are looking for in the form of the entrance to the hotel's basement car-park. The entrance is guarded by a barrier manned by an attendant in a box, but by walking hunkered down the boys pass under both the barrier and the eyes of the attendant.

They hurry down the ramp and find themselves in the car-park.

'Their security sure sucks,' says Shinji.

'It's only a hotel, not a gold reserve,' retorts Kenichi. 'Come on. The lifts are over there.'

'And what are we gunna do then?' inquires Shinji. 'Crash the party? We're not really dressed for a fancy party.'

'Yeah, but neither's Itsumi, so it must be okay,' says Kenichi. 'And anyway, think of all the free drinks you can help yourself to.'

'Yeah, I guess so.'

They discover a stairwell adjacent to the lifts and decide that this might be a safer option for their ascent. They climb the first flight and step out into a corridor.

'This looks like the service area,' says Shinji.

'Yeah, we're too far back. We need to go this way; towards the front of the hotel.'

'But what if someone catches us?'

'Don't worry. Just act like you're supposed to be here.'

This plan either doesn't work at all or works too well because the first corner they turn they run into a man dressed as a waiter, waistcoated and bow-tied. He stands with hands on hips, and looks annoyed, yet unsurprised at seeing the two young men.

'So there you are! About time you got here! I only took you two on as a favour to Lenny, and you can't even show up on time! We're short-staffed out there, so get yourselves changed, pronto!'

Now all of this, spoken in English, is so much gibberish to Kenichi and Shinji, but when the man curtly indicates for them to follow him, they comply, exchanging confused looks.

'What was he saying?'

'*I* don't know!'

'And where's he taking us?'

'I don't *know*!'

They are led into a changing room. Two waiter's outfits are lying neatly-folded on a table. The man utters another incomprehensible sentence. The boys look at him blankly. This reaction provokes an even more angry outburst, but this time with the man pointing imperatively at the folded suits of clothes.

The two look at each other.

'We've got to be waiters?' says Shinji. 'I didn't sign up for this!'

'Yeah but this could get us into that party!' argues Kenichi. 'That's where we want to be, isn't it?'

Kenichi starts to undress. Reluctantly, Shinji follows suit. They change into the waiter's outfits. They manage to successfully don the tight waistcoats, but the bow-ties prove a much greater challenge. After failing to tie their own, they attempt to tie each other's with equally unhappy results. Finally the irate overseer intervenes, rapidly tying both their ties while muttering words the boys don't need to understand to get the general gist of.

Their wardrobe complete, the head waiter leads them along another corridor and into a vast kitchen area. White-clad chefs mill around tables laden with cakes, canapés, and all manner of sweet and savoury snacks. The furthermost table is a sea of champagne glasses enfolding islands of ice-buckets; each island rising to a green-glass peak, its cork summit foil-capped. The head waiter picks up a tray of filled glasses and presents it to Shinji.

'Don't mind if I do!' says Shinji. He picks up two of the glasses and drains first one then the other. He smacks his lips appreciatively. 'Boy, that sure hit the spot! Nice bubbly!'

This provokes yet another angry outburst.

'Dumbass!' snaps Kenichi. 'He wasn't offering you a drink! We're supposed to carry these trays!'

'I'm not doing that!'

'Yes you are! Where do you think we'll be going with these drinks? Into the party! Our whole objective!'

'Okay, man,' sighs Shinji.

Chapter Seven
Bloody Party

The grand opening party, located in the Excelsior's vast ballroom, is in full swing; which is to say there are a lot of smartly-dressed men and women, standing around in groups, engaged in pretentious conversation (this *is* a literary festival!) while getting slowly drunk on sparkling wine. Soft music provides the backdrop. Some questioning eyes have been turned towards a Japanese woman, who, on entering the room, made straight for the snack tables, and even now is still loading her plate with edibles, rapidly consuming them, and then loading the plate once again. It's not so much the girl's voracious appetite that attracts attention, as the fact that her boots, cycle shorts and hoodie do rather clash with the prevailing tuxedo and ballgown *motif*.

Loath to entertain the idea of a party-crasher having breached the Excelsior's defences, people decide that she must just be an eccentric novelist.

Another, and in this case, genuine, eccentric novelist present is Franny Pie. Feeling awkward in a tight ballgown, she stands alone. Franny has not made many friends since her arrival at the convention. Her popularity as a writer has perhaps made her unpopular with her literary colleagues; or it might be that the intimidating presence of her agent, Lydia Luvstruk, has deterred people from approaching her.

The agent in question, weaving her way through the throng, breathlessly rejoins her client.

'I've found her!' she exclaims.

'Found who, Lydia?'

'Why, the very person you've been dying to meet: Betty Mudie! She's here!'

'She is?'

'Yes!'

Franny is delighted. Since her arrival at the Excelsior, Franny has so far been unable to meet her literary idol Betty Mudie, the author tipped to be the recipient of this year's Lifetime

Achievement Award. The veteran author seems to have been hiding herself in her room. Betty Mudie was due to have been the third guest on the afternoon talk show along with Franny herself and Henry Rollix, but had cancelled at the last moment, on account of being 'indisposed.'

Whatever it was, obviously she's better now.

'Come, Miss Fragrance; I shall introduce you!'

Lydia takes Franny by her silk-sheathed elbow and leads her across the room.

Meanwhile, Kenichi is in search of Itsumi, his progress annoyingly hampered by people who keep stopping him to take glasses of champagne from the tray he is carrying. Don't these people realise he has better things to do? He's on a mission of love! Why can't they go and get their own champagne? The kitchen's right through those swing doors!

He bumps into Shinji, bent on the same quest as himself.

'Any luck?' he asks.

'Nope,' is the answer. 'Can't see her anywhere.'

'You've given out a lot of champagne,' says Kenichi, observing the other's tray of empty glasses.

'Oh, I drank those,' is the casual reply.

'Dumbass!'

'Hey, this is thirsty work!'

Kenichi sighs. 'Okay. Let's split up and search some more.'

'Okay, dude. Y'know, I think I might even make it with one of these white chicks tonight! I've seen 'em looking at me, y'know? Looking kind of interested.'

'Jerkwad. If they're looking at you it's cuz they're wondering why you're hauling around a tray of empty glasses.'

'You think it's just that, huh?'

'Course it's just that. White guys go for Asian chicks, but white chicks don't go for Asian guys. Fact of life.'

'Yeah, I guess you're right.'

The search is resumed.

'That bastard,' says Natalie, downing another glass of bubbly, referring to one of those white guys with the sexual preference mentioned above.

She occupies a corner of the room with her friend, an unnamed minor character.

'Look, if you wanna get back together with the guy, just do it!' says the friend, rolling her eyes.

'Who says I wanna get back together with the guy?' demands Natalie, pouring herself another glass from the bottle she has commandeered.

'Because you keep calling him a bastard.'

'And that means I wanna get back with him?'

'It means you keep thinking about him, so yeah.'

'But how can I get him back?' she wails. 'He's got the hots for that girl band slut.'

'So what?' retorts the friend. 'Sure she's Asian, and looks all exotic to white guys like Lance; and yeah she's got that Japanese skin that ages slowly, so she'll still be looking good while you start looking old; and yeah in bed she's probably all submissive and "Please be gentle with me!" in a way that drives guys crazy—'

'Are you trying to make me feel better or not?' demands Natalie.

'Look, what I'm saying is now is your best chance. You know he hasn't been to Shinjuku to see that girl all week; he's been too busy here setting up the convention. He'll be starting to forget her. But you: he's been seeing you all the time. It's proximity that counts, y'know.'

'Yeah, he's been seeing me, but he's been seeing me giving him the brush off and telling everyone else what an asshole he is!'

The friend shrugs. 'He *is* an asshole. Show me a guy who isn't. But what you gotta do is let him know that even though he's an asshole, you forgive him and you wanna get back with him!'

'You think so?'

'I know so. Just finish off that bottle; it'll get you in the mood.'

'I've been reading your books since I was at school! I just loved *Furnace Flats* the moment I picked it up! And *The Giuoco Piano* is still my favourite book! It was because of you I wanted to start writing myself!'

'Is that so?'

Franny winces. She knows she's sounding like some gushing

fangirl, and that the people around them are smiling and trading glances; but it's Betty Mudie's monosyllabic responses that are inflicting the most discomfort.

'Yes...' says Franny. 'That was why I dedicated my first book to you...'

'Did you? Oh yes; I seem to recall...'

Betty Mudie wears an evening gown, her piled-up hair adorned with a tiara. Her face does not display all of her fifty-nine years, but Franny cannot help noticing that the neck supporting that face evinces more in the way of wear and tear.

'So, when is your next book coming out?' ventures Franny.

'Oh, soon,' is the reply. 'I don't like to rush these things. I'm not a production-line writer.'

Franny feels this to be a thrust aimed at herself and winces accordingly.

'Yes... I suppose with all the royalties from your old books you—'

'It's not about the money,' shortly.

'No, of course! I just mean that...' Franny trails off, unsure of what she does actually mean.

And then somebody else addresses the veteran author, and Franny finds herself out of the conversation.

'Come, Miss Fragrance.'

Lydia takes Franny by the arm and guides her away. Tears stream from Franny's eyes.

'I made a complete fool of myself,' she sobs.

'Oh, Miss Fragrance, you were not the one at fault,' Lydia tells her. 'That woman was being intentionally rude to you. I would have stepped on your behalf, only I knew you wouldn't appreciate my intervention on this occasion.'

'You think she was being intentionally rude?'

'I'm sure of it.'

'But why?'

'Because she is hostile to you, Miss Fragrance.'

'But why? She's never even met me before!'

'Professional jealousy, Miss Fragrance.'

'Jealousy? That can't be true, Lydia! How could the woman who wrote *King of Knaves* and *The Five Daughters* be jealous of my books?'

Lydia sighs. 'All of that woman's books you have mentioned this evening are amongst her early novels, aren't they? Why haven't you mentioned any of her more recent titles?'

'Well, I…'

'Because they're not as good, are they?'

'Perhaps not as good as the early ones, but still—'

'Her star is falling, Miss Fragrance; yours is in ascendance while hers is falling. That is why she is jealous of you.'

Kenichi comes upon Itsumi suddenly. A group of people move away and there she is, right in front of him. He has no time to turn away, recognition is instantaneous.

'Kenichi!' she cries, surprised but happy. 'What are you doing here? You never told me you were a waiter!'

'Yeah it's just for one night,' says Kenichi. 'They were understaffed…'

'It's long way from Shinjuku for just one night's work: Is it gunna be worth it?'

'Well, you know…'

'You don't seem surprised to see me,' proceeds Itsumi. 'Did you know I was here?'

'Yeah, I've seen you around the room. Would've stopped to say hi sooner, but y'know, too busy…'

'Sure. I understand.'

'You here on your own then?'

'Well I am right now,' says Itsumi. 'I tried to talk to some people, but nobody speaks Japanese. The buffet's good, though.'

'You just came here for the food?'

'And to kill some time. I'm seeing Lance later.'

'Lance Enders? He's here?'

'Sure he is! His PR company is running this whole convention!' Mystery solved.

'Is that so?'

'Yep.'

'And… you'll be going home with him?'

'Don't have to. He's got a room right here in the hotel.'

'So are you and him—' He breaks off. He has just spotted Lance

Enders! The man is scanning the room, presumably searching for Itsumi. 'Well, I better get back to work. See you around!'

He rushes off.

Moments later Lance joins Itsumi.

'What the hell are you doing here, Itsumi?' He looks nervous. 'I told you to go on up to my room!'

'I know, but I thought I'd just check out the party first. Isn't that okay?'

'No, it's *not* okay. Natalie's here somewhere! If she sees you…!'

'But she doesn't know what I look like, does she?'

'That's just it: I don't *know* if she knows. She might have looked you up online. *Please* will you just go on up to my room? I'll be right behind you. I've just got to have a quick word with someone, then I'll be right on up.'

'Okay!' agrees Itsumi cheerfully.

Where's Kenichi? Where's he got to?

The crowded ballroom has become a shifting maze to Shinji. People. People everywhere. Penguins and sequins. He has steered his way between them for what seems like hours, frantically searching for his friend. And his steering has become erratic by this time; he's starting to lose control of the helm, and he ploughs into more people than he passes. His head spinning, Shinji barely registers the protests and epithets directed at him, unintelligible in language but lucid in tone.

Of course he has given up all pretence of being a waiter. He dropped the last tray of drinks he attempted to carry. And worst of all, before he'd had chance to drink a single glass!

Shinji just wants to find Kenichi and get out of this place. He wants to go home.

He doesn't see the snack table until he barrels straight into it. Both man and table overbalance and come crashing to the ground. Shinji finds himself entangled in white linen tablecloth and plates of finger-food.

But then, friendly hands help to extricate him for the wreck and lift him to his feet. No. He soon registers that these hands are *not* friendly at all, and that he is being hauled across the room by people who do not hold him in high esteem.

After this it is all a whirl. He is in some other room. People are shouting at him. He is forcibly divested of his waiter's suit and then is clumsily dressed in his own clothes. Then there are more corridors; a forced march. And then he is pushed roughly through a doorway and into the cool night air.

When Shinji looks back on his evening in Daedalus Central, this is where his memories will stop.

Room 3111.

This is the one. Itsumi inserts the key card, opens the door. The lights come on as she enters the room. She is just turning to close the door when someone barges into the room.

'Kenichi! What're you doing?'

'I followed you up here,' declares Kenichi, a determined look on his face.

'What for?'

'I got something to tell you.'

'Okay, but can you make it quick? Lance'll be up here any minute. But then I guess he knows you're working here…'

'No he doesn't,' snaps Kenichi. 'Now let's get out of here before he shows up!'

Itsumi laughs. 'What do you mean "get out of here"? Why would I wanna do that?'

'Because I don't want you seeing that guy!'

Itsumi starts to see the light. 'Kenichi…'

'*I* like you, Itsumi! *I* like you more than he does!'

Itsumi sighs. 'I know you like me, Kenichi. I guessed from the way you're always at the noodle bar… But Lance is my guy right now…'

'He's no good for you, Itsumi!'

Itsumi pinches the bridge of her nose. 'Look… We'll talk about this; but not right now, okay? Lance'll be here any minute, so you should clear out before he sees you.'

'What? Clear out and let you spend the night with that guy?'

Itsumi's face now looks very close to being cross. 'That's up to me, Kenichi. Just go home and we can talk about this tomorrow.'

And she ends the conversation by turning from Kenichi and

crossing the room to what she takes to be the bedroom doors.

The room beyond them is indeed the bedroom and a sumptuous one. Inside, Itsumi removes her boots, discards her hoodie and pulls off her top. She is just stepping out of her cycle shorts when Kenichi walks in.

'Now look I—' He breaks off. 'What are you doing?'

'I'm getting undressed,' replies Itsumi. 'And if you're a gentleman, Kenichi, you'll go away right now. You're not my guy.'

'No!' insists Kenichi. 'I'm staying! I won't let you sleep with that jerk!'

Itsumi sighs, unclips her bra, takes it off. Her panties come next.

If Kenichi had wanted to prove himself that gentleman of whom Itsumi had just made reference, he would have vacated the room, or at least turned his back. But the sudden shock of seeing his idol stripping completely naked right in front of him freezes him to the spot a speechless spectator. And can you blame him? Body-fascists might criticize Itsumi for being a bit on the chunky side and for having a bit of a pot-belly—but for a J-fan, and this one more than any other, she is still a sight worthy of beholding with eyes respectfully extended on stalks.

Both flattered and annoyed at the audience reaction, Itsumi places hands on hips and is about to deliver some mildly sarcastic comment, when the sound of the outer door being opened interrupts her.

Lance!

For a split-second Itsumi and Kenichi trade dumbfounded looks; and then before Itsumi can offer any suggestion, Kenichi has taken the initiative and dived under the bed.

The bedroom door opens and Lance enters.

'Hi, gorgeous,' he says, admiring her naked form, although not as graphically as Kenichi. He has, after all, seen it before.

'Hi,' says Itsumi, looking as relaxed as she can.

Lance takes her in his arms, and even as she responds to his kiss, Itsumi feels that it's too late to mention that they are not alone; the moment has already passed. She should have said that Kenichi was hiding under the bed as soon as Lance entered the room. But now it seems like it's already too late; that she can't tell him now.

The idea of making out with Lance with Kenichi hiding under

the bed does not fill Itsumi with joy, either on her own account or on his...

But then the solution hits her. She'll just suggest to Lance that they take things into the bathroom to enjoy a romantic shower together. Yes! And that will give Kenichi the chance he needs to slip out of the room. He's bound to realise she is doing this on purpose so that he can escape.

'I need to take a shower,' says Itsumi, smiling coyly. 'Come with me so you can wash my back...'

'You don't need to take a shower, honey,' smiles Lance, annoyingly. 'I like you just the way you are, baby.'

'But I'm all stinky,' protests shyly pouting Itsumi.

'But I love your natural scent, honey,' persists Lance. 'It's you. And I love everything about you, Itsumi.'

At any other time, these would be sweet words to Itsumi's ears—but not right now!

'But... you know... I'm a Japanese lady...' says Itsumi, flicking Lance's neck-tie. 'Japanese lady always likes to be clean before making love...'

Itsumi may well have carried her point at this juncture, but the moment is ruined by another interruption: Someone else has just entered the suite.

'Lance?' calls a tipsy female voice. 'Are you in here?'

'Oh Christ! It's Natalie!' is Lance's strangled whisper. 'I forgot she's still got a key to this place!'

'You in the bedroom? I'm coming in!'

'Under the bed!' squeaks Lance.

Itsumi dives under the bed, grabbing her discarded clothing as she does so.

Lance turns to the face the doors just as they open.

'Natalie! Baby!'

Natalie, standing with her heeled shoes in her hands, cocks her head on one side. 'Well, I wasn't expecting this reaction,' she says. 'You actually seem pleased to see me.'

'Well, you know, you've been giving me the cold shoulder for three days now...'

'I know, Lance darling, and I'm sorry. We should have just talked this through; I was stupid to go around stone-walling you.

Let's make up and sort this whole mess out. Whaddaya say?'

'Sure thing, honey! First thing tomorrow—'

'No, silly! I mean right now! I mean let's make up and make out! Always the best way, right?'

She advances unsteadily towards Lance.

'Er, are you sure that's not just the booze talking, honey?' suggests Lance. 'I can see you've been enjoying the champagne at the party.'

'No, I thought of this *before* I got drunk,' says Natalie, half-truthfully. 'Now let's get down and dirty. Unzip me.'

She turns her back to Lance, pulls her hair aside.

'Y'know, honey, I'm really not in the mood tonight,' says Lance. 'I'd only be a disappointment to you, and then you'd probably take it personally and we'd be back where we started. Let's just take a rain-check on this, hey?'

Natalie swings round again, face clouded with suspicion. 'What's going on with you, Lance Enders? You're never "not in the mood" you old horndog. Are you hiding something?'

Her eyes range across the room.

'Hiding? What would I be hiding?'

She looks at him narrowly. 'You *are* hiding something. You can't fool me, Lance Enders. I know you.'

She stalks across the room and opens the doors of the built-in wardrobe.

'Okay sweetie, you can come on out,' she calls.

Lance joins her.

'Who are you talking to, honey? There's no-one in there.'

'That Japanese slut is who I'm talking to,' grates Natalie. 'Get out here, you little marriage-breaker!'

'I'm telling you, honey, there's no-one—'

'Can it!'

She sweeps aside the suits hanging in the wardrobe, but her aggressive search reveals no concealed person.

'You see! What did I tell you? Now why don't you—'

'She's somewhere else then!' declares Natalie. 'Of course! The bed!'

She springs to the near side of the bed, squats down and inserts an arm under the frame.

'Ah-ha!' triumphantly. 'Come on out you little whore!'

The detected intruder complies, but much to Natalie's (and Lance's!) surprise, the Asian who emerges sheepishly from under the bed is a young man.

A pregnant moment, and then Natalie turns to face Lance, interpreting his shocked expression as guilt unmasked.

'So it's Japanese *boys* now, is it?' she says, smiling ironically. 'You really have been bitten by the Japanophile bug, haven't you?'

Lance finds his voice. 'I swear honey, I didn't even know he was there!'

'You didn't, huh? Then what was he doing there?'

'Well, I… Look at his clothes! He's a waiter here! Yeah, he must have broken into my suite! Guy must be a thief!'

Natalie turns to Kenichi. 'Is that right? Don't they pay you enough around here?'

'He can't speak English, Nat.'

She pounces on this. 'Ha! And how did you know he can't speak English, Lance Enders?'

'Well, I just… I mean look: you can tell by his stupid expression that he hasn't got a clue what we're both saying.'

This is true enough.

Natalie takes Kenichi's arm. 'Well, I'll tell you what: I'll just take this handsome boy off your hands, shall I?'

'You don't have to hand him over to security, honey! I mean, just—'

'Who said anything about handing him over to security?' challenges Natalie. 'I'm taking him back to my room.'

She heads for the exit, Kenichi in tow.

'Now wait a minute!' protests Lance, following them across the lounge. On the have your cake and eat it principle, and although Natalie has become an encumbrance he would rather get rid of, Lance still jealously dislikes the idea of her getting together with anyone else. And especially with Kenichi! 'You can't just—'

'Can't I? Just watch me, Lance darling.'

Then, with the bewildered Kenichi still firmly in hand, Natalie is out through the door, slamming it behind her.

And so it seems that white chicks *do* sometimes go for Asian guys, after all!

Walk Y'self Sober.

It's like waking up from a deep, dreamless sleep, but instead of lying supine in your bed, you find yourself vertical and in forward motion.

This is what happens to Shinji. Suddenly he is conscious, and he is walking down a road.

How did he get here? He searches his memory
His recollections of the evening are at first clear and chronological: following Itsumi to Central, the ride in the taxi, being taken on as waiters... But then, befuddled by alcohol, those recollections become blurred, intermittent... And then they stop completely after his undignified exit from the Excelsior Hotel.
And then, nothing; nothing until this moment.

I've already compared Shinji to a heavy sleeper awaking in their own bed, but of course there is such a phenomenon as sleep-walking; and although genuine sleep-walkers differ from Shinji in that they do not usually wake from their dream while they are still in locomotion, a somnambulist can nevertheless awaken to find themselves in alarmingly unfamiliar surroundings, and this is certainly the case with Shinji.

He has no idea where he is.

He is walking at a steady place along the centre of a very straight road. Darkness reigns; not a light shows in any of the long, low buildings on either side; darkness and also silence. He has the feeling of being off the beaten track, completely alone.

Shinji stops to assess his situation. Somehow he feels that he is walking in the right direction, that is making his way home to Shinjuku. Or at least, his alcohol-poisoned mind during the period which is now a blank to him, believed that this was the right direction. He looks around and yes, there are lights on the horizon, back in the direction from which he must have walked. Daedalus Central? Yes, it must be. But then, the fact that he is walking *away* from Central does not necessarily mean he is walking *towards* Shinjuku. Daedalus Central is as its name implies, and there are districts radiating from it in all directions.

Why the hell hadn't his drunken self taken the train back? He bought that dayrider ticket, didn't he? What made him decide to walk? Shinji pats his jeans pocket. He pats another one. Nothing. His pockets are empty. The ticket had been in his wallet, and his wallet is gone. Then he remembers: when changing into the waiter's outfit he had taken his wallet, keys and phone out of his pockets and put them in his backpack.

He doesn't have his backpack.

He must have left it behind. It'll either still be in that locker room in the Excelsior or else it's been stolen by someone. Or maybe Kenichi has it…

And where the hell is Kenichi, anyway? His last befuddled memories of the party at the hotel are of himself searching fruitlessly for his friend. Where did that jerk get to? He feels annoyed at Kenichi. If it wasn't for Kenichi, he would never even have come out here at all! This all happened because Kenichi wanted to follow Itsumi like some creepy stalker.

(Shinji would be even more annoyed at Kenichi if he could see where he is right now.)

For a moment he considers retracing his steps, but those lights on the horizon look an awful long way off, and what if he goes all that way and can't find his stuff? He might be almost home where he is right now; it would be stupid to turn back.

He starts walking again. He sees nothing on the horizon ahead, but this is good. Nothing is just what he wants, if his destination is Shinjuku. Shinjuku is down from Daedalus Central; there will be the Shinjuku Drop to negotiate. His current location seems to be some kind of warehouse district; the buildings on either hand look like either factories or warehouses, albeit they have an abandoned look about them.

And then it hits him: this is the No-Man's land that lies between Central and the Shinjuku Drop: a wilderness of closed-down factories and disused warehouses.

So, he's just where he needs to be!

Shinji presses on, confident now that he is heading in the right direction. But Shinji is halfway between being drunk and hungover, a phase that most people prefer to sleep through; and on top of this Shinji is not exactly physically fit at the best of the times. His legs start to ache. His feet start to ache. His head starts to ache. And he feels the increasingly urgent need for a drink. Not a pick-me-up. Not the hair of the dog. Just a nice long draft of glorious rehydrating water is what he wants.

A floating shape appears, draws closer. A security robot, a flying dustbin with arms. The robot hovers in front of him, scanning him.

'Hey, you in there!' croaks Shinji. 'Is anyone watching? Can anyone see me? I need a ride back to Shinjuku! I lost my wallet and I'm totally exhausted, man! Can't you bring someone out to help me out? And I need a drink! I'm totally parched!'

The robot flies off, with not so much as a bleep to indicate Shinji's SOS has been heard. He walks on, at first vaguely hoping that relief might arrive, but losing heart as the minutes tick past without anything happening. He realises it might be hours before any human being views that robot's data, and the stupid tin-cans aren't programmed to act autonomously.

Finally he reaches the Shinjuku Drop, the steel cliff Craig and Dudley had descended by taxi on the night of their arrival. The Buffer Zone between the two districts, housing all the life-support systems. And Shinji's home is right in front of him. Straight down. He presses himself against the chain-link fence, looks down, sees only darkness.

Now that's he got here, is there any way down? He knows there are no roads: cars just float down. And what Shinji has performed—walking all the way from Central to the Shinjuku Drop—is not exactly common practice. So will there even be any pedestrian descent?

But there would need to be some kind of emergency access, right? A lift, or stairs…

Please be a lift. Let there be a lift.

After following the fence for some time, he comes to a breach, clearly deliberately-made. The mesh has been separated from one of the posts and pulled away like a curtain. Logic suggesting that no-one would have cut the fence at this particular place without a good reason, Shinji climbs through the breach. Stepping out onto a metal abutment, the roof of one of the utilities towers, he finds at it's edge not a staircase but a ladder.

And here is where Shinji's nightmare really begins.

Shinji is not good with heights. And although the ladder is enclosed in a tubular framework, descending a ladder several thousand feet above the ground does not exactly fill him with joy. But the breach in the fence seems to prove that there are people (probably the junkies and vagrants who haunt the Buffer Zones) who have used this method of entering or leaving the Shinjuku district.

He starts to descend; hungover, and already drained of energy, he starts to descend. The ladder proves to be in sections. Every few storeys it terminates on a ledge with an emergency door, and on the lip of the ledge begins the next section of the ladder. Thus, the whole experience soon becomes a nightmare of repetition and increasing physical pain for poor Shinji: Jumping off one ladder and lowering himself onto the next; an unending cycle of repetition. And those emergency doors always turn out to be sealed tight; after the first thirty or so, Shinji stops bothering to even try them.

On and on, on and on...

And then, later, much later, when a ladder deposits him onto not *terra firma* but just a substantially wider ledge, Shinji takes advantage of the available space to collapse with exhaustion.

He just lies there, breathing ragged breaths and hoping that the pain of his screaming muscles and his blistered hands will begin to subside.

The holographic sky begins to lighten with the coming of another artificial dawn. Artificial it may be, but like any lifelong resident of Daedalus Station, Shinji accepts it as the advent of day as any planet-dweller would the real thing. And with the brightening dawn sky and the blessed repose, he starts to feel better.

The sky takes on a lemon white hue as the sun slowly rises. Above Shinji, rise the grey towers of the Buffer Zone, receding in a dizzying perspective; those faceless pipe-festooned structures which supply the district's essential resources, cleansing and renewing the very air they breathe.

Shinji's head still throbs, his mouth is parched, his body dehydrated; but, lying on the rough concrete and resting his aching limbs, he does begin to feel better. Yeah, sooner or later he'll have to get up and resume his agonising descent, but he feels like he's on the home stretch, and knowing that makes a difference. He is close now to his familiar, comfortable environment.

Life's not so bad.

His life, down there in Shinjuku—it's not so bad. There's the music and those amazing girls who make the music. He has his cherished collection of girl-band records and merchandise. And the live houses where he can go and see his beloved bands perform are all pretty much right on his doorstep. He has his fantasies, but he takes it for granted he'll never make it with any of the girls. He's just not the type of guy girls want to get with; this is how Shinji sees himself. And then there's the alcohol, which will keep on making him feel happy until the day it kills him. Yeah, life's not so bad.

He rises to his feet, and putting his new-found optimism to work he tries this level's emergency door. And as if in response to his elevated mood, the door obligingly opens.

It opens and inside he finds a pitch-dark but otherwise perfectly serviceable stairwell. He starts to descend, using the bannister rail to guide his steps. His overworked muscles soon take up their song of protest, but the stairs are a tolerable purgatory compared to the hell of those endless ladders.

He begins to see a dim light below him. This light hails the end of his journey and at last Shinji finds himself on *terra firma* at the foot of the stairwell. His arduous descent is over.

Chapter Eight
Pregnant Fantasy

After the concert.

It has worked like a dream. Everything has come right this time for Craig and Mami. That disastrous first night is forgotten; some vast cosmic mistake that allowed two people who were destined for one another to get off to the worst possible of starts: that's what it was. But now the mistake is repaired, the stars back in alignment. Craig and Mami now just exist for the moment and in the light of each other's eyes.

'Please forgive me,' begs Mami, tears welling up in her soulful eyes. 'I treat you so cold that first time. I was nervous to meet you. I was so sad about it after. I'm so sorry, so sorry!'

She bows repeatedly.

'You don't have to apologise,' Craig assures her, in his most manly tones. 'I wasn't on top form myself. It was just one of those things. Let's just forget about it.'

'No! You must forgive me or I cannot forgive myself!' insists Mami. 'And I let that foolish man Carl join our table. That night was meant for you; I should not have let him stay.'

'Well, things weren't going too well between us and he was just someone you knew, wasn't he? A familiar face.'

'I should not have let him stay. Carl talk too much. He love the sound of his own voice.'

'Don't beat yourself up, Mami. We're together now and you know that I'm the only guy for you, right?'

'Oh yes! Yes! You are only man for me, Craig! You are my master! Please take me and make me yours!'

Before you know it, the jumpsuit has been discarded and Mami is in her usual position on Craig's bed. As he showers those glorious upraised buttocks with kisses, history's most immortal, most emotive words of love leap unbidden to his already busy lips. Adopting the appropriate French accent, he recites those words between his passionate kisses:

> *'Ah, I love you…! You set my soul on fire! It is not just a little spark: It is a flame—a big, roaring flame! Ah… I can feel it now…!'*

And Mami feels it too, as he moves from words to actions, and he penetrates deep inside her.

'Faster! Harder!' she moans. 'Be violent with me! Make me yours!'

Craig complies.

Back in the real world, Craig decides to end the fantasy before it reaches its climax. (And please don't tell me you hadn't worked out that that was all just another one of his fantasies!) He stops, releases his grip, relaxes… He doesn't want to diminish his reserves of that precious *crème d'amour*. He has fervent hopes that those reserves will be called into use before this night is over.

He lies back on his bed, waiting for the mood to pass; and this process of detumescence takes an encouragingly long time. It seems his libido has fully recovered from its recent psychological assault.

'Our first night out together since we got here!'

Synthetic night has fallen and Craig and Dudley bend their steps towards the Shinjuku Loft, the venue hosting this evening's very special gig, the Cosmic Rays' 'Last Show Before Maternity Leave,' and with the support line-up including Tokyo Rose and the Smut Girls, Craig and Dudley's respective favourite bands.

The two young men are in ebullient high spirits, Craig's chemically-enhanced, Dudley's the natural kind.

'Yeah, a lot's happened, hasn't it?' says Dud.

'It has,' agrees Craig. 'That it has.' He looks at his friend. 'Told your folks yet?'

'About Krevis you mean?'

'What else would I mean? Here you are, only just flown the parental coop and you've already landed yourself a woman, and let's face it: she's going to be just one of those examples of womankind your mum and dad aren't going to approve of. They're kind of conservative, your folks.'

'Yeah,' agrees Dud, embarrassed. 'I told them about Krevis. I sent them a picture of her…'

'Not one of her porny pics, I hope?'

'Course not!' blushes Dudley. 'A normal picture.'

'And?'

'And they haven't replied yet.'

'Still getting over the shock, I shouldn't wonder,' surmises Craig. 'They'll be getting onto me, next. You see if they don't. Telling me I'm letting their darling boy mix with the wrong sort of woman.'

'But Krevis is nice!'

'You don't need to tell me! But she's not gunna be your parents' idea of "nice," is she? But, look; don't worry. You don't have to answer to them anymore—you're out of that trap… I only wish things could have gone as well for me.'

'Yeah, I'm sorry about that, Craig…'

'Would you stop apologising, you silly sod? It's not like you've been rubbing your good luck in my face. In fact, I know you've been going out of your way *not* to do that, haven't you?' Craig exhales a deep breath. 'Yeah, I can't help feeling a bit jealous, but it's not like I'm holding your good fortune against you. And anyway!' clapping his hands. 'I fully intend to make up for that first disaster when I see Mami again tonight. This time things will work out! I know they will! I can feel it in my bones!'

'I hope things go well for you tonight,' says Dud. 'I really hope they do.'

'Thanks, mate. You know what my mistake was? Well. I mean I made several, actually; but the one I'm on about is that I thought Mami was going to be just like her image is. You know, how she is on stage and on her blog? And she always came across like that in her emails to me, an' all. You know: all cutsie and bashful. But she's not like that in real life; not exactly. Some of that cutesiness is just her stage persona. She's more down to earth in real life. I wasn't expecting that, so it put my off my game… Still! Tonight I'll know better!'

'Yeah. Just be yourself with her, Craig. The real you. It'll be great if you can get to have a good long talk with Mami without that Carl guy around. Maybe he won't even be there.'

'No,' solemnly. 'No, I've got to be prepared for every eventuality this time. I've got to act like I know the git *is* going to be there and that he's going to be all over Mami. And if he is, then I've just got to use my manly charm and charisma to convince Mami that she'd be much better off with me than with him. Trouble is, he's got that edge over me because he speaks Japanese, the git, and Mami's English isn't so good.'

'That shouldn't matter! Krevis doesn't speak English that well either! In fact she's helping me with my Japanese lessons. You could get Mami to help you like that.'

'Y'know, I'd much rather help *her* learn to speak English better. Much less hassle…'

'The sacred portals!' announces portentous Craig.

They have arrived at the doors of the Shinjuku Loft. Like a lot of the live houses around here, the venue's unimpressive façade is comprised of pretty much just a sign over a door.

'The first and foremost live house for the Shinjuku girl band scene,' proceeds Craig. 'A place we used to only dream about entering; and here we actually are, for the first time!'

'Well, I've already walked past this place a couple of times since we've been here...' says Dudley.

'Well yeah, so have I,' admits Craig. 'But we haven't actually been inside, have we? That's what I mean. We've never been to an actual girl band show in Shinjuku.'

'Yeah, we haven't,' agrees Dud. 'I can't wait!'

'Then let's go!'

The 'Loft' isn't actually a loft, but it is on the top floor of the building' so having paid for their tickets, Craig and Dudley ascend a narrow, winding staircase; the stairwell walls are adorned with a display of framed vintage gig posters.

'Comfort House!' exclaims Craig. 'They were one of the first generation of Shinjuku bands. They set the standard, they did...

'And there's Green Tea Candy! The band who were tragically taken away from us when their tour rocket crashed off Vega...

'Ah! Strawberry Panic! The first all-lesbo Shinjuku girl band...'

Finally, the stairs and Craig's running commentary come to an end, and passing through a pair of doors they enter the bar-room of the venue. The lighting is suitably understated and a lot of black paint has gone into the interior decoration. The actual bar is on their left; before them they see the merchandise stalls, a series of trestle tables displaying the merchandise of all four of tonight's featured bands: LPs, 45s, badges, posters, t-shirts, towels, jewellery, etc... Examples of the posters and t-shirts are pinned to the wall behind the tables. The stage itself is not visible, being in an adjacent room.

There are already a large number of people milling around, and of course they are nearly all men. The prevailing age-range appears to be 20s to 50s, but there are a few who look even older. From young men to greybeards, the J-fans are out in force. The only females amongst the attendees seem to be members of other bands who have come to support their friends.

Craig takes in all of this, but then his eyes lock onto a familiar blonde bob. Yes, it's Mami! There she is: standing over by the merchandise stalls chatting with her bassist Otome.

This is it! The past is a blank slate: Craig is ready to go in and greet Mami the way he should have greeted her the first time!

'Mami's over there,' he says to Dud, repressed excitement in his voice. 'Here I go then. No time like the present.'

'I'll leave you to it then,' says Dudley. 'Good luck, Craig.'

Dudley departs in search of his girlfriend. Craig moves in on his idol. Still chatting with Otome, who is seated behind the merchandise stall, she hasn't seen him yet. Mami is wearing her pale blue patterned jumpsuit, which is absolutely Craig's all-time favourite of all Mami's on-stage outfits. He's told her in their electronic communication that the jumpsuit is his favourite outfit of hers; told her how sexy she looks, the black flat-soled shoes forming an attractive contrast with the light-coloured material of the suit. In countless of his fantasies has he helped her out of this very jumpsuit. Even now, as she leans over the table to talk to her bandmate, the thin material stretches tautly over her abundant posteriors...

This has to be a good sign, right? That she's wearing her jumpsuit? A positive omen. And if that isn't enough, it looks like she has also had a hair-cut! Yes, she's reduced the length of her bob since the other night; and now it's at just the length that makes her look her so completely at her cutest! To Craig's eyes she is an image of female perfection; a tactile, living goddess.

Has she done this just for him? Is her appearing in what she knows to be his favourite of her outfits—is it her way of apologising and making up for the other night...?

That familiar blend of reverence and desire takes possession of Craig as he draws closer to Mami. There she is. All he has to do is tap her on the shoulder and say to her is 'Hi!' That's all! Just sound happy! And then maybe, maybe when she sees it's him, she'll throw her arms around him and give him that hug he has always wanted her to greet him with!

Alerted by Otome, Mami turns to face Craig just as he reaches her. Unsmiling, she thrusts out a hand for him to shake. The hand seems like a stop-sign, a barbed-wire fence against any notions he might have entertained about going in for an embrace. Confronted with this stop-sign hand and the unsmiling visage, Craig's buoyant mood and sanguine hopes collapse into a pathetic pile of rubble.

The hand-shake is perfunctory.

'Hi,' says Craig, limply.

'Hi,' says Mami. 'Thank you for coming.'

Nothing has changed. The same chilly air. The same raised barriers.

And then someone slaps him heartily on the back.

It is Carl.

'Hiya, buddy!' he enthuses, grinning all over. 'Good to see you again! How're you doing? This'll be your first live show in Shinjuku, right? Your first time being here in person, instead of just watching on a holoscreen. A major event, right? Looking forward to it?'

Craig mumbles something. Carl turns to Mami, a now-smiling Mami. They fall easily into smiling conversation, speaking in Japanese.

Without a word, Craig retreats in search of the men's room. He needs to powder his nose.

The opening act of the evening are Love Rumble. Sporting '60s fashions and hair-dos, they infect the crowd with their feel-good garage rock tunes, a combination of covers from the era and compositions of their own in the same style.

Craig feels his pre-arrival buzz return thanks to Love Rumble's energetic set, combined with the renewed chemical effects from having 'powdered his nose.' To complete his recovery, a Japanese girl—he thinks it might be the drummer from Raw Babes in the Country—has been dancing in front of him throughout the performance, her raven-black pony-tail bobbing up and down just under his nose. The girls in the audience at these shows may be a minority in terms of numbers—but, distinct from the male spectators, they can actually dance, rather than just vaguely swaying, shuffling their feet and nodding their heads.

Craig has never seen a Japanese woman's hair this close before and the whole experience is very agreeable. Thicker and heavier than Caucasian hair, but lustrous and beautiful in its perfect black colouring, and right now so close that Craig believes he can smell the intoxicating scent of it.

His beloved Mami always dyes her hair, and while Craig has always thought she looks cute with her blonde bob, at the same time he has always liked the idea of seeing her for once with her hair with its natural raven sheen.

Love Rumble conclude their performance to rapturous cheers and applause, and then comes that back-down-to-earth feeling when the lights come on and the much quieter piped music resumes.

Craig joins the general exodus towards the bar. He wants to see Mami again. He is not giving up just yet. He just needs to play it cool. Act natural. Don't seem too eager, too persistent. And try not feel pissed off with her. Yeah, you'd think she'd know to treat him better than she did last time, but with these Japanese girls, you can't really work out what's going on in their minds. Maybe she wants to act like that other night never happened…

And don't be pissed off if Carl is with her! The guy's just a dick. You can out-shine him, Craig Jenx. Don't let him throw you off.

Thoughts focused on this next stage of his campaign, he automatically side-steps to avoid an approaching patron, finds his move mirrored, side-steps the other way only to be blocked once more.

And then Craig sees who it is, and of course it's Fragrance Pie.

'Not you again!' he groans.

'Yes, me again,' is the unapologetic response.

'And what are you doing here?'

'Research! I told you before: I want to know what makes you J-fans tick. Can I ask you a few questions?'

'No you bloody can't. I'm busy!'

'It's him!' comes a new voice. 'The sex-maniac from the spaceliner!'

Lydia Luvstruk places herself protectively between Craig and Franny, her boardroom grey looking out of place in this environment.

'Don't you come near Miss Fragrance, you sexual predator!'

'I don't want to be near her! She just keeps getting in my way!'

'Actually Lydia, I did want to interview the young man…'

'And I don't want to be interviewed either! Piss off, the pair of you!'

'Just look at him, Miss Fragrance,' sneers Lydia. 'A degenerate masturbator. One of society's rejects. Brains addled by that raucous noise they like to call music. Clearly he's a paradigm of all of his type. All the research material you need is just written in his hollow-eyed unshaven face, Miss Fragrance.'

'You know what?' says Craig. 'I've just remembered I need to go to the bog. Excuse me.'

And he heads to the gents to powder his nose again.

'Hey, you love birds!'

Asuna, front-woman of Raw Babes in the Country (not performing tonight), her of the ash-blonde hair and tanned complexion and accelerated libido, and mother of that precocious youngster Hina, greets her bandmate Machiko, who sits with her—ahem—'boyfriend' Vern on one of the sofas which occupy the Loft's 'chilling out' area, a room situated midway between the bar and the auditorium.

Never did two people look less like 'love birds.' Asuna belatedly notices this fact.

'What's up, you guys?' she asks, dropping onto a neighbouring sofa.

'What's up?' echoes Machiko. 'Nothing's up! Is it, darling?'

She turns to Vern for confirmation. He manages a sickly smile.

Machiko's eyes narrow. 'I said nothing's up, is it, darling?'

'No, nothing's up.'

'That's good,' says Asuna. 'I'm so happy you two have got together!'

'Thank you,' replies Machiko. To Vern: 'Asuna just offered us her congratulations, darling. Why don't you thank her?'

'Thank you,' says Vern.

'So: you're not a virgin anymore!' says straight-to-the-point Asuna to her bass-player.

'No, I had that taken away from me,' agrees Machiko, with a ready smile. To Vern: 'Didn't I, darling?'

Vern studies his toe-caps.

'Didn't I, darling? I had my virginity taken from me, didn't I?'

'Yes,' mumbles Vern.

'Get me a drink, darling.'

Vern springs to his feet.

'Same again?' he asks.

'Of course.'

Vern turns to leave.

'Darling?'

He stops in his tracks, about-turns.

'Haven't you forgotten something?'

Vern looks worried. 'Er… Have I…?'

'Yes, you have, darling. Asuna. You haven't asked Asuna if she would like a drink.'

Vern smiles weakly. 'Sorry. What do you want, Asuna?'

'Thank you! I'll have a beer, please. And don't forget yourself! You've been sitting there with no drink! You look like you could use one. Loosen up a bit!'

'Oh no, Vern isn't drinking tonight,' Machiko informs her. 'Are you, darling?'

'No, I'm… I'm not drinking tonight…'

'Well don't just stand there, darling. Get going.'

Vern gets going.

Three J-fans:

'Love Rumble were looking good tonight.'

'Sure. Those '60s babydoll dresses were hot!'

'I dunno; I prefer the shift dresses they sometimes wear. They accentuate the figure, y'know.'

'Idiot! That's the point of the babydoll dresses! They leave more to the imagination!'

'Yeah, and you get that contrast between the totally covered up top half and then the legs underneath.'

'Oh boy, those legs! They were great legs; all six of 'em!'

'Yeah, and they sure looked good in those heels!'

'I'm hearing that!'

'Yeah, why was it they invented high-heels in the first place? Was it to give a girl more height or to make her feet look smaller?'

'To give her more height!'

'I dunno about that. I always thought they were to raise a lady's dress off the ground so's it didn't get dirty.'

'Oh yeah! Like those wooden sandals Japanese women used to wear!'

'High-heels are nice an' all, but those girls shouldn't wear 'em all the time; they can ruin your feet; make the veins stick out, y'know.'

'Yeah, that may be an issue to you with your foot fetish. The rest of us aren't so worried.'

'So tell us, connoisseur, who's got the sexiest feet?'

'Out of Love Rumble?'

'No, dummy. Out of *all* the bands.'

'Out of all the bands? I'd say Mami Rose.'

'What? Hers are really big!'

'Well I think bigger is better. I'm not into that foot-binding and tiny feet.'

'Foot-binding was Chinese, wasn't it? They never had that in Japan.'

'Are you sure? I thought they did.'

'Okay, I'm not *sure* sure, but I always thought it was just China.'

'Foot-binding wasn't just about keeping feet small, it was about keeping them soft and tender as well.'

'Ha! Like a little girl's feet, right? So it was a loli-con thing!'

'So what's the deal with big feet on a girl? Is it symbolic of female emancipation or something?'

'It's symbolic of having a big ass to go with 'em, in Mami's case! Why does she always wear that stupid jumpsuit? Someone should tell her it only makes her ass look bigger!'

'I think Mami kind of likes her big ass.'

'And so do you!'

'Well, sure.'

'Still, she ain't so big up top.'

'C'mon, that's pretty common with Japanese ladies. Mami's tits are still bigger than average. Y'know, the traditional Japanese woman's figure is just two little mosquito bites.'

'I think the traditional Japanese ladies' figure is meant to be pretty flat and straight all over, isn't it?'

'Ha! A little girl's figure! Back to the loli-con thing again!'

And of course it would have to be the above conversation that material-researching Franny Pie happens to overhear.

Listen to them! Just talking about the girls' bodies! Discussing them like they're lumps of meat! Not a word about the music! And as for that supposed respectful and submissive adoration of the girl bands—Huh! Didn't hear much of it there!

Just as she'd thought all along.
This will be going into the book.

(If Franny could have overheard a backstage conversation between the girls discussing the J-fans, she might have heard a very similar kind of dialogue, albeit with perhaps the notable difference of the physical assessment being confined to just one vital area.)

There she is!

Espying Mami in the crowd, our (once again) reinvigorated Craig zeros in on her, all ready to compliment her on her outfit and haircut. Casually complimentary, of course. Don't make it sound too obvious and rehearsed.

Mami turns and sees him. Craig turns on his most winning smile and opens his mouth to speak but Mami, pointing to her upper lip says:

'You have nose-bleed.'

Buggeration.

Craig dabs his own upper lip and sure enough sees a spot of blood on his fingertips.

'Are you okay?' asks Mami.

'Sure,' answers Craig easily. 'I just get these nose-bleeds now and then.'

'Well you would get them,' speaks up a grinning and hitherto unnoticed Carl. 'If you've got a "sniff," right?'

To clarify the allusion, Carl presses down on one nostril and sniffs loudly through the other.

They all laugh at this, with Craig at the same time silently damning Carl to hell for a smug fucking bastard whom he would dearly love to treat to one major fucking nose-bleed that most definitely won't have been induced by inhaling anything!

'Look, I'm only asking for her email address, asshole!'

'Don't asshole me you little turd! And you're not getting her email address!'

The speakers are Kenichi and Lance; the setting, the corridor leading to the backstage area. (Neither of them should be there.)

'And why not?' demands Kenichi. 'Me and her, we're like an item now. We slept together, y'know?'

'"Slept together",' smiling scornfully. 'Yeah, and that's all you did, wasn't it? Sleeping.'

'Whadda you mean? We were totally—'

'Forget it, loser. Natalie told me about the whole thing.'

A frown. 'Who's Natalie?'

'Oh for—She's the lady you "slept" with, genius. Her name's Natalie, and she also happens to be my girlfriend.'

Kenichi looks surprised. 'She is?'

'Yeah, she is!'

'But then, why did she—'

'—Why did she take you back to her room? One: because she was totally hammered; and two: she wanted to get at me!'

'Get at you?'

'Yes! Because she found you hiding under my bed—'

'I can explain that!'

'Don't bother; I know all about that one as well. I got the story from Itsumi. But Natalie didn't know why you were there. When she found you under my bed she just thought that you must have been my bedroom partner for that night…'

'What? No way! Even if I swung that way, I still wouldn't go with you!'

'Yeah, right back at you, buster. The point is that's the reason why she you took off with you. It was just to get at me. 'Cept that not a whole lot happened after that, did it? When she got you back to her suite, seems like you had yourself a major case of first-night jitters; and Natalie soon got bored of tryin' to coax some life out of you, so she just went ahead and passed out drunk. And then, when she woke up next morning, you'd already split, hadn't you? Just crawled off with your sorry tail between your legs.'

'Fuck you, man! Y'know, anyone can be like that the first time! But next time we get together—'

'*Forget it.* There isn't gunna be a next time. She'll have already forgotten you exist. Face it, loser; you had your one chance to get lucky—and most probably the only one you'll ever get—and you blew it.'

'Fuck you, jerkwad! I can go'n see that chick again any time I like! I don't need your fucking permission! And why's she your girlfriend anyhow? You shouldn't *have* a girlfriend! You're supposed to be stepping out with Itsumi! *She* should be your girlfriend!'

'Look, my private life is none of your fucking business, you little shit! You can't have Natalie and you can't have Itsumi! Got it? Just go back to jerking off to porno flicks in your apartment, sad-sack; that's the only action you'll ever see. This conversation is over!'

Lance turns to make a triumphant exit; but the gesture is over before it's started when he finds Itsumi standing in his way.

He's never seen her looking angry before.

'There's no respect at all,' says Franny. 'No respect for these women or for their art. It's just a lot of libidinous men wrapped up in their sexual fantasies about these girls, and coming to their shows just to leer at them, and in the vague hopes that they might get off with one of them.'

'Just as you suspected all along, Miss Fragrance,' confirms Lydia, eager to agree as usual. 'With your customary perspicuity, you had accurately assessed the situation before you even arrived here. I said all along you could have just started on your book without doing any on-the-spot research at all, and it still would have been completely authentic. They're still men, these so-called J-fans; and if there is one thing you understand, Miss Fragrance, it is the workings of the male mind.'

'Well, male minds aren't that hard to figure out.'

'Not for you, Miss Fragrance.'

Franny pauses. And then: 'You know what I've got in mind, Lydia?'

'No, I do not, Miss Fragrance; but I am eager to learn and convinced that whatever it is, it will be a good idea.'

'Thank you, Lydia. It occurs to me that all of this,' she indicates the room around them. (It is the interval before the headline band's appearance, and people are standing talking in groups.) 'is similar to the situation in nineteenth century Europe; I'm referring to the time when theatre actresses were always being chased after by so-called "gentlemen." They would go to the plays, they would loiter around backstage, sending gifts of flowers and jewellery to the actresses they wanted to make their mistresses... They didn't care about the women's art, those men; they didn't care how good at acting they were; they only cared about their good looks.

'So, my idea is to write a novel with two separate timelines running parallel: one with the Shinjuku girl bands here in the present day, and one with the theatre world of nineteenth century London.'

'An astonishing idea, Miss Fragrance!' enthuses Lydia. 'Only a genius such as yourself could have come up with such a plan!'

'You like it, then?' asks Franny, smiling modestly.

'Oh, Miss Fragrance; it will be your greatest novel yet! I am convinced of it!'

'And of course back in those days, the world of the stage was considered a very dissolute world,' continues Franny, warming to her subject, 'associated with loose living; not the respectable calling the theatre is today. And then here you've got this: the rock music world; and that has *always* been associated with casual sex, drugs and alcohol, loose morals, and what have you!'

'Absolutely, Miss Fragrance! Another point of comparison!'

'Yes, and I think with what we have here, we could go even further. These bands: all Japanese women. But look at the men in the audience; most of them white men. Historically, Asian women have always been perceived by Caucasian men as just being exotic and submissive sexual partners, as though these women were toys designed exclusively for their pleasure. And here: if you take away all those false trappings of musical appreciation and idol-worship, it's just the same thing!'

'You've got it all wrong, y'know,' says an unexpected new voice.

Shinji has been seated next to Franny and Lydia for some time, but Shinji is one of those individuals who often goes unnoticed, and consequently the two women hadn't noticed him. And moreover, being within the range of their translators, he has been able to understand every word of their conversation.

They look at him now; a skinny Japanese boy with the lazy smile, and clearly very much the worse for drink.

'And what have we got wrong, according to you?' asks Lydia, in the tone of someone not expecting to be convinced by what she hears.

'About the J-fans,' says Shinji. 'Sure, most of 'em are white an' they've got a thing for Asian ladies, but not in the way you just said. It's more like they idealise 'em, y'know? Like they think Japanese ladies, and especially the girls in the bands here are like the next step up the evolutionary ladder; like *homo superior* or something.'

'Ha!' laughs Lydia. 'We've heard a very good example of how much J-fans revere and respect the girl bands! Tell him, Miss Fragrance!'

Franny relates some of the conversation she had overheard earlier.

Shinji just shrugs. 'Well sure we'll talk about how they look: their bodies and what they're wearing over them. That's just natural, ain't it? Everyone does that. J-fans ain't some religious order with lots of dos and don'ts attached to what we say. But that's just guy-talk, what you heard there. But how we really feel… You can't really expect us to be talking about how we really feel about the bands, the girls… Even soft guys can't really express that kind of junk; not to each other… I couldn't even tell it to you right now. I wish I could, but I just can't find the words to go with those feelings, y'know?

'So you go ahead and write that book. I heard you talkin' about it and it sounds good. But I think you should be showin' that us J-fans are different to those Victorian swells, not the same as 'em, y'know? Like you said, those guys didn't care about the ladies' art. We do. We love their music and those of us who understand 'em love their lyrics, too. So it ain't just about guys looking for girls to get lucky with. I mean, look at me: I've been with this scene for years now and I ain't never been there! Sex-wise, I mean. I'm just not the kind of guy girls wanna get with; I know that. Surrounded by girls and I'll most probably die a virgin! But I'm okay with that.

'And yeah, I know some people criticise the girl bands cuz they sing about food, and cats and all that everyday stuff; and saying they're out of touch cuz they don't really do politics aside from a general "love and peace" thing. But y'know, that's cuz these girls are like from the future, right? They don't talk politics cuz they belong to a time way, way off, where there's no politicians, and no cops, and no armies and wars.

'Yeah, it's not the Shinjuku girl bands who've got it wrong, if you ask me; it's everybody else who's got it wrong. Those girls, they're the only folks in town who've got it right; and us J-fans we kind of see that, and that's we love them so much. Yeah, so that's pretty much it!'

Shinji laughs embarrassedly.

'Well thank you for explaining all that,' begins Franny. 'But don't you think—'

She stops. Shinji's head has nodded forward, his breathing has become stertorous, and drool trickles from his mouth. Having spoken his unusually long piece, Shinji has dropped straight back into character by passing out in a drunken stupor.

The labcoated, power-chord playing headline band the Cosmic Rays have taken to the stage to perform their set, rocking the house with their songs about string theory, super-fast particles, dark matter, etc.

The Last Show Before Maternity Leave! However, the band stick resolutely to their pet subject and not a word is sung concerning motherhood, labour pains and absconding biological fathers.

The heavily-pregnant Sayako has been playing seated, but now, after the final song, she takes off her guitar and rises to her feet in order to salute her cheering fans.

Her labcoat falls open, exposing her previously hidden belly.

Silence falls.

A blue sarong around her waist and a matching bandanna covering her chest frame a naked belly, its distended surface decorated with child-like crayon pictures of stars and rockets and planets.

The crowd stares. It is a mesmerising, hypnotic sight.

Sayako raises the microphone to her mouth.

'Thank you, Shinjuku!'

The cheers break out anew.

Sayako raises her arms aloft, and her nude belly, ripe with incipient maternity, asserts its presence still more; it positively *glows* under the stage lights. And as she basks in the crowd's adoration, this young, beautiful, bespectacled Japanese woman simultaneously projects something back at those spectators; something powerful and imperative that sweeps through that male audience, something nameless and beautiful and far older than time.

It permeates every pore of the men's bodies, this something. It takes control of their thoughts, their senses, their identities; stripping them down to a primaeval gestalt. All eyes are fixed on that swollen belly, seeing nothing else; and the cheering rises to an ecstatic, moaning crescendo, a sound dragged from the dawn of time; and then another climax occurs, simultaneously affecting every last man in that crowd, a white-hot eruption sweeping over mind and matter… And those moans dissolve to a collective sigh of blessed release.

'Thank you!' cries Sayako, once more. 'Thank you all for coming!'

Chapter Nine
This Love Sucks

I know what you're thinking.

What about poor Craig Jenx? He has gone to all the trouble of thoughtfully conserving his personal supply of that vital fluid on account of and for the benefit of his lady-love Mami Rose. Have those reserves now been compromised? Have the tanks shed their contents?

Fear not. Craig has escaped being part of the preceding epiphany by the simple fact of his not even being there to witness it.

It happened like this.

The Smut Girls have just performed and Craig sits alone nurturing dejection and self-pity in equal portions. He has completely failed to make any headway with Mami; he has completely failed to have anything even remotely resembling a meaningful conversation with her. And his frequent visits to the powder room are becoming steadily less and less efficacious. You can never quite recapture the buzz of your initial high; not on the same night. Craig knows this himself, but he has kept on at it anyway, and all he has to show for it are two very sore nasal passages.

And then two people sit down on either side of him. It is Dudley Moz and Krevis Jungle. Krevis is as tall as Craig and pleasantly hot and sweaty from her recent performance under the stage-lights. Introductions are made. Krevis seems genuinely happy to meet Craig, her boyfriend's best friend. Craig sees for the first time that those pugnacious lips of hers can spread into a very generous smile when they want to.

'Aren't things working out with you and Mami?' asks Dud.

'No…' says Craig. 'I just can't seem to hit it off with her. Everything I say seems to just fall flat. It's been a total bloody disaster.'

'She turn you down?' inquires Krevis.

'Turn me down?' echoes Craig. 'What do you mean?'

'When you ask her. She turn you down?'

'Ask her? You don't just *ask* someone if you can have sex with them!'

'Not for sex, *baka*,' says Krevis. 'Ask her *out*. Ask her to be your girlfriend.'

At first Craig looks dumbstruck, but then a smile begins to spread across his face.

'Ask her out… I never thought of that…'

'Ask now,' says Krevis

She points to the stage. Tokyo Rose are there, setting up for their performance.

'Ask her out…' says Craig, the wonderment still in his voice.

In all of those countless fantasies involving himself and Mami, Craig has never once played out the simple scenario of just asking the girl out. His fantasies have always been of the 'one thing leading to another' variety, ending up with them both in bed; and then only after that event, on awakening the next morning, deciding that they were an 'item'. (And in fairness to Craig relationships very often *do* commence in this way.)

But to actually just go up to her and ask her out…

'You should do it, Craig!' urges Dudley.

Yes, he should. It's a crazy idea—But it just might work!

Suddenly a man with a purpose, Craig rises from his seat and strides purposefully across the auditorium, the stage his destination.

Ask her out… Of course! What an idiot he had been not to think of that! Ask her out! Of course he should ask her out! If you don't ask you don't get! You shouldn't just wait and hope for things to just drop into your lap! No, you have to go out and grab them! (Metaphorically speaking.) Ask her out… Mami has probably been wanting him to do that all along! Yes, and those bad vibes between them could just have been her annoyance that he *hasn't* popped the question! What a fool he's been!

Ask her out…

Without hesitation or authorisation Craig mounts the stage and walks up to Mami, who is performing a last-minute tune up of her guitar.

She looks up at him, smiles demurely.

'Hello,' she says. 'Something is wrong?'

'Mami,' says Craig, down to business.

'Yes?' says Mami.

'Will you go out with me?'

She looked puzzled. 'Go out with…?'

'Yes! Go out with me! Be my girlfriend!'

'Your girlfriend…' Her head droops, an awkward smile forms around her overbite. 'But we only just meet…'

'Yeah, but we've been online pals for ages! We already know each other well! And you must have guessed that I love you! I do love you!'

'Well, you see…' She hesitates over her words. 'I don't really know you… Not well, I mean… So, I think now is not the right time for us to become a romantic couple…'

'You don't?'

'No… Too soon…' She brightens. 'But I very happy you ask me! Very happy!'

'Oh... Okay...'

Craig had stayed to watch Tokyo Rose's performance, but he hadn't enjoyed it. His favourite band in the universe and the long-anticipated event of him seeing them play live for the first time in his life—and he hadn't enjoyed it.

Without a word to anyone, he had walked out of the venue the moment they had finished their set.

'...And so at first I thought I was going to pack my bags and head straight back to Gameron. I mean, what was there left for me here in Shinjuku? The main reason I'd come here in the first place was because of Mami Rose and she obviously doesn't want me. That's how I felt. But then I thought, why would I be going back to Gameron? Did I think I'd feel better if I went back home? Well, yeah to start with I thought I just didn't want to have anything more to do with Shinjuku and the whole girl band scene. I thought I just had to get out of the place. But I've made this scene my whole life; what would I do without it? Yeah I know, you'd say no matter how bad I may feel right now, sooner or later I'd get over it and find something else to take up my time, some new interest—I know that; but then I started being honest with myself and I realised that by going home to Gameron, what I really wanted wasn't to get away from Mami, but for her to see that I'd gone; for her to see that because of the way she'd treated me she'd driven me back home; I'd do it cuz I wanted to make her feel guilty and upset so's she'd start sending me messages begging me to come back; or that she'd maybe even come to Gameron in person to take me back with her. Yeah, right! Like that would ever happen. So I'd be back home at Gameron waiting for something that was never going to happen, and when I'd finally realised that, what would there be for me back home? I never had that many friends, and more and more of them seem to be drifting out of my circles, you know? Turning away from the underground and heading into the mainstream. That's happening with a lot of the people I knew at school...

'Yeah, I should probably tell you about my school days: they were pretty crappy. I had this so-called friend called Justin Danz, and he was always trying to get one up on me, like it was some stupid competition we had going on. He would study and make sure he got higher scores than me on every test; if I started reading a particular book, he'd start reading it too and make sure he finished it before I did; anything I said in a conversation where I maybe wasn't on solid ground, he would go home and do his research and come back to school the next day with proof that what I'd said was wrong... He'd do just about anything he could think of to get one up on me; he was just doing it to bolster his own fragile ego at my expense; make himself look good by making me look bad. And of course it worked because I *did* start to feel inferior. Looking back though, I know I shouldn't have just taken it. Danz was nothing special himself; I mean yes, he did well academically cuz he was a swat, but he wasn't exactly the class alpha male or anything...

'Maybe I *am* drifting off the point a bit, here. I mean I'm way over Justin; haven't set eyes on the git for years. Dudley's my best pal these days; the guy I flat-share with. We weren't at school together; I only met him a couple of years back when I first started getting into the Shinjuku girl bands; I went online to see if there were any other J-fans living in Gameron City, and there he was. Yeah, he was still living with his parents and he was a bit backwards for his age, like those types usually are; so I kind of took him under my wing; and then in the end we decided to move out here, to be where the action is. Yeah, old Dud has only just flown his family nest, something I did years back, but I'm starting to feel like he's already overtaking me. For one thing he's been lucky since he got here, while I've been striking out: his idol is Krevis from the Smut Girls and they clicked from the start, those two; just like me and Mami bloody *didn't* click. I'll admit I was jealous and pissed off about it at first, but it's not his fault, is it? And Christ knows he's been going out of his way not to let me even think he might be rubbing my nose in it... Yeah, he's a better person than me, is Dud... Although, I did actually think he might be the—No, doesn't matter. I know it's not him now. That was just a stupid suspicion I had...

'So, yes, I think I'm gunna stay in Shinjuku for now at least; see how things pan out. I mean sometimes I feel *so* pissed off with that bit—I mean with Mami. Y'know, when she turned me down and said that my asking her had "made her very happy". Yeah right, I thought. That sounded completely sincere and heartfelt, that did. I mean, if she'd been happy that I asked her out, she could have accepted the offer, couldn't she? But she turned me down, the bitch! Sorry. Pardon me. I'm not saying all women are bitches or anything; not even all Japanese women. Your minds are different, right? I know that. You don't think the same way as the rest of us mere mortals. I mean you were never even my type before—you know, you delicate Japanese flowers. Not at all. My last girlfriend, she was a tomboy; very assertive... But anyway, how could she lead me on like that, saying "love Mami" in her emails, sending me GIFs with hearts floating up in the air, encouraging me to move out here, and then when I arrive she acts like she doesn't give a flying one about me? Like I'm just another J-fan. Now is that fair? I don't think so. And if she *has* lost interest in me, then how about an explanation? Is it something I've said or done? Or has she just dropped me cuz suddenly she's decided she likes someone else? Well, who is it? And why does she think whoever it is is better than me? I mean I'd think it was that arsehole Carl who's always in the way when I try to talk to Mami; but he's been away for about half a year; he only got back the day after I arrived here; so I don't see how she could have suddenly fallen for him when he was out backpacking and she wasn't even in touch with him—doesn't make sense, does it? So I'm back to thinking it's something I did wrong; something I said. But I can't think what. I checked through our emails to see. I'd sent her some pretty sexy messages in the past—I mean before I moved out here—but nothing too dirty, and anyway she always seemed to like them. I'm not one for serious online making out; I never even sent her a dick-pic!

'So what else can it be? I think it must be me; I mean the physical me. Somehow when we met face-to-face, something was wrong; somehow I wasn't what she was expecting. I dunno how, cuz she'd seen enough pictures of me; selfies I'd sent her... But something must have been wrong; something that made her turn all cold the minute she met me...

'And now, I just don't know. I know you'll say I should just try and forget about her, and I'll say I don't want to forget about her; I want to see if I can still salvage this; and then you'll say how it will seem hard for me to let go right now, but that will pass with time. I know all that. But I just… I just… I mean yeah, I know attraction has to be mutual for it to work; otherwise it's just unrequited love and if you try and force it, it becomes stalking; I know all that. But I just can't believe that we weren't meant to be; everything about us two just felt so right; I mean before we actually met it did. I don't like the idea of chucking it all in when maybe it can still all come right. But then, like I say, I just feel so bloody angry at her a lot of the time, right now. I need to cool off; I need to let all this stuff just settle down…

'And well, that's why I'm here, doctor. When things first started going wrong I turned to recreational drugs; you know, uppers. But after that gig two nights ago I feel like I never even want to look at those drugs again, let alone put them up my nose. So, I don't know, maybe you think a programme of counselling might help me…? With you, maybe? I mean I know you're a general practitioner but you seem like someone I could open up to, so maybe… Or if there's anyone else you can refer me to…?'

He trails off. The duty doctor, young and attractive, her coat as white and clinical as her consulting room, has been staring intently at him through bespectacled eyes, expression unreadable. She hasn't uttered a word. Now, seeing that Craig has finally come to the end of the lengthy description of his symptoms, she sits back in her chair and says, 'So.'

The intensity of her looks while listening to Craig has in actuality been caused by her desperate struggle to make any sense of what he has been saying. Right from the start, he seemed to have been talking complete nonsense; but then the doctor had slowly come to realise her translator must be malfunctioning. (It is one of the cheaper models on the market.) However, not wishing to interrupt Craig, she has listened on, determined to sift some sense from his garbled words. All the stuff about a urinating competition with elephants at high school she dismisses as a bad translation, but she has understood enough to know that the crux of his problem is an unhealthy fixation he has with his younger sister, who performs in a kettle-drum band. He wants to have sex with this girl, and she has quite properly rebuffed his advances. He apparently also entertains prejudicial opinions regarding Japanese women, deeming them to be subhuman creatures with impaired cognitive abilities…

'So,' she says again, having discreetly switched off the faulty device. 'You are depressed?'

'Well, yeah,' answers Craig.

'Good.'

She turns to the dispensary unit on her desk, taps the keyboard and out pop two labelled boxes. She slides them across the desk to Craig.

Pointing to the first box: 'Antidepressant; take one a day.' To the second box: 'Antipsychotic; take two a day. Make appointment at reception for medication review in thirty day. Thank you.'

'Okay…' says Craig. He takes the boxes of tablets. He looks at the doctor. She looks back at him. No mention of counselling. Perhaps she doesn't think it will help.

Someone else who could probably do with some prescription medication is Vern.

He has been summoned again.

Summoned to the abode of his 'girlfriend.'

Another afternoon session of condign punishment.

The last session of this ongoing programme of retribution had involved Machiko making use of Vern's face as a toilet. She had ordered him to lie down on the floor and, squatting over him, had performed a heavy bowel movement. Now, there might be a certain small section of the population who actually enjoy this kind of thing, who actually like to have faeces deposited on their faces: Vern is not one of that happy brotherhood. In this particular context, not even the close proximity of Machiko's genitals to his face could be considered a consolation.

This scatological punishment is just the latest stage of a rapidly spiralling situation. Remorseless Machiko seems intent on finding ever more refined tortures to inflict, new avenues for degrading and humiliating Vern.

And now Vern is just scared. All that guilt and self-pity have given way to good old-fashioned fear.

He just doesn't see any sign of this ending anytime soon. He doesn't see any way out. That's what scares him. Far from arriving at that frame of mind where she might consider vengeance satisfied and forgive Vern his crime against her, that desirable moment seems to be receding ever further into the distance. Machiko's hatred and contempt for Vern seem to increase with each new punishment she inflicts upon him. Without a doubt, she is getting 'carried away.' But then, that's just what he'd done in the first place, wasn't it? Getting 'carried away'? So, does he even have any right to complain?

Another thing.

Today happens to be Vern's birthday. He wonders if Machiko knows this. He wonders if she has concocted some particularly exquisite torture in honour of the day. He hopes that this isn't the case; hopes that she doesn't even know that today is his birthday.

So here he is, once again outside Machiko's apartment building, and the only thing that's stopping him from turning around and running straight back home is the knowledge that if he disobeys Machiko's summons she will only punish him all the more. Like most people, when it comes down to it Vern puts his personal reputation above almost anything else, and the idea that Machiko might start spreading the word around that he is a rapist, is for him the ultimate worst-case scenario. It is mainly this that prevents him from just packing his bags and quitting Daedalus Station.

There's also the possibility that, if provoked, Machiko might go back on her word in another respect and just hand him over to the civil authorities, which would result in much more widespread loss of reputation, not to mention the small matter of complete loss of personal freedom in the event of his being sentenced to a spell in prison.

Perhaps Machiko would consider she has gone too far with her own private course of retribution to belatedly bring the cops into the business, but Vern isn't sure of this, and he has no desire to test the theory.

Vern enters the building, and, arriving at the door of her apartment, he sees taped to it a scribbled note bearing the legend: LET YOURSELF IN.

Has she just popped out for something? Or maybe a longer excursion? Yes! Maybe today's punishment is for him to sit alone in his tormentor's apartment, not knowing when, or even if, she might return.

Vern can think of better ways of passing a pleasant afternoon, but on balance a spell in solitary is better than having shit all over your face.

Removing the note from the door, he enters the apartment.

The cats are home of course. They come and go as they please. He can see three of them, all curled up on the furniture, and none of them favouring Vern with more than a brief uninterested look from one half-opened eye.

'Come through to the bedroom,' calls out Machiko's voice.

So she's here after all.

Then why the note on the door? Why couldn't she just come and let him in? Is she busy doing something…? What…?

'Now, you pig!'

Obediently, Vern crosses the room. Twice before she has made him enter that room, the scene of his crime, and it wasn't for anything nice. He doesn't expect this occasion to be any different.

He crosses the threshold.

Today *is* different. But not for the better.

Machiko is naked on her bed. So are the three men with her. The men are muscular, tattooed; they look like street toughs or bikers; definitely not J-fans. One of the men is industriously copulating (or would you prefer 'making love'?) with Machiko, while she fellates the second. The third is just a spectator at present, gently masturbating to keep himself 'fluffed up' for the moment of being called into action. The three men all grin at Vern, but say nothing.

'Sit down,' orders Machiko, glancing briefly at him before returning the penis to her mouth.

A chair is very pointedly positioned facing the bed. So this is to be his ordeal for today. The latest refinement of torture. Vern feels his very soul plunge down into his lower extremities, and he finds himself starting to recall with fondness having his face covered in shit.

The most wretched man on Daedalus Station, he drops onto the chair in this room smelling of men and sex.

Machiko bursts into laughter, spluttering all over the member in her mouth.

'The look on your face!' she says, looking at him this time with a rueful smile. 'You really fell for it, didn't you? Just look at you...! I don't know...' shaking her head, 'This isn't what it looks like, foolish boy. These guys aren't my new boyfriends! That's what you thought, right? As if. I don't even know their names. I just saw them hanging around in the street and suddenly I had this great idea. I thought: "If I take these guys home with me, and then my darling boyfriend Vern walks in to find me in bed with them, he'll think I'm cheating on him!" That was the plan—and you completely fell for it didn't you! You really did… No, this is just an amusing joke, foolish boy! I could never cheat on you, my darling, my cherished boyfriend!'

And then, changing the subject: 'Oh, that's it! Faster! Harder! Oh yes! I'm coming! I'm coming!'

In commendable unison, the two men release their seed, the one inside her, the other over her face.

'Mmm… That was good…' sighs Machiko, smiling at Vern through her lathered face. 'I know what you're thinking, Vern darling: "A joke's a joke", right? I agree and I would stop this right now, but I have promised to pay these young gentlemen a very large fee for their services, so it would be rather a waste for me not to get my money's worth, right? And, you know, I think it'll be fun to see just how long they can last, don't you? Maybe these tough guys aren't the hot stuff they seem to think they are, yes? Let's find out. So you just sit right where you are, my darling, and don't you dare take your eyes off me.'

Machiko's conjectures regarding the virility of the three men turn out to be unfounded; all three of them proceed to display commendable endurance, and lucky Vern gets to watch the marathon right through to the end; watching the woman who, until he had stolen her virginity, had jealously guarded her body from male hands, now making out with three complete strangers, and men of exactly the type whom Machiko would normally be supremely contemptuous; low-brow toughs from a world completely alien to her own. They never say a word, these three young stallions; their silence is part of the arrangement. And Machiko doesn't hold back; she is all over them, caressing their muscular bodies, sucking their testicles, fingering their anuses, and worst of all, kissing them hungrily on their mouths.

The musky smell thickens in the air; the men sweating and reeking as they exert themselves. Machiko's moans and grunts provide the soundtrack, each sound stabbing Vern to the heart.

…But… all good things…

The men unhurriedly dress themselves. Machiko, satiated, stretches out on the disordered bed.

Attired, the three men, still compelled to silence, look questioningly at Machiko.

Machiko raises her head, looks at the men then at Vern.

'Aren't you forgetting something, darling?' she says. 'I promised these men, in return for their kind assistance with this little joke, the sum of 20,000 credits. Each. Pay them.'

Vern opens his mouth to voice a protest; a look from Machiko silences him.

He pays the three men. They depart.

Machiko stretches luxuriantly.

'Oh!' she says. 'Isn't it your birthday today? Yes, so it is. Happy birthday, darling.'

Franny still recalls reading her first Betty Mudie novel, *Furnace Flats*, recommended to her by a supportive English teacher who had told her she could do much better than just reading horror novels all the time. Franny was fifteen at the time and had wondered whether she was going to enjoy a novel which didn't appear to belong to any specific genre of fiction and didn't even appear to have much in the way of a plot; but in fact, even when reading horror or juvenile fiction she had always had the faculty for appreciating strong characterisation and dialogue; and this novel abounded in both.

Reading Betty Mudie for the first time, young Franny had felt like she had finally come home. She felt like she was reading the kind of book she had been destined to read; and that all those other books had just been so much light, preparatory material leading up to this moment.

Of course the first thing she had done was to devour the rest of Betty Mudie's books. After this she had started to turn to other authors, and the first authors she had turned to were unsurprisingly some of those immortal nineteenth century novelists whom Mudie often referenced in her own books; and again, her horizons had been opened even further.

And for a girl like Franny it had been a short step from reading this kind of fiction to wanting to write it herself. She had the potential which had been noticed by her English teacher, and she also had that which has been determined to be the essential characteristic of any good novelist by that respected student of the literary art, Marquis de Sade: to wit, her being much more an acute observer of life than an active participant. Even at school she had been like this; looking on with an amused interest—inevitably mixed with a measure of disdain—upon the activities of her classmates: who was asking out who, who was splitting up with who, who was cheating on who, who was sleeping around; the unrequited loves, the sharing of boyfriends, the violent jealousies… The whole business of sex and lies, the everyday world of love and lust in which we often treat our friends far worse than we would our enemies…

But who are authors to complain about this side of human behaviour? That eternal and inexhaustible source of material!

Yes, Franny was as much through circumstance as through choice no active participant in that whole school dating ritual. A shy, awkward and eternally bespectacled girl, her few close friends as inexperienced as herself, she was inevitably an outsider. The boys never looked twice at her. Franny herself had had a number of crushes during her school years, but she always kept these hormonal fixations to herself; and not least of all because, considering what a stupid and immature shower her male classmates were, she was annoyed at herself for even experiencing feelings of attraction towards any of them; she looked upon it as a deplorable weakness.

An attitude which has followed Franny into her adult life.

And so, Franny had started to write serious fiction, her powers of observation put to good work alongside that other essential quality any writer worth their salt possesses; namely an innate understanding of human nature. (I think it was another writer with a handle, Lord Lytton, who pointed out this one.) And it was the fresh and sardonic style Franny quickly cultivated which (combined with a healthy dose of that other essential, dumb luck) led to her first novel being published when she barely eighteen.

And now Franny, at thirty, has twelve novels under her belt, having published one every year since her debut. And she owes it all to her literary idol, Betty Mudie. At least Franny believes she owes it all to Betty Mudie—her agent Lydia Luvstruk always doing her utmost to disabuse her of this notion. And here she is, an invited guest at the annual Intergal Literary Festival, right along with her inspiration and favourite author. An inspiration and favourite author who seems to be going out of her way to avoid Franny.

Which is why find Franny sitting alone this evening in the Excelsior bar, nursing a gin and tonic. The flush on her cheeks suggests that this drink is by no means her first. Her glasses, sitting on her nose at a wonky angle, look like they've had a few too many themselves.

The bar is very quiet this evening, which suits Franny. She isn't in the mood for company, and with this in mind has given her agent the slip.

Across the room sits another solitary drinker. One of the men from the PR firm organising the event; Enders or Enderby or something... This guy's personal problems have become common knowledge around the Excelsior: it seems he's a closet J-fan whose girlfriend and co-worker found out he's been playing around with one of the Shinjuku girl band musicians. Franny remembers seeing the guy at the Shinjuku Loft a couple of nights back, so it appears the stories are indeed true. This evening the man is sporting a black eye. Franny wonders who has decorated him with this award: the girlfriend or the bit on the side?

That's what you get for playing both ends against the middle, mister.

Lydia says that it's jealousy. That jealousy is responsible for Betty Mudie seeming to avoid contact with her colleague and admirer; and likewise for the woman's dismissive coldness on the one or two occasions when they have exchanged any words.

Well, her books *are* outselling those of her idol at the present time; an undeniable statistical fact. But sales figures aren't everything; Franny knows that and she would have imagined that Betty Mudie would have thought the same way. Sales figures are no index of literary merit; there are plenty of authors whose books outsell those of both herself and Betty Mudie put together, but they damn well *aren't* better authors! And then there is that ever swinging pendulum of popularity; sometimes an author, through no fault of their own, can just go out of vogue…

No, it can't be professional jealousy… None of her own novels are as good as Betty Mudie's best work, regardless of what Lydia Luvstruk might say. Even the idea of Betty Mudie succumbing to something as unworthy as professional jealousy, a subject the author herself has perceptively tackled in at least two of her books, is a disillusioning one. She has always imagined her idol as being above such meagre feelings; as one looking down on from above upon the eternal human comedy…

And the conversations she had dreamed of having with Betty Mudie! All those talks about those great Victorian authoresses: long conversations in which they would discourse upon the relative merits of Mary Braddon and Margaret Oliphant; the rampant sexuality of Ouida; and how Ellen Wood seemed to have a thing for schoolboys…

Just dreams, it seems… Unless something changes radically for the better, she's never going to be enjoying those longed-for conversations… Oh, what a mess she's made the first time she's spoken to her! Sounding like some silly gushing fangirl… *That's* what has put her off! *That's* why Betty Mudie is avoiding her! She just doesn't want to be subjected to a repeat of that embarrassing moment…!

'Miss Fragrance! There you are!'

Franny groans. Her keeper has tracked her down.

'I've been looking for you everywhere!' announces Lydia, stalking across the room. 'You disappeared without a word!'

'You're not the boss of me!' snaps Franny. To emphasise the point, she downs the rest of her drink in one gulp.

'Not at all, Miss Fragrance!' Lydia assures her quickly. 'But if you wanted to have a drink or two, you could have just called room service! We could have shared a bottle of wine!'

'I wanted some time alone, okay?' Franny, belligerently.

'Of course, of course! But we don't want to get into the habit of being a solitary drinker, do we now? I mean look at that sad man over there!' indicating Lance Enders (who hears her clearly).

'What's wrong with being a solitary drinker?' retorts Franny. 'I *like* being a solitary drinker! Gives me time to think…'

She trails off.

Lydia sighs. 'I understand perfectly, Miss Fragrance, but don't you think you've done enough thinking for tonight? Come on, let's go back to our suite…'

'Okay…' agrees Franny.

Lydia escorts her charge out of the bar to the elevators, and thence back to their suite.

'I need the loo,' mutters Franny, and slouches into the bathroom.

And then, when she emerges: 'I'm going to bed.'

Lydia proffers a pint glass of water.

'Drink this first, Miss Fragrance,' she advises.

'Don't want it.'

'But you must! I implore you, Miss Fragrance! This drink could be the only thing between you and splitting headache when you wake up tomorrow!'

'Alright.'

Franny downs the pint of water, shuffles into the bedroom. She awkwardly divests herself of her clothes and gets into bed.

'Turn the light off on your way out.'

The room is plunged into darkness, but Lydia Luvstruk hasn't actually departed. Franny realises this fact when her agent, divested of her clothes, wordlessly climbs into the bed with her.

'Whadda you want?'

'To comfort you, Miss Franny,' is Lydia's breathless response. 'I know why you've been drinking. I know why you're upset. Let me be your consoler.'

Franny, vaguely wondering if 'consoler' is even a proper word, allows herself to be embraced by Lydia. But the impetuous literary agent's hands are soon wandering into forbidden areas, stroking and caressing. Franny pushes her away.

'Get off me!' she snaps. 'You're just like a man: thinking you can solve everything with sex!'

'But, Miss Fragrance—'

'Get out! Get in your own bed!'

Crushed, Lydia retreats to the neighbouring bed.

Silence falls. But then Franny discerns a sound. The sound of sobbing.

Sighing, she throws back her duvet, and climbs into Lydia's bed. Lydia lies on her side, presenting her back to Franny, the turned back of good intentions spurned, of the wrongdoer who feels herself the victim.

'I'm sorry, Lydia,' says Franny, touching the woman's shoulder. 'I didn't mean to yell at you…'

'I just wanted to…' sniffles Lydia.

'I know. Come on; turn around and face me. And just hold me, Lydia. That's all I want; just hold me…'

Chapter Ten
Someone Make a Monkey Out of You

Lunch at the Osaka Noodle Bar.

Itsumi is on duty. She brings Craig and Dudley their steaming noodle bowls. Craig has met Itsumi before, but not since that night Mami turned him down. He cannot but wonder what Mami might have been saying to Itsumi about himself. He has come to the conclusion that Mami has some reason of her own for strongly objecting to him, and that therefore she will have surely been bad-mouthing him to her bandmates. He also assumes that Itsumi, having long been friends with Mami, and knowing him hardly at all, will accept everything Mami has said against him, and will now also not like Craig.

Actually, Itsumi feels sorry for Craig for having been turned down by Mami. Itsumi has known Mami for twenty years, has been in Tokyo Rose with her for fifteen; she knows that Mami is flighty and can sometimes be thoughtless, and that it did sound like she had been leading Craig on a bit back when they'd just been internet pals. So, she does feel sorry for Craig and would have liked to express her sympathy—but then, when she presents him with his noodle bowl, he greets her smile with such an inhospitable look that she feels repulsed, and consequently says to him nothing more than the obligatory 'Please enjoy your food.'

Craig breaks open his chopsticks and looks down at the steaming bowl. Japanese food is renowned for coming in small portions, and this is generally true; these noodle bowls are an exception to the general rule. The bowl is huge, filled with ramen noodles and—in Craig's case—tofu and mixed vegetables; the whole of it swimming in broth. There are even a couple of eggs floating on top.

Silently, he commences his meal.

'What's up?' asks Dudley. 'You're quiet today.'

'Oh...' says Craig. 'Stuff.'

'Like what?'

'Her for one thing,' indicating Itsumi, now serving another customer at the counter.

'Itsumi? What about her?'

'Well, you saw the look she gave me when she brought our food...'

'No, I didn't notice anything,' says Dud. 'What kind of look did she give you?'

'Oh, I dunno. All standoffish. Like she thinks I'm dirt.'

'I don't think she looked at you like that, Craig. And why would she think you're dirt?'

'From Mami, of course. She's probably been bad-mouthing me to the rest of her band.'

'Why would she do that? Just because you asked her out...?'

'Well, not just that, maybe. I did send her some angry emails...'

'Did you? Just because she turned you down—'

'No, I mean *before* that; after that first time we met.'

'Oh, I see. Well, I know you were upset then, Craig, but you should have waited till you'd cooled off a bit before you sent her any messages. You only say things you'll regret later when you do that.'

'I know that, but I had every right to be angry,' insists Craig. 'You admitted yourself she treated me badly that first night, didn't you?'

'Well, yes. I don't think it was nice of her to start paying more attention to Carl, when it was you she was supposed to be meeting... But no-one likes getting angry emails, do they?' Dudley is thinking to himself that these angry emails may provide a compelling clue as to why Mami turned Craig down when he asked her out.

'Yeah, I know…' sighs Craig. '"Do unto others as you would do unto yourself" or however it goes. Well I've stopped that now. Lately I've been sending her these more friendly emails.'

'Well that's good! Has she replied?'

'Nope.'

'Oh… Well, maybe you shouldn't push it too much, Craig. Just leave it for a while…'

'Yeah, I know. I don't want her to feel like I'm pestering her… But if I leave off, then I leave the field open for that git Carl, don't I? For all I know, he's already dating her.'

'I don't think she is. I asked Krevis, and she hasn't heard anything like that.'

'Yeah, but I bet he's still trying. I bet he just wants to get Mami cuz he knows *I'm* after her. That bastard's had it in for me since the day we met. He's the bane of my life.'

'You shouldn't let him bother you,' advises Dud. 'There's nothing special about him. If I was Mami I'd definitely go out with you, not with him.'

Craig looks at his friend with genuine gratitude. 'Thanks for that, mate…' And then: 'You know what's been bothering me?'

'What's that?'

'You.'

'Me?'

'Yes, you. I haven't seen you sucking your thumb much lately. Have you finally kicked the habit?'

'Well, sort of… It's Krevis: she… she doesn't want me doing it in public. Says she doesn't want anyone laughing at me…'

'So you *have* quit.'

'Pretty much… But sometimes, I mean when I'm alone with Krevis, she likes me to…' He tails off, blushing.

'Yeah, I think that's as much as I need to know about that one,' says Craig.

Vern receives a surprise visitor this evening: Asuna from Raw Babes in the Country. Arriving unannounced, she says she wants to have a talk. Vern invites her to sit. Her unexpected arrival makes him feel uneasy. Has Machiko gone back on her word and told Asuna? Told her the whole story? He's always understood Asuna to be a close friend of Machiko's and the very first person she *would* tell if she needed to confide in someone. And if Machiko *has* told her, what has Asuna come here for? To tell him what she thinks of him? To show him her utter contempt and to order him to get packing and leave town?

Her first words disabuse him of this notion.

'I wanna know what's going on with you and Machiko,' she says.

'Going on?' hedges Vern. 'What do you mean?'

'I mean,' says Asuna, firmly. 'You two are supposed to be an item. But you don't look like an item. You look like an arranged marriage; like two people forced to be together. Machiko seems cross all the time and you seem depressed.'

Vern shrugs. 'Well, you know... We're just going through a bad patch...'

'Why? You only just started dating,' retorts Asuna, unimpressed. 'Come on: spill the beans. Something's wrong with you guys. What's going on?'

Vern attempts belligerence. 'Even if there was anything going on, that'd be between me and her, wouldn't it? It's none of your business, Asuna.'

'Well, I'm *making* it my business,' says Asuna. (The unassailable response!) 'Machiko is my friend and part of my band. I don't like to see her like this. Or you. Machiko even snapped at *me* when I tried to ask her what's wrong.'

'Did she?'

'She did. So now I'm asking you. And from you I want a straight answer.'

Vern rubs a hand over his face. 'I can't tell you,' he says simply.

'Is it a secret? Did you make a promise or something?'

Vern thinks about this. 'No... I don't think she actually made me promise not to tell anyone. She probably didn't think that was necessary...'

'If there's no promise then you can tell me,' insists Asuna. 'It's like Machiko's got something on you. Some hold on you. What is it?'

Vern looks at Asuna, searching her tanned features; that face that usually smiles at the world, but right now looks upset and concerned. Could he tell her? Could he tell her the truth? Could he dare to do that…? But what would she think of him? Would she start to hate him?

Part of him feels like it would be a relief… Just to get it all off his chest… To share it all with someone else… He so desperately wants a shoulder to cry on…

But how can he expect any sympathy? How can he expect any sympathy from any woman?

Tears start to stream from Vern's eyes. Blearily, he sees sympathy in Asuna's eyes as she studies him, head cocked on one side.

'Just tell me…' she says, her voice low and enticing. 'This thing's eating you up from inside. I can see it is. Just tell me…'

Vern wipes his eyes, swallows the frog in his throat.

'Okay…' he says. 'It started that night I met up with Machiko. After the pub, I walked her home. She invited me up for a tea— No, she didn't invite me; I asked; said I'd like to see her cats. She agreed, but she said it was *just* for the tea and seeing the cats; nothing else… So we went up to her flat. She went to get changed while I was in the living room with the cats; and she came out of the bedroom just wearing this short black dressing-gown; a Chinese one…'

'And…?'

Vern glances up at her, looks away again. 'Well, she made the tea and then… One thing led to another. I was drunk; we both were…' His voice rises. 'I mean I thought she wanted it as well! That's what I thought! She…'

Asuna sighs. 'And so you raped her, right?'

'I suppose I did,' says Vern, quiet-voiced. 'I mean, I didn't see it that way at the time, but she did…'

'Yeah, that's how it usually is with date-rapes,' says Asuna, dryly. 'I think I know the rest. What Machiko is doing to you now; how she treats you: this is her revenge, yes?'

'Yes… I had to agree to it; it was either that or she'd call the cops…'

'And how long is this revenge to last?'

Vern shrugs helplessly. 'Until she thinks I've been punished enough and she's ready to forgive me...'

'And what does she do? Not just bossing you around, I'm thinking. What other things does she do when you're alone together?'

Vern gives her a brief résumé of some of the indignities he has suffered over the past few days.

'I see,' is Asuna's calm response.

Vern looks at her.

'Do you hate me?' he asks.

'No, I don't hate you,' replies Asuna. 'You did a bad thing and now you are paying for it. Machiko must feel very bitter to do all this to you. You betrayed her; she expected better from you...'

'I know... So... do you think you could speak to her...?' ventures Vern. '...Maybe get her to ease off a bit...?'

Asuna shakes her head. 'You raped her. She's entitled to her revenge. And you know, it might be even worse for you if she discovers you've told me these things...'

Vern's head sags. Has he just made things worse by unburdening himself? At least Asuna says she doesn't hate him, but does she really mean it? Perhaps, deep down, she—

He looks up. Asuna stands before him. Vern is stunned at how quickly and silently she has managed to take off all of her clothes.

'...I can't stop your punishment,' she says, taking up the thread of her discourse. 'But I can give you a break from it...'

She smiles and softly strokes his hair.

Henry Rollix is an aggrieved man. He is beginning to realise a woman he was sure he'd clicked with has actually just been making a jackass out of him! Jesus Christ! What is it with these women? A guy does his damnedest to be the sensitive male feminist, but the bitches keep laughing at him!

And just five minutes ago he'd felt so good! He'd put on his best tux, slapped on his fanciest cologne, and was on his way down to the Excelsior bar to meet up with a lady. She was a journalist for some holoviz station out on Sirius: a black chick named Martha Dillon. He'd only met Martha for the first time this very afternoon when she had asked for a quick interview with him; but it felt like they'd developed an instant rapport, you know? She was clearly a lady who understood him and his writing.

But then, getting out of the elevator, he'd bumped into Fragrance Pie and her psychopath of an agent.

'And what are you looking so happy about?' demanded the latter, smirking at him.

'And why shouldn't I be looking happy?' retorted Henry.

'I told you, Miss Fragrance,' said Lydia. 'Absolutely no sense of irony.'

'Irony?' said Henry. 'What's irony got to do with anything?'

'Your holoviz interview with Martha Dillon this afternoon,' said Lydia.

'What about it? That happened to be a very good interview. For one thing it didn't have you around to start hitting me over the head with chairs. I bet you didn't even see it, did you? Well, whoever told you it wasn't a good interview is a goddamn liar.'

'No-one told us. We *did* see it.'

'Well, then! What the hell are you talking about? It was a good interview! That lady understood me; she brought out the best in me!'

'Oh, she *understood* you alright,' grinned Lydia. 'Only too well. And as for "bringing out the best in you": it's called "leading you up the garden path," you lummox. She just egged you on to say the stupidest things she could get out of you, and you fell right into it. And you thought she was sucking up to you, didn't you? When all she was doing was mocking you! And you didn't even see it, did you? You were blinded by your stupid male arrogance.'

'That's bullshit!' declared Henry.

Lydia exploded into laughter. 'You still don't see it, do you? That's priceless! I'm telling you: Miss Fragrance and I were laughing fit to burst when we watched that broadcast! The whole galaxy must have been rolling around on the floor!'

Henry folded his arms with a look of satisfied superiority. 'Leading me on, was she? Making me look stupid, was she? Well, if that's the case, how come she's agreed to meet me for drinks, huh? Answer me that one, smartass!'

'She agreed to meet you for drinks?' asked Lydia.

'Yep. That's where I'm going right now! I'm meeting her in the bar. So, if Martha was so set against me, why would she do that, huh? Haven't got an answer, have you?'

'We've just come from the bar,' spoke up Fragrance. 'I didn't notice Martha Dillon there.'

'So? That only means she's not turned up yet.' Henry looked at his watch. 'Yeah. It's only turned seven just now. I'd've been a couple of minutes early if I hadn't stopped to listen to this crap. So if you ladies don't mind, I'll be getting along now. I don't want to keep my date waiting.'

'I think you'll be the one doing the waiting,' had been Lydia's parting shot.

And she was right. Henry has now been sitting at his solitary table for ten minutes, and no sign of his journalist date.

He's been stood up. Not just stood up: set up.

That "irony": he begins to see it now. Looking back on that interview, he can see the mockery in what he took to be compliments; the sardonic curl of the lips in what he had taken to be smiles of approbation.

'Mind if we join you?'

He looks up. It's that PR guy, Lance Enders and one of his cronies. He has been vaguely conscious of them sitting at an adjacent table.

'Well, I dunno,' confesses Henry. 'I *was* expecting a lady, but I'm starting to think she ain't going to show.'

'Who's the lady?'

'Martha Dillon.'

'The reporter for Sirius Broadcasting? I'm sorry to break this to you, but Martha and her team checked out of the hotel about an hour ago.'

Henry nods his head. 'Figures.'

He'd asked her to join him for drinks right after the interview, but she had said she had a couple more interviews to do, so had put him off for a couple of hours. Just the time she needed to make a clean getaway and leave even more egg on his face.

'You look like a guy who needs a drink,' observes Lance. 'And if you want some non-feminine company, me and Roland can join you.' He indicates his friend, a small, roly-poly guy with one of those loose-lipped, double-chinned faces usually described as 'sensual' (and not to be confused with 'sensu*ous*', which is another ballgame entirely and not a description you would apply to Roland).

'Sure you can join me,' answers Henry. 'But I'll pass on the drink. Never touch it. That stuff's poison, man.'

'Well yeah, we all know that,' agrees Lance. 'But sometimes you need to unwind, right?'

'Not with alcohol,' dissents Henry. 'Not this guy. If I need to unwind, I just hit the gym and pump some iron.'

Each to their own,' chuckles Roland. He performs his own favourite exercise, the right elbow-lift, and downs his scotch on the rocks.

'Well, unless you want to head off there right now,' says Lance, 'how about a fruit juice at least? Just to be sociable.'

'Sure, why not?' agrees Henry. 'Just to be sociable.'

Lance turns to Roland. 'I think it's your turn to hit the bar, right? I'll have the same again, and get a *fruit juice* for Mr Rollix. You know the one I mean?'

'Right. A *fruit juice*. I got you!'

Chuckling inanely, Roland heads for the bar.

'No offence, but your pal seems like a jerk,' says Henry, when Roland is out of earshot.

'None taken,' replies Lance. 'He is. But he's the only member of my team who'll even speak to me right now. Shows you how low I've sunk.'

'Oh yeah,' says Henry. 'I heard about your woman troubles.'

Lance grimaces. 'The whole fucking hotel has heard about them, thanks to that bitch Natalie.'

'Natalie… She the one who gave you that?' indicating Lance's black eye.

'Yep.'

'Women, huh?'

'You said it. I mean, it's not like we were even going out, me and her. Well, I guess we *were* going out; but we'd never talked about setting up home together, so it wasn't what I'd call a really *serious* relationship.'

'An open relationship.'

'Well, yeah; that's how I always saw it. But I guess Natalie didn't see it that way. Not that she's got much room to talk, not after what she tried on a couple of nights back. But she's got her excuse, of course. They always have, right? Yeah, she was all ready to sleep with this other guy: payback for what I did, she called it. She was entitled to that, apparently. Ha! One rule for them, another rule for us, right?'

'I'm hearing you, man.'

Roland returns with the drinks, placing a tall glass in front of Henry.

'Thanks. This is the tropical juice, right? I've had this before.'

Roland explodes into mirth.

Henry frowns.

'What's so funny, mister?'

'Oh, ignore him,' says Lance, shooting his friend a warning look. 'He's already had a few too many tonight.'

'Well, that's your funeral,' Henry tells Roland as the latter takes his seat. 'And I mean that literally, cuz you're slowly killing yourself with that poison. Rots your brain, rots your liver, poisons your blood. Don't you read the health warnings?'

Roland just grins. 'So, you've never drunk alcohol?' he asks.

'Never?'

'Uh-uh. Not me. *This* is the stuff to drink,' pointing at his glass. 'Fruit juice. This stuff purifies your body. Has to be fresh-squeezed, though. Don't drink the concentrate. That's just too much fruit. Fructose overload. That'll give you heart disease.'

Henry downs the contents of his glass.

He pulls a face. 'Jesus Christ! That was awful! Tasted like it was so old it was starting to ferment! I'm gunna complain about this shit!'

'Relax, feller,' says grinning Roland. 'It's not like you paid for it.'

'I don't care who paid for it!' Henry slams a brawny fist down on the table. 'No place should be selling shit like this to its customers! Least of all a place like this! "The Excelsior" my ass! I'm gunna complain!'

'Look, I'll sort it out, Henry,' says Lance hurriedly. 'I'm the PR guy, remember? If the drinks are off during this convention, then I guess I'm the one at fault.'

'No!' says Henry firmly, this time slapping the table with the flat of his hand. 'You are *not* the one at fault here. It's those jerks at the bar! I will *not* have you taking the blame for their lousy standards and practices! I'm going over there and I'm gunna give 'em a piece of my mind! And don't try and stop me!'

Henry stands up, totters, and sits back down again, rubbing his head.

'Woah. Major dizzy spell. What the hell's happening to me? Only those skinny, out-of-condition guys get head rushes like that when they stand up too fast. I *never* have them! Never, I'm telling you!'

Roland explodes with laughter.

'What's so damn funny, mister?' demands Henry. 'Cuz if you think... think...' Henry sniggers. 'Yeah, I guess it is funny... Stupid fruit juice...'

Henry starts to laugh.

Lance and Roland are quick to join in.

Dud is seeing his girlfriend tonight, and as Craig was feeling too wired to just sit in the flat and read or watch the box, he has decided to come out for a quiet drink.
And, seeing that Craig has only just started on a programme of antidepressant and antipsychotic medication, having 'a quiet drink' isn't the best of ideas. Alcohol and medication of this type often do not mix well (read the label), especially when you've only in the initial stages of taking the latter. The most common side-effects of combining booze and meds are either drowsiness or else becoming very intoxicated very quickly.

Craig is experiencing the latter.

His mind is still lucid, but only because it's a step or two behind his body in getting drunk. To use the correct terminology, his motor functions are impaired. He's not exactly lurching around as he saunters through the neon streets, but he is having to walk with that concentration one requires if one doesn't want to *start* lurching around.

It seems that Craig is concentrating so much on the act of walking, that he is paying little attention to *where* he is walking; either this or his intoxicated legs have their own ideas about where they would like to be; because when Craig finally pauses to take stock of his surroundings, he discovers that he has wandered into the middle of Shinjuku's famed red-light district.

Most of the illuminated signs are in Kanji or Hiragana, but the illustrations on the illuminated boards are enough to give Craig the picture: old-fashioned cheesecake art; backlit images of sultry, glamorous Japanese ladies, smiling and reclining...

The district is mostly pedestrianised and the pavements are thronged with people: business men in suits letting their hair down; prostitutes plying their trade; transgenders and crossdressers strutting their stuff; cute girls handing out fliers to entice customers into the establishments they represent; gangsters in designer threads and sporting lots of jewellery, strutting around like they own the place. Which they do. Everyone knows that the local Yakuza basically own and run the red-light district here in Shinjuku.

Craig hadn't meant to come here; he's never thought of coming here. But now that he *is* here... Could he find solace in one of these places? He wonders... It's not so much sex he wants right now as just some female company; and he knows that some of these places have 'hostesses' or whatever they call 'em, whose job it is just to sit with you all evening, listen to your stories, laugh at all your jokes, and basically act like they actually enjoy being with you...

It would be nice...

But one the debit side, Craig also knows that these places will fleece you mercilessly, and Craig's credit balance is a bit on the low side... And then of course there's that whole moral issue regarding the fact that by frequenting these places you're financing and maintaining organised crime...

A hearty slap on the back and a, 'Hey, buddy!'

Recovering from the impact, Craig looks at the perpetrator, a young salaryman in his off-duty attire: jacket slung over shoulder, top shirt button undone, tie askew. Clearly the better for drink, he smiles at Craig.

'Erm... Do I know you?' asks Craig.

'No, I don't think so,' is the reply. 'I just saw you lookin' around like you weren't sure where everything is, so I thought I could maybe show you around. Name's Sato. You're one of those J-fans, right? I can tell by your threads. That and the fact that you're a white guy. What brings you to these parts? Lookin' to try something new? Is that it?'

'I just ended up here by accident really,' explains Craig.

'What's your name, buddy?'

'Craig.'

'Well Craig, now that you're here, I reckon you should have a look-see,' declares Sato. 'See that place over there?' he points. 'That's a real nice club. Really cute girls. Come on, I'll take you there.'

'I dunno…' says Craig. 'I don't have that many credits…'

Sato waves a dismissive hand. 'Don't worry about that. I can get you in as my guest. I'll even stand you a drink.'

'That's nice of you,' says Craig. 'But will they let me in like this?'

He indicates his jeans and lumberjack shirt.

'Your threads? That's no problem. Sure, I mean some of the classy hostess clubs have dress codes, but place I'm thinking of is just a strip joint. Pole dancin' and stuff. You don't have to be dressed smart for this place. Wanna come?'

'Okay!' decides Craig. 'Thanks!'

Sato slaps him on the back again. 'That's right! We all gotta unwind sometimes, yeah?'

He guides Craig across the stone-flagged street. They stop at one of the illuminated doorways with its smiling female attendant.

'Hiya, Aoi,' Sato greets her. 'This is my pal, Craig. He's my guest for tonight, okay?'

'Sure. He wanna sign up?'

Another dismissive wave. 'Maybe later, maybe later. He wants to check out the joint first, y'know? See what the action's like.'

Aoi smiles her assent, and they go inside. Craig has never actually been inside a strip club before, but like most people he's seen them represented on movie and holoviz dramas often enough to know what to expect.

They enter a room dark and smoke-filled, with islands of coloured light marking the circular pole-dancing stages; these are placed at intervals around the room, each surrounded with a ring of chairs and tables.

And the music, played with the bass track pumped up, is reassuringly familiar to Craig: It's the Smut Girls, no less! Craig feels sure the band would be pleased to know that their music is being put to such worthy use.

'Look, there's Kimiko,' yells Sato, pointing to one of the dancers. 'She's real hot stuff. She has this kinda serious look I reckon you'll dig. Not all cute and smiling like some of the others. Come on.'

Craig follows Sato and they sit themselves at a vacant table close to the raised podium. A waitress appears and Sato shouts out an order, but Craig doesn't hear what he says; his attention is fixed on the stage.

Kimiko is hot stuff alright. Framed by silky bands of long black hair her perfect Oriental face holds a severe, even disdainful expression, the effect accentuated by expertly-applied make-up. Her thick lips are vivid and glossy; her disdainful eyes framed by lashes far too long to be genuine; a vivid beauty mark artistically applied just below and to the left of her mouth, completes the effect.

She wears a bondage outfit, all straps, buckles and big boots, but with her breasts and buttocks left tastefully exposed. The breasts are small and conical, dominated by nipples dark with large aureoles; the buttocks are sleek and rounded, one of them graced with a heart-shaped birthmark.

She moves to the music with fluid, aggressive eroticism, occasionally deigning to cast a supercilious glance at her audience, and displaying much more reverence for her phallic pole than for her flesh-and-blood admirers.

'Not bad, hey?' shouts Sato in Craig's ear.

The waitress returns with two drinks on a tray.

Sato passes one of them to Craig.

'Here you go, pal. *Salut!*'

Craig raises his frosted glass, drinks, winces. Scotch on the rocks. Craig usually prefers his liquor with a mixer. The pure spirit burns his throat and gives him a headrush.

His eyes settle on a pole dancer across the room: a woman with glasses, dancing under a green light. Where has he seen that enticingly expressionless face before…? In a completely different context, he is sure. Not like this, dancing round a pole in stockings and suspenders. But where…? Where was it…?

Then it hits him.

The duty doctor at the surgery! The one who listened so attentively to his problems and prescribed him his medication! It's her! It's bloody her!

'I love you guys! I fucking love you! You're just… You're just the greatest, dammit!'

People would be surprised to hear the cult author Henry Rollix speaking words such as these. Henry is not known for being the most demonstrative of people; and as for using the word 'love' in relation to anyone except female sexual partners…! Why this is in stark contravention of his image; an infringement of his masculine, muscular dignity!

But it's surprising what a couple of glasses of 'fruit juice' can do for a guy; especially when the guy in question is unaccustomed to drinking the particular 'brand' he is being plied with tonight.

Having made the above pronouncement, Henry wipes a manly tear from the corner of his eye. (Whoever said this guy was not sensitive?) Lance and Roland, the recipients of these tender sentiments, being much less drunk, offer the usual ironic reciprocation.

'You know what I wanna know?' proceeds Henry.

'What's that?' encourages Roland.

'I'll tell you what it is,' declares Henry. 'Now, you two…' He points at his auditors to emphasise that it's not some other 'you two' who are being tabled here. 'You two, you're running this show, right?'

'I wouldn't say we're "running" it, per se,' says Lance. 'It's more like we're just here to make sure everything goes smoothly.'

'Yeah, so you're running it,' says Henry. He fixes his eyes on Roland's chubby face. 'So… what I'm thinking is… you guys must know who's gunna be winning that Lifetime Achievement Award, right?'

'*I* don't know,' answers grinning Roland. 'But *he* does.'

Henry transfers his gaze to Lance. 'You do?'

'I might be privy to that information,' says Lance. 'But it's very confidential, you know. If you're asking me to tell you—'

'No, no, no!' interjects Henry quickly, hands raised, palms outwards. 'I'm not asking you to tell me or anything... No. Uh-uh. But... well, there's this rumour going round that the award's *not* going to Betty Mudie. Y'know, the one most people were sayin' is gunna get it...'

'Well, like I said, Henry, I can't divulge—'

The 'stop signal' hands come up again. 'No no no! I'm not askin' you to divulge *anything*... *Uh*-uh. But... I was just wonderin'... if it's *not* Mudie who's gunna be winning the award...' He looks around, then fixing Lance with a hopeful look: '...is it me?'

'Y'know, Henry,' answers Lance, slowly. 'I think I can safely say, without breaching any confidence, that no, the winner is *not* going to be you.'

The hopeful look crumbles. 'It's not, huh?'

'Nope.'

'Not me, hey?'

'Definitely not.'

'Hmm.'

'Maybe next year!' says Roland encouragingly.

'So...' continues Henry. 'Betty Mudie *is* gunna get the award...?'

'Can't say, Henry, can't say,' replies Lance.

'...It's not...' proceeds Henry, '...It's not gunna be *Franny Pie*, is it...? That's what some people are sayin'.'

'Can't say, Henry,' repeats Lance.

'Ah, man,' says Henry. 'That'd just kill me... That'd just kill me if *she* won the goddamn prize...'

'Why's that, Henry?' asks Lance. 'I'd heard that you liked Franny Pie.'

'Like her?' flares up Henry. 'Like that fucking bitch? Who said that?' And then: '...Yeah, I like her...'

Henry subsides into dolour. This admission has clearly humbled him.

'Franny Pie?' utters Roland, in a tactlessly incredulous tone.

'Yeah, and why not?' demands Henry, flaring up again.

'Nothing, nothing!' Roland quickly assures him. 'It's just... I mean, she's a bit *plain*, isn't she?'

'She is *not* plain!' retorts Henry.

'A bit mousy, maybe,' ventures Roland, shovelling away.

'I'll give you mousy!' roars Henry with a threatening gesture which seems to imply that 'giving someone mousy' involves a punch in the face.

'No, no, not mousy!' back-pedals Roland hurriedly.

'Right,' says Henry. 'She's a nice-looking lady.'

Lance and Roland make the appropriate noises of concurrence.

'Appearances aside,' continues Lance. 'I wouldn't have thought Fragrance Pie would be your type, Henry. Personality-wise, I mean. She's very anti-man; one might even say misandristic.'

'One might even say *what*?' from Henry, confused.

'Misandristic,' repeats Lance. 'A man-hater.'

'Well, yeah; she's got some issues,' allows Henry. 'But I could help her work through those.'

'And have you talked with her on the subject?' inquires Lance, knowing full well that Fragrance Pie detests Henry Rollix.

'I would if she'd give me the time of day!' replies Henry, angrily.

'Won't give you the time of day, huh?'

'No! Not a chance!' confirms Henry, aggrieved. 'I mean how's a guy supposed to get his point across if she always walks out on you?'

'Maybe you just haven't found the right way to connect with her,' suggests Lance. He smiles. 'You know what I'm thinking, Henry? I'm thinking now might be a good time for you to give it another try.'

'You think so?'

'Sure. I don't know why, but you seem to be in a very good mood this evening. Much more forthcoming. Not so reserved about expressing those delicate feelings. What do you say, Roland?'

'Ooh yeah,' agrees Roland readily. 'You've definitely unwound more than you usually do.'

'Have I?'

'Sure,' says Lance. 'You need to take hold of the moment, Henry. Right now would be a very good time for you to go and see Fragrance Pie and lay your cards out on the table.'

'Yeah... Maybe you're right...'

'I know I am. You should just go in there and tell her how you feel!'

'Yeah!'

'You need to overwhelm her with your masculine charm!'

'Yeah! I'm hearin' that!'

'She'll soon submit to a real man!'

'You think so? That's just what I always thought!'

'Then go on!' urges Lance. 'Tonight's the night to make those dreams a reality!'

Henry gives the table a resounding thump. 'You're right, dammit!'

'You know where she is right now?'

'I'm pretty sure she's in her room!'

'Then what are you waiting for? Go and see her now! It's now or never!'

'Right! I'm gunna do this! God dammit, I'm gunna do this!'

Henry rises from the table and exits the room like a man on a mission.

'I think it's going a bit *too* well.'

'What do you mean, Miss Fragrance?'

'These peace talks,' says Franny. 'One minute Deveron was stamping its hooves, saying it was going to attack every planet in the sector. And now they've suddenly rolled over, agreed to these peace talks with the Federation and they seem to be conceding to everything that's being demanded of them: weapons inspectors, disarmament, release of political prisoners; everything. It's such a complete U-turn I think people ought to be suspicious.'

'Much as I hate to differ with you on any point Miss Fragrance, I think the situation we see here is very understandable. These rogue planets are always all bark and no bite. They like to strut about, flexing their muscles, make their noisy threats and ultimatums, but then, when it comes down to it, they know that the moment they made any hostile move, the Federation would retaliate; and they know that their own war-machine would never stand a chance against the united Federation forces. Why, it's just typical male bravado, Miss Fragrance! The very thing you lampoon in your books!'

'Well yes, that's true enough,' concurs Franny. 'This military posturing is all very masculine and childish… But there were those rumours going round that Deveron had developed some new weapon of mass destruction…'

'Empty rumours, Miss Fragrance,' declares Lydia. 'Circulated just to make people worried. How could a tin-pot planet like Deveron come up with any weapon the Federation couldn't easily deal with? Even with all the money they pour into building up their military machine, they just haven't got the expertise.'

Franny and Lydia are watching the holoviz news in the lounge of their hotel suite; an optimistic report from the peace negotiations on Deveron providing the source of the above dialogue.

Lydia excuses herself to go to the bathroom.

There comes a knock at the apartment door, unexpected and urgent.

'I'll get it,' calls out Franny.

She goes to the door, opens it, and finds herself confronted by Henry Rollix. And it's a very different Henry Rollix from the one she had met in the lobby only an hour or two before. His face is red, his eyes glassy, and an unaccustomed smile sits above his lantern jaw, leering at Franny.

'You've been drinking!' bursts out Franny, astounded.

'Who's been drinking?' retorts Henry. 'I never touch the stuff. Just had a couple of glasses of fruit juice with the guys, that's all!'

'Drinking with the guys,' says Franny. 'So she did stand you up then!'

'Who stood me up?'

'That reporter; Martha Dillon!'

Henry swats an imaginary fly. 'Forget her! It's *you* I'm interested in!'

'Me!' squeaks Franny.

'Yeah!' Henry stretches himself to his full intimidating height. 'You and me have got some unfinished business!'

'We have not!' retorts Franny, taking a step back. 'I don't remember ever even *starting* any business with you!'

'Whether we started it or not, we're gunna finish it right now!' insists Henry, with irrefutable drunken logic. 'So let's get to it right now!'

Seriously alarmed, Franny tries to shut the door on Henry.

'No you don't!' Henry slams the door into the wall, sending Franny staggering backwards. 'Don't fight it, honey! We'll both feel better afterwards!'

'Speak for yourself!'

Franny retreats into the lounge.

'Lydia!' she cries. 'Help me!'

'You have called at a rather awkward moment, Miss Fragrance,' comes Lydia's voice from the bathroom. 'Can I beg your indulgence for half a minute?'

'Just hurry up!'

Henry Rollix lurches towards her, and here Franny makes the tactical error of retreating into the bedroom. Following her, Henry interprets this move as acquiescence and gleefully pounces on Franny, pinning her down to the bed.

And this is the sight that greets Lydia's eyes when, moments later, she rushes into the room. Her beloved star client, writhing on the bed, with the panting, muscular form of Henry Rollix looming over her.

'Well don't just stand there!' yells Franny. 'Help me!'

'Oh, Miss Fragrance!' blurts Lydia. 'I am torn between my duty to rush to your aid, and my guilty desire to see your delicate body being ravished by this savage brute!'

'If you don't bloody help me,' retorts Franny, 'I shall be advertising for a new agent tomorrow!'

'Oh very well, Miss Fragrance!' sighs Lydia. She goes to find a chair to hit Henry Rollix over the head with.

They're in a room, sitting on a leather sofa.

Craig can't seem to remember how they got here. Sato is still by his side, his tie now adorning his head like a bandanna. The room is very dark and full of people sitting on sofas. The women are all semi-naked and form the majority. The men are wearing suits. Everyone is drinking, smoking and laughing.

Are they still in the same club? Or have they moved on somewhere else?

'...And that's Melon-chan, the AV actress,' Sato is saying,

indicating a woman with huge breasts.

Craig moves his head to look, and feels dizzy. Right now, the slightest move he makes brings on this sensation.

'Wow, they've got to be implants,' slurs Craig.

'Uh-uh. You'd think so, but they're not!' Sato tells him. 'One hundred percent natural. Some Japanese ladies do have big tits, y'know? They don't all have mosquito bites!'

'Yeah... Craig thinks maybe he should namecheck some of the girl-band members who are more well-favoured in the chest department, but his mind is fuzzy and he somehow can't quite remember whose breasts are whose...

'And you see that lady with the blonde hair and big biceps?' proceeds Sato. 'That's Ichiko, the pro wrestler.'

'Wrestler, huh?' says Craig. 'Wouldn't've thought she'd work in a place like this...'

Sato laughs. 'She doesn't work here! She's a customer! She's a lesbo, y'see?'

'Oh, right...'

Craig slowly scans the room, squinting through the carcinogenic haze.

'Can you see... a lady with glasses...? She's my doctor...'

'I keep telling you, man, that wasn't your doctor!' says Sato. 'No way a lady doctor would moonlight in a place like this. She must have just looked like your doctor.'

'If I could just see her...'

'She's not here, man.'

Someone slides into the vacant seat on Craig's right. Another dizzying head movement and the features of Kimiko, the pole dancer from before, swim into focus. She leans in close to Craig, her expression as unsmiling as it had been on stage, but Craig sees an inviting glimmer in those heavily-lashed eyes, and her glossy lips are slightly parted...

They ascend to a room with a futon bed and wall panels illustrated with eighteenth century Shunga art; images featuring ludicrously over-endowed feudal warlords making violent love to white-faced women who, for the most part, just look bored with the whole business. (Only the woman being pleasured by the octopus actually looks like she's having a good time.)

Craig sinks onto the futon and lazily watches as Kimiko removes the buckles, straps and thigh boots that form her attire. This done, she slides onto the mattress and coils herself around Craig.

'You never been with Japanese lady, Japanophile guy?' she purrs. 'I'll be your first. Once you taste real Japanese woman you not want any other kind.'

Craig plays with her long, silky hair.

'You're beautiful…' he murmurs.

'That's right… You like exotic raven hair beauty, right? Oriental lady with black eyes and yellow skin. Only the best for you, Japanophile guy…'

She starts to relieve Craig of his clothes; and although Craig, inert and recumbent, does little to assist, she performs this office deftly and with practiced ease.

She straddles Craig's chest, looming over him.

'Taste my wet pussy, Japanophile guy,' she says. 'Japanese lady taste different down there. You know that, right? Yeah, we taste better… Much better…'

She lowers herself over Craig's face, smothering him with her heat, her smell, her hair and her moist tender flesh…

Overwhelmed almost to unconsciousness, Craig performs clumsy cunnilingus.

After a minute of this, the woman rises.

'Now we go all the way,' she says. 'You make me yours. Impale me on your manhood, Japanophile guy…'

She eases down Craig's body, but then—

'Hey! What's this?' she demands, handling Craig's offensively flaccid member. 'What's going on? I not good enough for you or something?'

She angrily manipulates Craig, but his stubbornly limp penis remains proof against even Kimiko's manual dexterity. If anything, it starts to shrink even more, in sympathy with its miserable owner's desire to curl up in a ball and disappear.

'I'm sorry…' he moans wretchedly. 'The medication…'

'I not give crap about your medication!' snaps Kimiko. 'You insult me, you *gaijin* piece of shit!'

And she sinks her teeth into Craig's penis. Now this *does* elicit a result: a violent scream of pain from Craig.

'Serve you right!' snaps Kimiko, contemptuously spitting his blood from her mouth.

'You can't do this...!' protests Craig feebly. 'It's not like I'm here to satisfy *you*...'

'Shut face, dickless wonder!' snaps the spurned woman. 'You pay up now!'

'But we didn't...'

'You still got oral!' Without stopping to clarify whether this 'oral' refers to her having sat on Craig's face for a minute, or her taking a chunk out of his penis (or indeed both), Kimiko starts rifling Craig's clothes in search of his wallet.

She throws them aside, now even more angry.

'You don't even have wallet with you, freeloader!' she spits.

'I do!' says Craig, alarmed now. He makes the effort to sit up. 'It's in my jeans pocket...!'

Kimiko throws the article at him. 'Show me!'

Craig dizzily explores the four pockets. They yield nothing save his apartment key.

'It must have fallen out...' he says. 'It must be on the floor somewhere...'

A quick search fails to discover the missing billfold.

'Then I've been robbed!' exclaims Craig. 'I know I had it with me...!'

Kimiko turns from Craig and starts shouting at the top of her voice; a stream of angry Japanese.

In response to this, heavy footsteps thunder up the stairs and several women burst into the room, at the head of the group Ichiko the wrestler.

'This piece of shit trick me! He got no dick and no money!'

The looks on the women's faces show clearly how they sympathise with the unforgivable nature of both offences. Fists raised, the pro wrestler advances towards Craig.

'Now wait a minute!'

Craig feebly tries to scurry away but only succeeds in cornering himself.

And then comes the numbing pain—slightly muffled by his

intoxicated state—as Ichiko briefly but efficiently pummels his naked body... Now, Craig is lifted bodily, and head swimming, he feels himself being carried down the stairs and along a series of corridors...

...And then, through a door and Craig is hurled into a rubbish-filled alley... He lies there, naked and stunned while the women administer the final condign punishment of the felon by spitting on his bruised and battered body... As the women file back inside Craig vaguely registers the light glinting off a pair of glasses...

The door slams shut.

Craig will lie there for some time, feeling too ashamed of his battered and bitten nudity to attempt leaving the shadows of the alley—but fortunately for him assistance will finally arrive in the form of a drunken officer worker, who, stepping into the alley to relieve himself, will discover Craig's discarded but still living remains, and being of a kind-hearted nature, this man will phone for an ambulance to come and pick up the mess...

Chapter Eleven
Goodbye My Roller Girl

Japanese women!

Sure, they may look nice enough; but they're so bloody enigmatic and inscrutable you never know where you stand with them!

In thinking these bitter thoughts, Craig thinks not so much of the ladies of the red-light district who had robbed him, beaten him up and dumped him naked in an alley—he's fairly sure of where he stands in *their* estimation—but more of his fatal *inamorata* Mami Rose of Tokyo Rose fame.

Alright, you might say she'd made her position clear enough that night she had declined going out with him—but he hasn't heard a word from her *since* then; not a single reply to his messages. That's what's bugging him.

Craig *had* still entertained the hope that in spite of the whole being turned down thing, that Mami would still be up for hanging out together, meeting up and going to places, etc... Just as friends, of course.

A nice idea, but it looks very much like Mami isn't even up for taking that first step of even agreeing to meet up with him.

Well then, why can't she just bloody say so? Why can't she just come out and say what she's thinking, what she's feeling?

Craig, dismally wandering the streets of Shinjuku, has finally come to the realisation; has been confronted with the heart-crushing truth: Mami is just not interested in him. He has been wilfully blind to this simple fact, avoiding the nagging truth, always looking to circumstances and to other people to blame for his lack of success.

He has blamed the fact of their disastrous first meeting, believing that if that meeting could be negated or rewritten, everything would go swimmingly. He has blamed Carl (the git!), transforming him into a rival whose removal from the scene would result in his winning Mami's heart.

No, Mami will never be his, and Mami had been the main reason for his moving to Shinjuku in the first place. He remembers the anticipation he felt when the move from Gameron was imminent; all those air-built castles, the sanguine belief that everything was going to pan out exactly the way he imagined it would...

If he could just have contented himself with the fact of being in Shinjuku, with just being where the action was; the home of his beloved girl bands... But no, he had to go and believe that his fantasies and aspirations regarding one in particular of those girls were bound to come true; and now that that has fallen through, he feels so bitter about it all that he is starting to develop an aversion the whole bloody Shinjuku scene, to question his ideals, to scorn the very things he had once held in reverence...

For a start, there's that whole business of the girls being completely apolitical and oblivious of social issues, both within their art and outside of it. Back at the beginning, when Craig had first got into the Shinjuku scene, he had liked this characteristic of the girls; admired it, even. After all those angry punk bands on Gameron with their politically-fuelled lyrics, he had found the Shinjuku girl bands and their complete lack of interest in all that stuff a refreshing change. They just never went there. Sometimes they might sing songs with a general 'love and peace' message, but they never elaborated or went into specifics and Craig had liked that.

But thinking about it today, it just pisses him off. Burying their heads in the sand; that's what it is. Trivially focussing their thoughts on food, cute things and themselves, forgetting that there's a universe out there, with a lot of serious shit going down in it. Do they even know about those peace talks taking place on Deveron and how close this whole station was to being targeted by that warmongering planet?

Of course not! They never even watch the news. 'It makes me so sad,' they'd probably say as an excuse. And that's just it. They always talk about being happy, these girls; about what makes them happy. That's all they bloody care about! They just want to be happy all the time, so they blot out anything and everything that might cause them any *un*happiness. Again, this was once something Craig had admired in Mami. Before they had ever met, when he was still on Gameron, he had asked her if she was really always as smiling and cheerful as she appeared to be. Her reply had been a confirmation of this: Yes! Always smiling, always cheerful. At the time he had admired this about Mami; it was something new to his experience, and he had even felt envious of her ability to maintain such a cheerful outlook on life…

But now… What's the point of being happy, if you have to shut out the universe and everything that doesn't please the senses in order to achieve that…? This is how Craig feels now…

She's selfish, that's what it is. She's never really thought about him for one minute, not seriously. Perhaps at one point she had considered him an amusing diversion, but if she had, his novelty has since that time clearly worn off…

…Yes, he needs to forget about Mami Rose. (He tells himself for the hundredth time.) An unrequited love should be abandoned, lest it fester and turn sour. Yes, he will have to let go, and that will involve letting go of her band as well. Maybe that won't be so hard. Their last couple of albums haven't been as good as their early stuff, and in his heart of hearts he has been concerned for some time that Tokyo Rose might be on their decline as a band…

It's Bon Festival time in Shinjuku, the traditional Japanese

Festival of the Dead. Craig has already walked through Hoko Park where they are hanging the paper lanterns and setting up the booths which will house attractions like target shooting, ring tossing and goldfish scooping—while others will dispense such delicacies as candy floss, takoyaki, chocolate bananas, etc... And then the evening's events will culminate with a fireworks' display and a dance. As good a way as any to remember your ancestors, muses Craig.

Walking the streets, he has already seen a number of girls and women wearing their brightly-coloured yukatas, walking along with those mincing steps.

One woman in particular catches his eye, advancing towards him along the busy pavement, her brilliant white yukata patterned with sapphire flowers and tied at the waist with a sapphire obi-sash. Her apparel and the artificial sunlight of her blonde hair, elevate her from the crowd.

It's Mami. Mami Rose.

Her path lies in a direct line with his; there is no way for Craig to avoid her unless by making a deliberate effort. He feels a sudden, intense self-consciousness of his injured face; he doesn't want Mami to see him looking like this; doesn't want her to see these marks of his humiliation...

But it's already too late; she has caught sight of him. She smiles at him, shy, hesitant.

The moment he saw and recognised her his heart had taken that familiar leap, and now as she comes to a halt before him, all those wise resolutions about letting go are scattered to the winds; the old familiar feelings flood back over him, asserting themselves. Mami Rose; once again, she stands before him an ecstatic vision; unalloyed perfection in Craig's eyes. The broad, manga face, framed with its bobbed hair and neat bangs; the large, deep, glimmering eyes; the strong, even teeth displayed by her smile; the high cheek bones, the sheen of her perfect skin... She glows, she positively glows... She just has to cross his path, she has to stand before him and he is hopelessly in love all over again... Seeing her, he can think only of her virtues: her genius songwriting, her amazing musicianship, her beautiful singing voice; her personality, both childlike and wise; her boundless energy and love of life...

'Hello,' she says, hesitantly. She stands slightly pigeon-toed in heavy sandals and white tabi socks.

'Hello,' replies Craig, with a desperate smile.

What's she thinking? Is she worried I'll start an argument with her? That I'll take her up about her not replying to my last message?

'You look great,' says Craig.

Oh, that came out terribly! It sounded forced. And 'great'; what kind of a compliment is that? You should've said 'cute'! Japanese ladies like to be told they look cute, you idiot! *Kawai!* You should know that by now!

'Thank you,' she replies, displaying once again her freshmint overbite.

'Oh Christ, Mami; I still love you. I'm crazy about you. I love you so much it hurts. Let's start over. Let's give this another try. *Please.*'

Out loud, he says: 'So you're going to the festival tonight?'

'Yes,' she replies. 'Are you?'

'If I can go with you, Mami. I'd be proud to go anywhere with you, to let the whole world see us just walking side by side. Just you and me. You and me.'

Out loud, he says: 'I'm... not sure yet...'

'You...' says Mami, touching her own face to indicate his: '...You hurt yourself...'

'Yeah, I lost a fight with a lady wrestler,' says Craig, grinning weakly.

Mami looks surprised. 'You lose fight with...?' Then she smiles. 'Ah! A joke!'

She giggles.

I made her laugh. I actually made her laugh.

First time that's happened!

'So... I maybe see you later?'

'Forget later, Mami! What about now? Let's just go somewhere; anywhere we can be together. I still love you, Mami.'

'Craig...' Tears well up in Mami's eyes...

...And then the connection is finally made and they are locked in each other's arms. Craig holds her tightly, his mouth and nose in her hair, breathing in the scent that both soothes and enflames. At last he is holding her in his arms. He knew it would happen sooner or later; it *had* to happen sooner or later: that connection, that union of souls destined to be together. He holds her tightly, desperately. He has a hard-on and he doesn't even want to use it; just to feel her warm, living body against his; to inhale her, to absorb her; that is all that he wants…

'Oh, Mami…' he sobs.
Back in reality, he says: 'Sure… I'll see you later, maybe…'
'Goodbye!' smiling.
'Goodbye…' dismally.
Mami walks on.
Craig walks on.
That's it.
Gone.
He feels like he's just blown the last chance he'll ever have.

And now a leaden gloom settles over Craig. It hugs him in a cold embrace that stifles every warm emotion, freezes every hope left inside him… And with it the tears start to fall. Just as they had at the end of that first disastrous night; that ill-starred night at Sex on the Beach, the tears start to fall. You can call them tears of self-pity if you want. Craig wouldn't argue with you on that one. He wouldn't argue, because, as far as he is concerned, he has every right to feel sorry for himself; every right. How can anyone *not* feel sorry for themselves at a moment like this? At a moment when he sees everything that gave his life meaning vanishing beyond the horizon…

This is it. The end. There's no way he can stay here. He has to go back to Gameron. Not ostentatiously; not in the hope of being called back here again; there's no hope of that—he just has to go. He can't carry on with this anymore. It's time to let go. He *has* to let go. Of Mami. Of Tokyo Rose. Of the whole Shinjuku music scene. Of everything. His whole damn life for the past couple of years.

There's nothing left for him here except bitter memories.

And he *will* go; he'll go right now. Today, if there's a flight. All that real estate he has picked up in Fool's Paradise: it's time to start selling out.

Craig arrives back at the apartment to find that Dudley has a guest. Walking into the living room, he sees the back of one dark head seated on the sofa, while near the window stands a figure with long blonde hair and wearing a white dress.

Stacey, of course. Figures. Stacey seems to have been slowly but surely taking Craig's place in Dud's life anyway. And, considering the bombshell he is about to drop, maybe it's just as well.

'Hi, Dud. Hi, Stacey.'

Giggles are all the reply he receives. Searching for the source of the joke, he looks again at the figure by the window.

And he realises.

It's Dudley. Dudley, wearing Stacey's wig and dress. Stacey, seated on the sofa in male attire, turns his head to smile at Craig.

'Okay, you got me,' says Craig, managing a weary smile. 'You two *do* look alike.'

'Are you okay?' inquires Dud, noticing Craig's strained looks. 'You look upset. Has something happened?'

'Yeah, something's happened...' says Craig. He sighs. 'Basically, I'm going. I'm leaving and I'm going back to Gameron.'

Dudley looks stunned. He stares at Craig. 'You're going back to...? B-but why...? I mean... when are you planning to go...?'

'I'm going right now, Dudley. There's a flight to Gameron going out tonight, and I've booked a seat on it. I'm sorry, Dud; I know this'll seem very sudden, but... I... I've got to get out. Right now. I can't stay here anymore, I just can't...'

Stacey has risen to his feet. 'I think I'd better leave you two to talk this through,' he says. To Dudley: 'I'll come back for my stuff later, okay?'

'Okay...'

Stacey departs.

'Come on. We can talk while I pack.'

Dudley follows Craig into his bedroom, where Craig takes his suitcase from the wardrobe, sets it down on the bed and starts packing his clothes, piling them into the suitcase anyhow.

'So… You're really going…?' says Dudley

'I'm going,' confirms Craig.

'What about me…? Do I… do I have to come with you…?'

Craig can't help smiling at this. 'Of course you don't, you wally!' he says. 'You don't have to go just cuz I'm going! You don't have to do anything you don't want to! You're independent now, remember? No mate, you just stay right where you are; you've got Krevis now, haven't you? Or have you and her split up since I went out this morning?'

'No, we're… we're still going out… So… is this about Mami? Why you're going, I mean…?'

'*Of course* it's about Mami,' snaps Craig. 'What else would it be about?'

'But… but… you're wrong about her and Carl, you know. They're not going out. I asked Krevis again, and…'

'They might not be going out right *now*—anyway, it doesn't matter. Even if Carl wasn't in the picture, it still wouldn't have worked with me and Mami. She doesn't fancy me. Simple as that. And there's nothing I can say or do that would make her *start* fancying me, either. "Now is not the right time for us to become a romantic couple." That's what she said when I asked her out that nigh—but what she really meant was that there'd *never* be a right time. I've just been kidding myself, thinking I could get things back on track. Back on track. They never *were* on track in the first place. There's just no connection there between me and her. Nothing. We just didn't click… and we… we never will click either…' His voice falters. 'I've gotta get my stuff from the bathroom…'

He rushes past Dudley, out of the room.

His suitcase packed, Craig wheels it out into the hallway.

'You… erm… haven't packed your records,' Dudley reminds him, nodding back towards the living room.

'Yeah, I… I don't wanna take them… Not right now, anyway… Too much to lug around. You can send them on to me, okay? Once I've got sorted out back on Gameron.'

'Yeah, where *are* you going to stay? You moved out of your old flat…!'

'I know. I'll have to find a new one, won't I? Till then I'll just put up in a hostel or something…'

'So… you're really going, then…?'

'Yep, I'm really going.'

'But—'

'We were a right pair of idiots, you know,' cuts in Craig, forcing a laugh into his voice. 'Mooning over our favourite rock stars like a couple of teenage girls. Thinking we could just come here and make our dreams come true. And you, well you've been bloody lucky, you have: your dream *did* come true. Things worked out for you, and the odds were all against them working out for *either* of us, never mind *both* of us!' Craig shakes his head, smiling sadly—an affected gesture that rings hollow.

Dudley following, Craig wheels his suitcase along the hall to the front door.

'Well, I think I've got everything…'

'You're going right now? Do you want me to go with you to the spaceport? I don't mind—'

'No, it's alright, Dud. I'd rather be alone right now. I wouldn't be very company.'

'Okay,' says Dudley. 'I'll-I'll miss you, Craig… It won't be the same…'

'Cheers. Well, you'll be alright. You've got your girlfriend to look after you, right? And then there's Stacey just downstairs, if ever you need anything…'

'Yes, I'll be alright…'

Craig opens the door. 'Well, see you around, then.'

'See you, Craig. You'll call me when you're back on Gameron, won't you?'

'Sure, I'll call you. So long.'

And then Craig has gone.

Dudley has barely had time to make it back to the living room when a brisk knock at the door sends him back down the hallway, wondering if it's Craig who's forgotten something or if Stacey has come back already.

It is neither: Dudley opens the door to find himself confronted by a middle-aged man and woman. A horribly familiar middle-aged man and woman.

'A transvestite!' shrieks the woman. 'He's become a transvestite! Do you see this, husband? Do you see what our son has become?'

'I see it, but I can't believe it,' is the grim reply.

His parents.

Dudley becomes a crossdressed picture of abject horror; and if the ground beneath his feet does not open up and swallow him, then the ground performs him a great disservice.

A blue sky over Daedalus Central. Holographic skies are always blue, with just the occasional cotton wool clouds added for effect. Observing this sky from her fiftieth-floor window, Franny Pie feels that it doesn't seem right. By all rights the sky over Central ought to be dreary and overcast this afternoon, in sympathy with both her own state of mind and the prevailing atmosphere here at the Excelsior Hotel.

On its final day, the Intergal Literary Festival has been abruptly terminated; the scheduled closing ceremony, including the much-anticipated presentation of the Lifetime Achievement Award, will now not be taking place.

Betty Mudie, the veteran author and anticipated recipient of the above award, has taken her own life. She was found by a maid this morning, hanging by the neck in her hotel suite.

To add to the prevailing sense of gloom, ominous news comes from nearby planet Deveron. Or rather an ominous lack of news. The first sign of trouble was that the off-world journalists had been barred from the Conference Hall. No reason was given, but rumours began to filter through that the Federation delegates at the conference had been detained by the Deveron military; some whispered reports even hinted at something worse.

And now, the journalists themselves have fallen silent. Not one of them can be reached by their respective holoviz stations or news organisations. And Deveron itself has ceased all communication with the outside universe. They have made no response to the Federation's increasingly forceful demands for information regarding their delegates.

Lydia Luvstruk now enters the room, and Franny turns from the window.

'One piece of good news at least, Miss Fragrance,' she says, quietly. 'There is a flight leaving for Gameron early this evening. I've booked us both seats.'

'Well that's something,' says Franny. 'I just want to get out of this place as soon as I can.'

'I understand,' replies Lydia. 'And there's no need for us to just hang around here until this evening, either. We can check out right now if you would prefer, and have our luggage sent on to the spaceport. I think you would be better off outside instead of cooped up here. We could find a restaurant somewhere and have a quiet afternoon tea, perhaps.'

'Yes,' agrees Franny. 'Yes, let's do that.'

Lydia nods her head. 'I will see about the luggage right away.' She turns to execute this task.

'Lydia?' says Franny, stopping her.

'Yes, Miss Fragrance?'

'About the Lifetime Achievement Award...' says Franny. 'What you were saying before we got here... *Wasn't* the award going to go to Betty Mudie...? I mean, is *that* why she...? Did she know it wasn't going to her...?'

Lydia sighs. 'No, Miss Fragrance. The award *was* going to go to Betty Mudie. I've just heard this confirmed. I believe she must have known this herself, and I think it was precisely for this reason that she killed herself... Don't you see? A Lifetime Achievement Award. It must have brought it all home to her; that all her achievements were in the past; that there were never going to be any more; that she had lost her touch as a writer... I think this is why she did it. I'm sorry, Miss Fragrance...'

The pig!

How dare he not answer the phone when she wishes to summon him to her presence? His complete submission to her will is one of the terms of the contract! And now he is ignoring her calls! How dare he? The pig!

Does he think that he has been punished enough? That is not for him to decide! Does he think that her punishments have become unfair? Unfair? Perhaps he needs to be reminded where he would be right now if she had just gone ahead and summoned the authorities that night!

The punishment will continue until she is ready to forgive him! *Those* the terms of the contract!

And now, for making her walk all the way to his apartment... *Nothing* is too bad for the wretch to endure!

She hammers on the door.

Unexpectedly, Hina, the daughter of her bandmate Asuna, opens the door.

'Hello!'

'What are you doing here?' demands Machiko.

'Watching cartoons,' is the reply.

'I want to see Vern,' says Machiko. She pushes past Hina into the hallway; the sounds of the holoviz set issue from the living room at the far end. 'Where is he?'

Unruffled, Hina walks past Machiko and opens the bedroom door on the left.

'Vern's in here,' she announces.

Machiko steps past her and into the bedroom.

Vern *is* here; but he's not alone. The bed is occupied by Vern and Asuna. They are both naked and have clearly been interrupted in the midst of sexual foreplay.

Machiko freezes, thunderstruck.

The lovers look back at her, Vern alarmed, Asuna smiling a friendly greeting.

'Machiko's here to see you,' says Hina, rather superfluously.

'Hello, Machi-chan!'

Ignoring Asuna's greeting, Machiko turns to Vern who—quite literally in one area—wilts under her furious gaze.

'Speak! What have you got to say for yourself?'

Nothing, apparently. He looks to Asuna for assistance.

'What's wrong, Machi-chan?' she asks.

'What's wrong? What's wrong?' rages Machiko. 'What are you doing in bed with... with my...?'

'Your what?' challenges Asuna, with a wry smile. 'He's not really your boyfriend, is he? That's just a cover-story, isn't it? Vern's explained it all to me.'

Machiko looks at her. 'He's told you? What—everything?'

'Yes.'

'Did he mention the small detail that he raped me?'

'Yes, he did. I was very cross about that.'

'Really? But you seem to be offering him consolation. You think I shouldn't be punishing him the way I am? Is that it?'

'I'm not saying that. I think you're entitled to revenge yourself in whichever way you see fit. But...'

'But what?'

Asuna sighs. 'Oh, Machi-chan. Don't you see what this is doing to you? It's not just Vern; you're becoming bitter towards everyone—even me, and that makes me sad because you're my best friend. I don't want your revenge to start warping your personality. That's all.'

Machiko has cooled down. She looks downcast. 'So... You think I should forgive him and forget about it? Is that it?'

'Forgive him whenever you're ready to,' answers Asuna with a shrug. 'But right now, I think what you should do is get into bed with us.'

For a pregnant moment, Machiko makes no response.

And then, with a sigh of her own, she starts to undress.

Dudley Moz is having to pack his bags, renounce his new life, his new-found freedom, and return to Gameron at the behest of two very angry and self-righteous parents.

Craig had sanguinely believed that Dudley had finally shaken off the parental yoke. For that matter, Dudley had entertained some ideas along those lines himself. But that was when his parents had been half a light-year away and he was enjoying a new world of freedom beyond their sphere of influence.

Now those parents have actually turned up on his doorstep, and once more in their imperious and imperative presence and without Craig there to back him up, Dudley soon found himself yoked and back under their thrall as if nothing had ever changed.

'We haven't arrived a moment too soon! Out of our sight for one week and look what happens to you! Going out with some delinquent exhibitionist from a rock band, and now you're a transvestite to boot! Did that creature you call your girlfriend put you up to this? Did she? Well? What have you got to say for

yourself?'

'I... I... I...' was the best he can manage.

'Well, the first thing you can do is to change out of that disgraceful costume, and then you can start packing! You're coming back home with us, young man! I should never have let you go off with that reprobate Craig Jenx in the first place!'

The trouble is that they've got him too well trained, have Mr and Mrs Moz, the latter especially. Dudley has been obeying her every command for twenty-odd years now; and habits as ingrained as this cannot be shaken off in an instant. And so, when his mum had ordered him to start packing his bags, he had started packing.

He doesn't want to leave. Yes, he is upset and confused about everything that has been happening with Craig, but even so, he doesn't want to go back home. For one thing, there's his girlfriend, Krevis Jungle. He is in love with Krevis. His parents, on the other hand, consider Krevis to be the most urgent reason for removing their son from this region of the universe. She is a 'bad' woman. She is shameless. She is violent. She uses foul language. She is morally corrupt. She is in every way the wrong woman for Dudley Moz.

This is what Mrs Moz has been drumming into Dudley's head for the past couple of hours, supported by occasional interjections from her husband. And the worst thing is, Dudley is starting to believe what they are saying. 'Mother knows best' is another one of those ingrained lessons. He still loves Krevis, but he is starting to doubt himself; to believe that his parents may be right; that Krevis is the wrong woman for him. Is he really cut out for this life? To inhabit Krevis Jungle's world? Or is just trying to fit himself in somewhere a milksop like him was never meant to fit in?

And if he's not cut out for this, if he's not made of the right stuff, maybe Krevis herself would come to realise this. Maybe she would start to reject him… Maybe she would start to get fed-up with him and would find some guy better suited to her way of life…

So maybe it would be better just to give it up now, before it all turns sour. His parents think he should leave, and they are older and wiser than himself…

Stacey had stopped by a while ago, to pick up his wig and dress.

When he saw what was going on, he didn't seem to think that Dudley should be just leaving like this. However, when he had ventured to speak out, Dudley's mum had peremptorily shown him the door; and Stacey, being himself not the most assertive of people, had walked meekly through it.

And now they are ready to leave. A taxi has been called and has just arrived outside. Carrying Dud's luggage, the family group descend to the ground floor. Dudley remembers he has to surrender his key to the manageress. He knocks on the door, and after the usual delay she appears, and without a word (also as usual), holds out her hand to accept the key, as though she has been expecting it.

Outside in the gathering dusk the cabbie waits beside his vehicle. It's the rasta guy of course. (Do I even have to tell you this?) He recognises Dudley.

'So it's you!' he says. 'One of the J-fans from Gameron. You leaving this fair city already? And I'm thinkin' I only just brought you here a week back! You look very sad, my friend. You have a falling out with that pal of yours or somethin'?'

'I don't see that that's any business of yours,' interjects Mrs Moz, before Dudley can open his mouth. 'Please put our son's luggage in the boot. We need to be at the spaceport before eight o'clock.'

The cabbie bows ironically. 'Your wish is my command, good lady. And I will certainly deposit you at the spaceport in good time for your flight.'

He stows Dudley's luggage. Just as this has been done, a large motorbike arrives noisily, pulling up just behind the taxi.

Dudley's heart flip-flops. It's Krevis! (Alerted to her boyfriend's predicament by a concerned cross-dressing neighbour.)

Mrs Moz also recognises the culprit.

'It's her!' she shrieks. 'That woman! Get in the taxi at once, Dudley!'

Dudley, starting to cry, has stepped forward to meet his idol, who remains seated on her machine. She looks cross.

'Where are you going?' is her curt inquiry.

'I... I... I've got to go back... to Gameron...' whimpers Dudley.

'Got to? Who says you've got to go back?'

'My mum and dad… They say… that I—'

'Do you want to go back?' demands Krevis. 'Do you love me or not?'

'Yes I do!' blurts Dudley. 'But I… I…'

'Stop talking to that woman and come here at once!' orders Mrs Moz. 'I forbid you to listen to anything she says!'

Dudley looks back at his parents.

'Do as you're told, boy!' snaps Mr Moz, crisply authoritative.

'Dudley Moz!' says Krevis, drawing his attention back to herself. 'Make your choice. Your parents or your lover. Come with me. Or go with them. Do it now!'

She revs her bike's engine, indicating her imminent departure.

'Let her go!' orders Mrs Moz. 'You don't need her! Come with us. Come home with us!'

Dudley's eyes, imploring, are fixed on Krevis. Her eyes are fixed on his. Her pugnacious features relax in a smile.

Dudley smiles back.

The connection is made, finally severing another once and for all. Dudley, light as air, jumps onto the back of Krevis's bike. He locks his arms around her waist and holds tight as the machine springs into motion.

'Dudley!' screams Mrs Moz.

The motorbike swiftly vanishes down the street.

Chuckling, the cabbie climbs into his vehicle.

'Where do you think you're going?' demands Mrs Moz.

'Why, I am going to follow that fine young man of yours to his destination so that I can deliver him his luggage,' is the smooth reply. 'But worry not; I shall call one of my colleagues to pick up your husband and yourself. You'll still make your flight in time. Have yourselves a pleasant journey home!'

And the taxi moves off, gently mocking the speechless parents with an impish twinkle of its tail lights.

The spaceport departure lounge. Craig, navigating through the crowd, finds himself dancing the pavement two-step once again—and with his usual partner.

'Not you again!' exclaims Franny Pie.

'Right back at you,' says Craig.

Where there is Franny, there is Lydia. 'It's him! This is stalking! This man is definitely stalking you, Miss Fragrance!'

'I'm not stalking anyone! I'm catching a flight to Gameron, that's all I'm doing.'

'But *we're* booked on that flight! You see, Miss Fragrance? He *is* stalking you, he is! I will call security at once!'

'Oh, leave the poor boy alone, Lydia. Can't you see he's upset?'

'I can see that he's been in a fight. Some drunken brawl, no doubt!'

'It wasn't a fight. I just got beaten up.'

'And richly deserved, I'm sure!'

'Lydia! Please!'

I'm really not in the mood for this, thinks Craig. He removes himself from the conversation, striking off across the lounge. He looks at his watch. Still thirty minutes till boarding time.

The departure lounge is vast, high-ceilinged, brightly lit; the busy hub of the spaceport. Across the room from the vast holographic display of departures and arrivals, a floor to ceiling observation window occupies the outer wall, looking out upon the skyline of Daedalus Central.

Skirting round the busy seating area, Craig makes his way up to the observation window, more to be alone with his thoughts than with any idea of enjoying the prospect. A digital coating on the window's surface shields it from light reflection, thus the nocturnal cityscape is unobscured by any mirror-image of the room behind him.

What's she doing…? What's Mami doing right now…? Oh, of course, she'll be at that festival that's going on in Hoko Park. The Festival of the Dead… He'd told her he'd be seeing her there… Will she even notice he hasn't turned up? No… she'll probably just think she's missed him in the crowd… If she even thinks of him at all…

What will Mami think when she finds out he's gone completely, gone back to Gameron? Will she feel any regret, any guilt…? Or will she just be glad…?

One of Craig's fondest fantasies of Mami, one that didn't end up with the usual facedown on his bed scenario, was this cosy daydream of their lying side by side on his living room sofa, and just embracing and soothing each other, smiling into one another's eyes.

The sofa in these fantasies is always the one in Craig's old apartment back on Gameron, and like everything else in that apartment, including the interior dimensions, the sofa was small, and probably could not have comfortably accommodated two people lying at full length. Craig had never attempted the experiment; he had often shared that sofa with his former girlfriend, but this had usually involved them just sitting side by side on it while watching the holoviz. Admittedly the sofa had been utilised for sex on a number of occasions, but never for horizontal sex.

This fantasy of Craig's had always commenced with Mami coming to Gameron just to visit him; an arranged visit and involving her staying at his apartment. (And he had in fact suggested the idea of her paying him such a visit on one or two occasions; this was before he had arrived at the realisation that the Mountain could just as easily come to Mohammed, the journey being the same distance in both directions.) This fantasy was a creation of Craig's more depressed and lonely moods, and involved Mami arriving to find Craig feeling in low spirits. And of course because the Mami of Craig's fantasies intuitively understood all of Craig's various frames of mind and what needed to be done to make him happy when he was feeling sad, she would, having divested herself of her clothes (well, you have to expect that even Craig's more innocent fantasies of Mami are going to contain at least *some* sexualised content), lie down with him on this sofa, and they would just hold each other and look at each other and she would speak soft words in her velvet voice that would caress and comfort him...

And it had worked. Even just as a daydream, a fantasy, Craig would often feel consoled by replaying this scenario when he was in one of his more downhearted frames of mind...

But now... now that fantasy has now gone; it has slipped beyond his grasp. Craig can still call it to mind, but only as a recollection of something that never happened, a memory of a memory... It has gone; it has gone completely; drifted out of his reach...

Makes sense. Any comfort he used to derive from the fantasy came entirely from his own head, and fantasy has been overwritten by reality, the reality of a Mami Rose who can never offer him that kind of comfort.

A haze of light has appeared behind the towerblock skyline, at first noticed only by the eye and not the cognitive brain. Only as it grows in intensity, throwing the starscrapers into relief, does the light assert itself over Craig's introspection.

What is it? Sunrise? But it's not even tomorrow yet; it's still today! But wait a minute: is this a holographic night sky or is it the real thing…? Yes, Central is right at the apex of Daedalus Station; maybe at night they extinguish the holosky and show the real thing, actual outer space… But that light, it's still getting brighter, and Daedalus is way out on the edge of this system; there's no way the sun could look that big from out here…

He hears murmurings behind him, bewilderment edging towards alarm.

'What on earth is it, Miss Fragrance? A comet?'

Franny Pie and her agent, standing at the window, off to Craig's right. Did they follow him over here…?

Brighter, ever brighter grows the light, spreading itself over the horizon. The towerblocks become silhouettes.

And now klaxons ring out, filling the air, loud, imperative.

'EMERGENCY! EMERGENCY! ALL PASSENGERS PROCEED TO THE SHELTERS! ALL PASSENGERS PROCEED TO THE SHELTERS!'

Pandemonium erupts. Screaming. Running. Trampling.

'It's Deveron! It must be! They've fired a Nova beam!'

'Then let's hurry, Miss Fragrance! We've got to get to the shelters!'

'Shelter? There's no shelter from a Nova beam! Look at it! Look at it!'

The light, overwhelming, spreads rapidly towards the observation window, devouring the whole sky, blinding, burning, annihilating.

Tonight is the Festival of the Dead.

Suggested Further Listening

TsuShiMaMiRe – Sex on the Beach (FlyingStar Records – VICB-60055)
Shonen Knife – Free Time (P-Vine Records – PCD-25106)
Detroit7 – Fever (Getting Better – VICL-63532)
Lolita No. 18 – Fubo Love NY (Sister Records – CRCS-1005)
Kokushoku Elegy – Kokushoku Elegy (Super Fuji Discs – FJSP-419)
The Go-Devils – Super Stuff (Majestic Sound Records – MSCD-079)
Nippon Madonna – Band Yamero (Redrec – RACP-003)
Kinoco Hotel – Marianne no Yuwaku (Yamaha Music Communications – YCCW-10187)
The Molice – Catalyst Rock (Velour Voice – VV-013)
The Girl – UR Sensation (Felicity – cap-159)
Seagull Screaming Kiss Her Kiss Her – Give Them Back to Me (Hate it, Damn it Records – HDR-001CD)
Red Bacteria Vacuum – Dolly, Dolly, Make a Epoch (Guzguz Records – LTSF-001)
Mescaline Drive – Ideology Cooking (King Records – KICS 973)
The 5.6.7.8's – Teenage Mojo Workout (Time Bomb – BOMB CD 68)
54 Nude Honeys – Drop the Gun (UK Project – UKCD-1075)
Noodles – Cover Me Shakespeare (AAD Records – BUMP-023)
Go!Go!7188 – 569 (BMG – BVCR 11109)
Sekiri – Take Me to Sekiri (Alchemy Records – ALPCD-5)
OXZ – Along Ago: 1981-1989 (Captured Tracks – CT-293)
Les Vivian Boys – Jigoku no Vivian (Austin Records – ARR-0023)
LAZYgunsBRISKY – Quixotic (July Records – DDCB-14002)
Bo-Peep – Is it Good for You?!! (3rd Stone – JHCA-1005)
That's a No No! – Yes or No? (Sazanami – SZNM-1044)
Toquiwa – Toquiwa (Scopitones – TONE CD 047)
Zarigani$ – Avocado (Natural Hi-tec Records – XQJR-1077)
Titan Go King's – Ultrasonic Wave 01 (Benten Label BNTN-

044)
Beardsley – Double Frenzy (Captain Records – CAP-1033-CD)
Mummy the Peepshow – Electric Roller Girl (Benten Label – BNTN-051)
Kyah – 1984-1986 (SS Recordings – SS-920)
Yellow Machinegun – Father's Golden Fish (Howling Bull – HWCA-1002)
SiX – COBB (Seez – SEZ-3022)
Kokeshi Doll – Ichi Kara Yon (JPT Records – SHIKEKO005)
Super Junky Monkey – Parasitic People (Sony Records – SRCL 3484)
Supersnazz – Diode City (Time Bomb – BOMB CD-59)
Puffyshoes – Finally the Weekend (Papercake – KOCA-65)
The Pebbles – First Album (Sympathy for the Record Industry – SFTRI 498)
Who the Bitch – Toys (DCT Records – XQJS-1003)
The Highmarts – Early Recordings (Sazanami – SZNM-1058)
The Flamenco a Go Go – The Flamenco a Go Go (Wonder Release Records – WRR19)
Spookey – Spookey Cat (Killer Records – KS007)
The Let's Go's – Heibon Cherry (Label 222– L222-001)
Akabane Vulgars on Strong Bypass – The Rumps Smoulder at the Gloom (Kizuna Media – KM-120001)
Theee Bat – Official Theee Bat Club (Radio Underground – RUC-25)
Zelda – Carnaval (Philips – PHCL-8025)
Pugs – Chimato Kubiki (Wax Records – TKCA-71612)
eX-Girl – Endangered Species (Alternative Tentacles – VIRUS 313CD)
Blacklab – In a Bizarre Dream (New Heavy Sounds – NHSCD040)
Papaya Paranoia – Captain Years (Solid Records – CDSOL-1355/56)
Wapperin – Wa (One By One Records – OBOCD-32)
Kana – Animal Human (Reveil – TECN-29729)
Eiefits – Genetic Memory (Mangrove – Root-071)
Zibanchinka – Discontinued (Call and Response – CAR-87)
Soapland Momiyama – Kedamono Damono (Benten Label –

BNTN-058)
Afrirampo – Afriverse (Supponpon Record – SPP003)
Limited Express (Has Gone?) – Tell Your Story (Less Than TV – CH-169)
Love Pigs – Pokin' the Pork Pie (God's Pop Records – SMGP-4003)
Lulu's Marble – Afro Girl (Sexcite Records – ALCA-5149)
Anokoha Wombat – Jisoku 40KM (not on label)
Galapagos – Flowers (Eastworld – TOCT-6331)
Akai Kurage – Voice (House Support K-in – K-IN-1001)
Pappys – Jigokudemoero (KOGA Records – 137)
United Banana – United Banana (Sazanami – SZDW-1052)
The News – Do!Do!Do!Do!Do! Luxury (Explosion Works/ING Label – EXP-ING 252088)
The Madame Cats – No Control (Sazanami – XQGX-1007)
Oddly – Loaded EP (Smooth Records – SM-004)
The Mash – First (Acid Rain – DDCR-1012)
Ni-Hao!/Garorinz – Ni-Hao Vs. Garorinz (Gal Gal Records – GAL-001)
Jaco:Neco – Jaco:Neco (Meldac – MED-57)
Orange Kandy – Lick it! (AJA Records – AJA-60005)
Me-ism – Sunshine Dori of Your Love (ING Label – ING-ME2500-1)
Mizutama Shobodan – The Virgin's Prayers - Da! Da! Da!/Sky Full of Red Petals (Shoh – SHOH 119)
Skirt no Naka – Chikotan (Redrec/Sputniklab Inc. – RCSP 0028)
Falsies on Heat – meaTone (not on label – CR001)
Atomicfarm – The World of Atomicfarm (Sazanami – SZDW-1007)
China Chop – Apes on Frontier (M&I – MYCD-30344)
Jamic Spoon – Bug (East West – AMCM-4344)
Tetsuko – Curl (Sazanami – SZDW-1112)
The Pen Friend Club – The Pen Friend Club (Sazanami – SZDW-1105)
Loves – JM (Felicity – cap-103)
Mady Gula Blue Heaven – O (Gyuune Cassette – CD95-11)
Megababe – Speak Japanese or Die (Babystar – BM001)

Samurai West

disappearer007@gmail.com

Printed in Dunstable, United Kingdom